KATHRYN COWLING

Fairly Jane

Published by The Conrad Press in the United Kingdom 2018

Tel: +44(0)1227 472 874
www.theconradpress.com
info@theconradpress.com

ISBN 978-1-911546-42-9

Typesetting and Cover Design by:
Charlotte Mouncey, www.bookstyle.co.uk

The Conrad Press logo was designed by Maria Priestley.

Printed and bound in Great Britain
by Clays Ltd, Elcograf S.p.A

Fairly Jane

for Tim

1

The man I knew as my father, Michael Rosental, was a quiet, solitary man, most of the time. To me, it seemed he was at his happiest when he was tramping around the Irish countryside with his flask of tea and his binoculars. He loved bird-watching; I think he enjoyed the peacefulness and quiet. Michael rarely spoke about his past, but one evening, as we all sat around the fireplace, he began to tell me how he had come to be living in Northern Ireland when it was not the place of his birth.

I was aware my father did not talk with an Irish accent but, in my childish mind, I never questioned why this was. Sometimes, when he was having one of his flashbacks, when he thought he was still a prisoner in the Burmese Jungle, he spoke a language that was totally alien to me. I later learned it was German. On this day, his voice was so quiet; I had to lean closer to hear what he was saying. His eyes were brimming with tears as he began to speak.

Michael explained, in a halting voice, how he and his elder brother had fled from Germany in 1932. He spoke of the shock of their departure, how his neighbours and friends turned on them. He revealed that his actual name was Maciej, pronounced Ma-Chay, and his brother, my uncle Len, was actually called Levin. They had changed their names when they arrived in Ireland to help them integrate into their new country. They could not, however, bring themselves to drop their surname.

Michael believed that his parents had sacrificed their lives so that he and his brother could escape and both boys wanted to hold onto their surname as a mark of respect for their courageous act. When he had finished his story, his eyes were dry once more. His face looked emotionless, as though he was wearing a mask. There were a few more times when he spoke about his life before he came to Ireland and I remember feeling really sad that he had to run from the only home he had ever known.

I tried to imagine how frightened my father must have been. He was only a few years older than I was then and he lost everything he had ever known and had to flee to a country that was totally foreign to him. I don't think the trauma ever left him.

2

I was born Jane Fairly on April the fifth 1943 in Bristol. My parents were Susan Bromley and James Fairly, known as Jimmy. My mother was working in a Strachan & Henshaw Munitions factory assembling parts for aeroplanes. She told me she felt that she needed to help with the war effort and this was her way of doing it. She was originally from Cornwall and often told me that she always thought of Cornwall as her home.

I'm writing this in 1975, at the age of thirty-one. One summer day in 1959, when I was sixteen, Susan, my mother, described to me how my birth and adoption had come about. She began by telling me something about her own childhood. Susan explained how she was forced to flee from her home, in Treruth, when she fell pregnant with her eldest daughter Edith. Her own father was a violent alcoholic and her mother, Peggy, had abandoned them both when Susan was very young.

She recalled how she was, mainly, taken care of by the other villagers and kindly neighbours but all these people lived in fear of her father. When my mother became pregnant, she was unmarried and feared her father might actually kill her. She and the father of her child, Edward Bromley, to whom she is now married, were spirited out of the village in the dead of night with the help of family and friends.

They moved to Bristol, where they eventually married and had another daughter, Iris. Everything I had heard about

Susan's father, John Penhaligan, from the villagers of Treruth, made me feel that she had suffered a terrifying childhood. Her father was over six feet tall and a bear of a man. When he was drunk, his temper took over and no one challenged him.

My mother's face took on a dreamy hue, though, when she spoke about meeting my father, Jimmy Fairly. It was 1942 and Bristol was enduring heavy bombing raids. Susan's husband was away fighting and had been for more than eighteen months. By 1942 her two daughters, Edith who was then fifteen and Iris who had just turned nine had been evacuated. Both had been sent to Cornwall to live with Edward's parents because of the bombardment Bristol was suffering.

I can still hear the joy in my mother's voice and see her face, lit up by the most wonderful smile, when she talked about meeting my father. She told me she had just finished a shift at the factory and, with some friends, was looking forward to an evening at the pictures. But before they had a chance to get there the air raid siren whirred into life. As they hurried towards the nearest shelter, my mother spotted my father. She told me that, at first, he brought out the maternal instinct in her; he looked so lost and afraid. He was standing very still, looking up into the sky.

She said she could tell right away that he was an American airman. His uniform was pristine, unlike the faded ones worn by the British military, and he wore a 'wings' motif on his shoulder. She laughed as she told me how she raced over and told him that he needed to get to an air raid shelter, still he stood, and she had to physically push him to safety.

When the planes sounded overhead, the poor guy was obviously terrified, so my mother tried to comfort him as best she could. He told her that he had only arrived in England that morning and had become separated from the rest of his crew. My mother told him about her children in Cornwall and her husband fighting abroad. My father, in turn, told her about his wife, Maria, and three-year-old son, Donnie.

My mother was pleased to notice that talking about their families had made Jimmy calm down a little, and soon they were showing each the small black and white pictures they carried of their children. When the raid had finished, everyone in the shelter got stiffly up and dusted themselves down. Stepping over broken glass and masonry, my mother and her friends decided it was too late for the cinema, so they chose to head to the nearby pub.

She giggled out loud when she told me how incredulous Jimmy was when he heard them discussing their evening out after what had just happened. He couldn't understand how they could all carry on as normal when they had just been sheltering from the German bombs that had seemed to land so precariously close to them. My mother explained that this was the only way they all managed to get through the war. She said my father told her how much he admired their spirit and bravery.

Jimmy Fairly told my mother that he had come to Bristol with the Eighth Bomber Command and was one of the first contingents of the United States Air Force personnel to arrive in England. They were known as the Eighth Air Force. He was stationed at RAF Filton at the time, which was close to where my mother was living.

With the help of my mother and her colleagues, my father was finally reunited with his crew and he and my mother went to the pub in a large crowd of people. At first, she explained, she and Jimmy were just two lonely people who enjoyed each other's company. She agreed to go to the cinema with Jimmy because he told her how homesick he was and frightened about going on his first bombing raid.

As time went on their feelings for each other became more intense, and they began to a secret love affair. She likened their romance to a shipwreck. She said that it felt like they had been thrown together on a desert island and they only had each other. As time went on though, they realised though that the relationship could not continue because both of them had families who they loved and couldn't bear to hurt so they had to part.

My mother told me how it was so very important that no one found out about her affair. She had a husband away, fighting for his country, and she was only too aware she would be vilified, by everyone who knew her, if anyone discovered her secret.

Her face clouded over when she explained that, after a while, they both came to their senses and decided to end the romance. Three months later my mother discovered that she was pregnant. Jimmy Fairly had now been posted to another base, along the coast, and my mother had no idea how to contact him. It was here that her own mother stepped in and offered her a way out of her predicament.

Susan explained how she and her mother Peggy Combellack had met a few months earlier for the first time since Susan was a small child, when Peggy had left Susan with her husband, John Penhaligon. Peggy had not wanted to abandon her daughter but her husbands increasingly inpredictable mood swings and heavy drinking had left her afraid for her life as he sometimes became violent. He had never, however, directed any of his anger towards

Susan. With nowhere to go, her mother decided that she would be better off with her father. A decision that proved to be the worst one she could make. Sadly, the reunion was not a happy one as Susan found it hard to forgive being abandoned, by her mother, when she was such a young child.

Now, however, there was a chance she could help her. My mother went to visit Peggy Combellack at the home she shared with her friend Margery. Susan was relieved to find that her mother was only too willing to help and offered to raise me as her own child.

The spoke in the wheel was that no one could know that my mother was pregnant. All of her friends and colleagues knew that her husband had been away fighting for almost two years. Here, one of my mother's factory mates stepped in and told her she could stay with her relative in Ireland, before her pregnancy started to show, then bring the baby back to Bristol for her mother to care for.

This plan worked very well. My mother got the chance to see me often, on the pretence that she was visiting her own mother and her secret was safe. Jimmy Fairly returned to Bristol when I was six weeks old. When he saw me, with my mother and grandmother in the local Lyons tea shop, he knew, immediately that I was his. I had his colouring and features and he also knew how long my mother's husband had been away.

My father managed a couple of furtive visits to see me before tragedy struck. When I was three months old, Peggy Combellack's house took a direct hit from a German bomber. Although we were all down in the cellar, she was killed. She used her body to shield me, saving my life.

Susan and Jimmy realised that it was not safe for me to

remain in Bristol. My mother returned to Ireland and I was adopted by Lucy Rosental and her husband Michael. My poor mother cried as she told me how she pined for me and longed to hold me but knew she had to let me go.

Two families were at risk of being broken up by my mother and father's love affair and neither of them wanted that to happen. Around the same time that I was born, Susan's eldest daughter, Edith, gave birth to twins; she told me that every time she held them she imagined it was me.

To some extent I can understand why my mother had an affair. Her husband had been away for more than two years and her children were living miles away. She must have felt terribly lonely. She told me how she used to write short stories and poetry. She had a few of her stories published in *Woman's Own* magazine. Susan explained that her writing allowed her to escape from the horrors of war, if only in her mind.

What I didn't understand was why my adoptive mother, Lucy, didn't tell me the origins of my birth, as soon I was old enough to understand. When I later questioned her about this, she told me that she was afraid I would stop loving her if I knew that she was not my biological mother.

When I was eighteen and I learned the truth, I felt as though someone had pulled the carpet from beneath my feet and left me flailing around on the floor, unable to get up.

3

My second vivid memory is from when I was about ten or eleven years old and was so frightening, I can remember every detail. I loved my father Michael, but when he began to shout loudly, in a strange language, I would run to find my mother. She explained this was because he had suffered a lot while fighting in the war and when he remembered it, it made him angry and that's why he shouted. She said we must do our best to love him.

I tried but I'd always known he was different from other dads. I was proud because my father was one of the few Jewish refugees to be permitted to fight in the British army. He was not, however, sent to fight the Germans. Instead he was posted to Burma to fight the Japanese. What he suffered there never left him.

I remember watching him while his wide eyes darted from side to side but I didn't know what he was looking at. It seemed to me he wanted to escape from something but whatever it was, I couldn't see it. My mother said it was because of what had happened to my father during the war. She said it was much too terrible and too scary for my father to talk about. That wasn't always true though.

Most of the time, he would sit quietly. Sometimes he would hold onto his teacup so tightly that his fingers turned white and I thought he would smash it to pieces. But when he drank whisky or brandy he would change from a quiet person into a very loud one.

My mother always used to put any alcohol at the back of the shelf inside the sideboard. I think my father must have been an alcoholic. By hiding the alcohol I think she was trying to save him but it didn't work, if my father wanted to drink, he would. When he drank though, he talked as though he needed to say everything really quickly, before someone tried to stop him.

I remember, it was a Saturday morning and I was chewing on my pencil and really concentrating on my colouring-in book; at the time, it was important to me that I got the yellowy brown of the owl's chest, in my picture, just right. My father was sitting opposite to me at the kitchen table looking down at his newspaper but not really reading it. I knew this because his eyes were fixed on one spot. My mother was behind me slamming the kitchen cupboard doors open and shut and she sounded angry:

'What's the matter, Mum?' I asked, because I thought that was what she wanted me to do.

'I haven't got enough flour for the pastry, will you be all right if I go next door to Granny Gerta to borrow some?' she said as she tugged her apron off.

Mostly, my mother didn't leave me alone with my father and I was glad because he was so unpredictable. One minute he would be silent then suddenly he would spring to his feet and scream out. If I'm honest, I didn't like being on my own with him but I really wanted to finish my picture. When I looked up at him, he seemed to be in a kind of daydream so I nodded and carried on with what I was doing. I remember Mother kissed the top of my head then she walked out, pulling the kitchen door behind her.

She had only been gone a few minutes when my father looked up from his newspaper. I watched as he walked over to the window and glanced out quite furtively. His hand then disappeared into his inside pocket of his jacket and he pulled out a metal flask. I watched as he unscrewed the lid and started gulping down the contents, I knew it was either whisky or brandy because I had seen him drink it before.

I watched it drip down his chin and I turned up my nose because I didn't like the smell of it. Very quietly, I slipped off my chair. I knew had to go and fetch my mother because she didn't like my father to drink alcohol. I had almost reached the door when my father darted around and stood in front of me:

'Where are you going now?' he asked me, then he knelt down so our faces were almost level, smiled and said, 'Would you sit on my lap and I'll tell you a story?'

I could hardly believe it when I saw my father was smiling. He looked really happy. It made him seem like a different man. I remember really wanting to hear him tell me a story and I nodded excitedly. I couldn't stop the grin from spreading across my face as I followed him over to his chair.

He patted his hand on his lap and I jumped on straight away. Wrapping my arms around his neck I rested my head on his shoulder. His hair smelled like shampoo. I felt like all my friends must have felt all the time. They always talked about how their fathers sat them on their knees when they came in from work. They told me he would read them stories while their mother cooked the tea.

Looking back now, I think my father wanted to unburden himself and might have found it easier to share his experiences with his little girl. My mother never wanted to listen and always seemed to slap him down. If he started talking about what happened during the war, my mother would tell him to shut up and not to talk about in front of me. I think, now, if she let him talk, he may have not felt the need to end his life the way he did.

I felt normal, like my friends were. I smiled even more widely when my father slipped his arm around my waist. The smell of the whisky he was drinking made me feel sick but I knew he really liked it. My Granny Gerta used to call it 'the devil's poison' and she always made the sign of the cross on her chest with her finger every time she said it. When my father stopped drinking, for a moment, he looked down at me and smiled sadly, then said:

'I went to Burma once, I was in the army.'

I listened as he said this. I felt uneasy. I knew my mother didn't like him to talk to me about what happened when he fought in the war. Hazy memories of my father shouting and screaming out, in the night, came into my mind. I know now my mother was trying to protect me from what my father wanted to reveal as it was very harrowing, especially for a ten-year-old girl. I am very sure, now, if she allowed him to share his experiences with someone, it would have helped him and, maybe, saved him. He carried on talking:

'Shall I tell you about it, do you want to know what it's like in Burma?'

I really didn't care about a place called Burma and didn't want to know anything about it but I did want him to make him feel better. I thought after he has finished telling me his story we might walk down the lane together. I wanted everyone to see me rambling around the village with my father holding my hand.

I thought if some of my school friends saw us out tramping around the Irish countryside together they would stop saying unkind things about him. They said he drank too much and was a bit mad. I knew they were right but I wanted him to change, to be a normal father.

I told him I really didn't want to know about Burma and asked if I should I get my story book. It seemed as though he hadn't heard me:

'It was a terrible, terrible place.' My father whispered, so quietly I nearly didn't hear what he is saying.

His face looked odd and I began to worry. I think I asked again, if I should get my story book, I said that we could read it together. He seemed to look straight past me, as though I was no longer in the room and neither was he. My father was scaring me but he didn't realise it, he was so lost in his own misery from the past.

He looked towards the window, into the distant fields and whatever it was he saw, obviously upset him. He gulped at his drink and when he squeezed close his eyes, tears dropped down his cheeks. I couldn't bear seeing him cry. I leaned forwards and kissed his face. My father looked so wretched. He shook his head and said:

'Nobody cares what happened to me, nobody wants to know.' He spoke with such dejection on his face, I wanted to cry.

'I care, I want to know,' I told him. He sat down and pulled me closer to him then he kissed my cheek.

'You're a good girl,' he told me and I smiled at him as he

began to talk quietly:

'The heat in Burma was like nothing I'd ever felt before, it burned so much, and it felt like I was on fire… I swear it sapped all the energy from my body. My legs, they were covered in sores, blood all over them… nobody cared or helped me, we didn't have enough food or water… I was always, always hungry and thirsty, it scares me to think about it.'

He stopped and pressed his hand over is mouth. When more tears fell from his eyes, I used my sleeve to dry them. He started to scratch at his legs then stroke and them over and over again. I didn't want him to but he started talking again, I wanted to cover my ears but I was scared I would upset him even more. He started speaking again, quietly still but now more urgently:

'I could hardly sleep, the nights were so cold and there was nothing to keep me warm. I shivered so much… I thought I would never see you or your mother again, the two of you kept me alive, I promised myself then I'd get back to Ireland, just the thought of seeing you both again helped me get through long nights and days and they were so long: I thought they would never end.'

My father began to sob really loudly, it sounded almost like he was choking. I started to feel very afraid; I remember really wanting my mother to come back. Sweat and tears were making my father's whole face damp. He was holding me so tightly that I thought I wouldn't be able to breathe if he squeezed me anymore:

'I always thought the Japanese guards were full of evil: I didn't think they could even be human. They treated us like it didn't matter to them if we lived or died: they just wanted us to build a railway. If one of us dropped dead, they threw the body in a ditch and if any of stopped working we would get beaten or even worse, killed.'

I didn't know much about the Japanese, just that we had fought them in the war, my teacher had told me. My father put the flask, of brandy, on the table then pressed both of his hands into his face. I wanted to pick the flask up and pour the contents down the sink but I was so scared I barely moved. I remember hoping he would forget I was there if I sat quietly enough.

My father then started crying even louder. He suddenly stood up and pushed me off his lap then he picked up his drink and began gulping it down quickly. His whole body was trembling. His crying then turned into a high-pitched, howling sound. I backed away from him towards the kitchen door; I had almost reached it when he suddenly looked up and shouted at me but I knew it was not me he was seeing, I think he thought he was back in Burma. The alcohol he was drinking seemed to be making his mind play tricks on him:

'I'm not staying here; I've got to get out, I am not dying in this stinking hole!'

He shouted so loudly I covered my ears. Now, I couldn't stop myself crying no matter how much I tried. I turned quickly and ran towards the kitchen door. My father spun round and screamed 'no.' He then hurled his metal flask at me; it hit me on the back of my head and I cried out in pain. I begged my father to stop shouting. I could feel blood running down the back of my neck. I was trembling from head to foot.

My father had a funny, faraway look on his face. He began to walk towards me. I screamed at the top of my voice for my mother to come and get me. No one came so I raced over to the table and pushed myself under it, as far into the corner as I could get myself.

My father walked slowly towards me and leaned down. His face was red and angry. I thought his bulging eyes were going to pop out of his head. I cried out louder as he reached in and grabbed at my ankles. I kept kicking my feet out so he wouldn't be able to get me and squashed myself further and further into the corner.

It really hurt when my father clamped his hand around my leg. As he pulled me from underneath the table I pleaded with him to leave me alone, this seemed to make him even angrier. He slid me out and I lay on the floor with my hands over my head. As he loomed over me, I covered my face and tried to curl myself into the tiniest ball I could, I remember feeling a terror so intense I thought I would be sick.

I can't explain what happened next but it seemed as though a light been switched on in my father's head and he had woken up. Suddenly, without explanation, he let go of my leg. I watched as he stepped back and shook his head from side to side really hard. Getting up as quickly I could, I backed myself into the corner of the kitchen and watched him. He had his back to me then he started to sway from side to side, his legs seemed to buckle.

I thought he was going to fall over so I quickly ran over to him and hooked my arms around him from behind. I gently rested my head on his back. He turned and leaned, partly on me and partly on the table. I looked up and I could see he was crying pitifully, as though his heart would break. I bit my lip so I wouldn't cry too and upset him even more. After a while he ruffled my hair and I tried to smile at him, to reassure him, but I was too scared. He spoke so quietly I could barely make out what he was saying:

'You don't need to know, Janie darling, you don't need to know,' he whispered then turned and walked out of the room.

I watched as he left the house, through the open back door, and headed towards the shed in the back garden. He always went there when he was sad and I felt sad too and I was still shaking uncontrollably, I had no idea what I could do to help me father.

That was the first time he had ever hurt me. When my mother returned and found me hiding, once again, under the kitchen table, she leaned in and scooped me up in her arms. As she held me close she promised she would never leave me alone with my father again. I remember making her swear on Granny's life that she would protect me from him and take more care of me and she promised she would.

4

The next significant event which I remember took place a couple of months later. It is seared into my brain as surely as I had been branded. All through my early childhood I could remember hearing muffled sounds coming from parents' bedroom at night but couldn't really work out what they were so I would just go back to sleep. This particular night was different though. I remember feeling comfortable and warm snuggled under the covers in my little bed. I loved feeling the weight of the blankets on me, they made feel safe and secure in my own little world.

It felt to me like the bedding somehow shielded me from my father's increasingly dark moods and sudden, unexplained outbursts of anger. I was quite sure the shouting and screaming sounds I could hear were coming from the monsters in my dream, at first they seem to be a long way away. Suddenly the monster seemed closer and I woke with a start. My room was very dark. I realised the noises were not from my dreams but were coming from the direction of my mother and father's bedroom.

Sitting up in bed, I waited because everything became silent again; I remember thinking my mother must have been having a dream because all was quiet for a moment and she must have gone back to sleep. Then a loud, piercing scream rang out, scaring me to death. My heart felt like it was going to jump out of my chest. I hurriedly climbed out of my bed and felt my feet touch the bare floorboards.

Hastily, feeling my way in the familiar darkness, I reached the door and opened it. I heard peculiar noises coming from my parents' room. I walked quietly across the small landing, every tiny bit of the child in me wanted to run back to my warm bed. As I got nearer I could hear my mother, she was now clearly crying, I was almost sure, or was she choking?

Suddenly, I knew she was in danger; I felt as though my feet had grown wings and I raced forward and shoved the door open. The pale moonlight was faintly lighting the room. I could make out the silhouettes of my parents.

My father was sitting astride my mother. With one hand he was hitting her and the other was around her throat. My mother was struggling frantically to escape but she was trapped underneath my father's body. I don't know why but he suddenly took his hand away from Mother's throat and started to beat her even harder. Mother was crying and begging him to stop. I couldn't stand it, I couldn't bear it anymore! Lifting both hands I pressed them over my ears to shut out the noise but I could still hear it. I shouted as loudly as I could with my eyes squeezed shut:

'No Dad, please don't hurt Mum, please, please stop it!'

It was now quiet and I slowly opened my eyes. I could see my father looking at me, as the moon became brighter. His face looked odd; he dropped his head to one side and leapt from the bed. He reminded of Shere Khan, the tiger, in my *Jungle Book* story, jumping out at Mowgli before he realised he was a man cub.

My father was running towards me, I screamed for my

mother but he moved too fast and hit me a glancing blow. I started to stumble backwards. I tried to grab the bannister to stop myself from falling but my father pushed me so hard that I felt myself flying through the air. My head hit something very hard then I could see nothing at all but blackness.

It felt like somewhere in my head I could hear a voice but it sounded really quiet. It sounded like someone sobbing and begging. Sometime later, I don't know how long, my mind seemed to clear, as though some imaginary clouds had been blown away and sunlight had broken through. The voice was clearer now, it was saying:

'Please Jane, wake up, Oh God, please, Jane, please, before he comes back.' I thought it was my mother talking although she sounded a long way away.

I shook my head to try and get rid of the fuzziness. It hurt so much I felt as though I was being stabbed with a thousand daggers. I groaned in pain then I definitely heard my mother whisper 'thank God.' My mind started to clear, like mist the lifting on a grey day. I used all my strength to try and wake myself up, all the time I could hear my mother whispering:

'Hurry, hurry Jane, please hurry, my little love.'

As I lifted my head up it hurt so much that the blackness almost came back but I fought to keep it away. I opened my eyes and saw my mother's face very close to mine, she kissed my forehead. Her tears were mixed with the blood coming from her nose and head and there were tiny pink rivers running down her cheeks. She looked so frightened. I knew I had to wake up properly:

'It's all right Mum, don't worry, I'm fine.' I told her but I didn't feel fine.

My mother helped me to sit up and then I struggled to stand. Together we staggered out of the open front door. The moon was now a big, golden ball in the early morning sky and it lit our way to the next door, where Granny Greta lived. It was not very far but I felt like each step was ten because my legs felt so heavy and my head was pounding. While still holding onto me, my mother banged on the door, not too loudly in case my father was still lurking in the shadows. I heard her cry with relief when she saw the hall light come on through a small pane of glass.

The door opened, and Granny Greta pulled us both quickly inside. She didn't need to ask us why, we had come to her for sanctuary many times before. Mother and I stumbled towards the sitting room while Granny put her full weight into closing the door and shoving a heavy bolt across to secure the house. I always felt safe when I heard the lock sliding into place. When Granny came in we all cuddled together.

My mother and Granny were crying but I couldn't cry anymore. I often felt I had cried more tears in my ten short years than most people had cried in their whole lifetime. Mother then slumped into the armchair and Granny went into the kitchen. All I wanted was not to feel afraid all the time and not to have to run or hide.

Granny's sitting room was lovely. I really liked the feel of the soft, blue, velour material that covered the chairs and sofa. It was small but very cosy and warm, and above all, safe. Granny returned with some water in a bowl and a large wad of cotton wool, she dipped it into the water and started dabbing at my mother's face and head.

Once I was sure that Mother was being taken care of I headed for the cupboard in the hallway and pulled out the bedding that we always used when my dad had been unwell. My head was still aching and I felt sick. All I really wanted to do was lie down and go to sleep. As I put my hand on the door knob, I heard Mother and Granny whispering, my mother was saying:

'Oh Gerta, I thought he had killed Jane this time: she was lying at the bottom of the stairs as still as death, it terrified the hell out of me.'

'We have to talk to him Lucy, my love,' Granny said back, 'He's getting worse, not better, bless his soul, we have to make him see that he can't go on like this.'

I barged into the room and the talking stopped, I couldn't help sighing angrily. Mother and Granny had talked, begged and pleaded with my father so many times before to get help but he would not do it. Each time, he just sat there shaking his head crossly then either stormed out or started to cry and nothing changed. I lay the blankets and pillows onto the floor and crawled into my makeshift bed.

It felt like not only was my head was hurting but my whole body; I longed to be in my own warm, soft bed. I felt like crying but couldn't see what good it would do. There was a big lump on the back of my head which was digging into the hard floor. I remember wishing my father would leave so we could all be safe then immediately feeling guilty and bad. I knew it wasn't my dad's fault he had an injured mind but I really wanted him to get better. I closed my eyes and waited for sleep to come, fearful about what the future would bring.

5

As we all ate breakfast the next morning I was really relieved that the throbbing pain in my head was not as bad as it had been and I only felt a little bit sick. It was different for my mother though. One of her eyes was almost closed because it was so swollen and pink; her bottom lip was bulging out and had dried blood all along it.

I could see that she was in pain because she winced when she chewed her food. I wanted to cuddle her, to make her feel better, but I didn't think it would help. I didn't really know what would. I remember I slurped noisily at my porridge, that morning, but my mother didn't tell me off like she usually did.

We all started to walk back to our house when we had finished eating. I thought my father was probably in the shed at the back. I don't know why but he liked it there. The wood was so rotten that the whole place was falling apart and bushes and brambles grew on the inside of it.

We were all scared. I knew this because Granny was turning the lock in the door as slowly as she could so it wouldn't make any noise and her hand shook. She pushed the door ajar, really gently, so that it hardly opened at all and called my father's name. I grabbed hold of Mother's hand when I heard the sound of wood creaking. I was frightened because I thought it might be my father wandering around, Mother squeezed my hand really tightly.

Granny stepped forward and pushed the door open even further. I heard a tremor in her voice as she shouted my father's name a little louder. When the door was fully opened, my mother started to scream really loudly. I followed her eye line and looked towards where the creaking sound was coming from.

I could see my father; his boots were polished so brightly I could almost see my face in them. Mother had told me a long time ago my father was overly tidy and fussy because when he was in the army they taught him to be really neat. He had two long creases exactly in the middle of the front of each trouser leg. His belt was shiny and spotless and buckled directly in the middle of his waist. I turned to look at Granny, tears started spilling down her face as though her eyes were taps and my mother kept on screaming.

I looked up and found I couldn't stop staring at my father. He was hanging from the banister with a thick rope around his neck.

6

My father's body was swaying gently making the wood creak and groan. His lips were a light grey colour and his eyes looked as though they were going to pop out of his head.

My gaze remained fixed on him; I don't know why but I couldn't turn away. His neck looked broken and strange but his eyes were no longer looking around wildly like they always used to do. I knew my father was dead and I felt nothing but relief, so much so that so, I found it hard to breathe. Alongside my overwhelming relief I felt massively ashamed for not being upset.

I let go of my mother's hand and ran outside into the garden. I felt an awful urge to be sick and the next minute my breakfast was spewing from my mouth onto the front doorstep. When I had finished I sat on the grass, it was still damp from the early morning dew.

I thought about all the times my mother had tried to explain what was wrong with my father. She told me lots of men came home from the war with broken arms and legs that could easily be fixed. She said my father had a broken mind which was much harder to cure. I was always puzzled when she told me we must both love him,. as much as we could, because that's what I always did, even when he frightened me. I wonder now if she was trying to talk herself into loving him.

Sometimes when my father smiled and cuddled me I didn't

know what to do. He got upset really easily and, occasionally, when I tried to put my arms around him he would push me away. The grass smelt sweet and I rubbed my hands into it. I felt the warmth of the sun as it began to shine through the thin layer of clouds. The birds were singing and I thought it was going to be a very warm day.

I didn't realise I was smiling, for a while, and when I did, I stopped right away. I knew it was wrong to smile when my father had just died but I also knew I didn't have to be afraid anymore. I would no longer have to tiptoe around the house in case I disturbed him or hide in my room when he started shouting. Never again would he hurt Mother. Inside and out I felt very peaceful and calm.

I walked slowly back inside. My mother and Granny had got him down by now. My father was now lying on the floor; his unseeing eyes were staring at the ceiling. I put my two hands around my mother's to try and comfort her, she had stopped screaming. I squeezed her hand a little tighter. As I did this I heard Granny cry out then gasped as she fell to the floor. Mother mumbled something then knelt, quickly, down beside her. She was cupping granny's wrinkly face in her hands and telling her she would be all right. Granny was making a rasping, choking type of sound. Mother turned to me and shouted:

'Oh God Jane, run for the doctor sweetheart, as fast as you can: tell him Granny's had a fall, be quick Jane.' She shouted as she stroked Granny's soft hair.

I turned and raced out of the door. Our house was on the edge of the village, it usually took us ten minutes to reach it but I ran it in less than five. The doctor's house was in the centre of a terrace near the village square and as soon as I reached the door I started pounding on it as loudly as I could.

All the time, I had the picture of Granny falling, playing over and over again in my mind and I could still hear the terrible sound she was making. I was breathless and trembling when Dr Sheldon's wife opened the door. I fell into her arms and screamed that my father was hanging and Granny had fallen. Mrs Sheldon called for her husband and he rushed out. She quickly relayed what I had told her, the doctor knelt in front of me:

'You're a very brave girl,' he told me. 'Now, now, you mustn't worry, doctor's on the way.'

I knew he was trying to make me feel better but I could tell he worried by the tone of his voice. Mrs Sheldon appeared at his side carrying his big, black medical bag. He took it from her and hurried towards his car as fast as he could. He was quite slow because he looked to me like a very old man but I guess now he wasn't much older than fifty.

I watched as his car disappeared along the track. Mrs Sheldon then led me inside by my hand. I told her the doctor didn't need to rush because I knew my father was dead and I thought my Granny had died too. She put her hand up to her mouth and pulled me into her arms.

7

I loved the warmth of her body and I snuggled into the folds of her clothes. Her closeness was making me feel a lot better, not so panicky. After a while she took me into her kitchen and when I was sitting at the table she poured me a big glass of creamy milk. I sipped at it and it tasted lovely. She then offered me some buttered bread. I was so hungry I swallowed it down really quickly and she gave me a second slice. As I finished my milk I heard the door open. Mrs Sheldon walked towards it then stood aside as the doctor and Mother walked in. I watched as he shook his head sadly at his wife:

'Would you make young Lucy a cup of tea my dear, she's had a nasty shock, plenty of sugar, maybe a little whisky if needed,' he suggested as he helped Mother into a chair.

I stared at my mother, she had lost the entire colour from her face and her skin was as white as my porcelain doll. She must have been crying a lot because her eyes were very red and even more swollen. Doctor Sheldon reached into the cupboard and pulled out a bottle of brandy. He poured some of it into a glass and drank it quickly.

In my mind I could see my granny making the shape of the cross over her chest with her finger. It made me smile and as he poured himself another I pictured her shaking her head again and telling him to leave the 'Devil's poison' in the cupboard. The doctor began to talk. It was like he had forgotten there was anyone else in the room because he seemed to be talking to himself:

'I should have tried harder: I should have made sure he got the help that he needed, now look what's happened: I didn't do my duty. I neglected that poor family.'

He finished his drink and told his wife he had to go and do the 'necessary', regarding registering the deaths. He then turned to me and asked if we had any relatives. I told him about my uncle Len and Auntie Violet who lived in Bristol. Mother just sat looking ahead; she didn't touch her tea or answer any of the doctor's questions.

It seemed a long time before she appeared to realise where she was and muttered a thank you to Mrs Sheldon. The doctor drove us home sometime later and when we got there my father and Granny were gone. The rope still hung from the stair rail and I could still smell Granny's lavender perfume.

8

For a few days, it may have been three; I sat at home with Mother. I made her cups of tea, which she drank but she didn't eat any of the steak and kidney pie I gave her. Three days after my father and Granny died, she said I had to attend school to get some normality in my life. I couldn't see how it would ever be normal again. I didn't really want to leave my mother alone but she insisted I go.

As I sat at my desk, chewing my pencil, I couldn't really concentrate on what Miss Rushmore, my teacher was saying. I thought to myself and was glad I was at school because Mother cried a lot and I couldn't do anything to stop her. At the same time I didn't think she should be on her own, I constantly worried about her.

I knew I should be feeling upset because my father had died but I was just glad he was gone and Mother and I would be safe. This thought made me feel mean all over again and I silently begged Granny's God to forgive me for thinking bad thoughts. When I was not worrying about Mother I was thinking about Granny.

Both she and my father had the same staring eyes when they were dead. I remember thinking about Granny's face and it made me want to cry. All of a sudden I wanted her to wrap her arms around me and tell me that everything would be all right. I wanted to squeeze my arms around her thick waist and bury myself into her apron; now I wouldn't ever be able to do that again.

I closed my eyes and tried to remember her living face but I couldn't, just the lifeless, dead eyes:

'Oh please Granny, don't be dead, who's going to look after me and Mother?' I asked, without realising that I had said it out loud.

Miss Rushmore rushed across the classroom towards me. When she reached my desk she gathered up my books and handed them all to me. Placing her arm around my shoulders, she walked me to the classroom door. I knew that all the other children were looking at me. I felt silly for crying in front of my school friends but I couldn't stop the tears from coming. Once Miss Rushmore had closed the door behind us, she knelt down in front of me.

The school corridor echoed because it was empty, that is what I felt like inside. She took her hanky from up her sleeve and dabbed my face. She told me to blow my nose, which I did. She pushed the hanky back into my hand when I tried to give it back to her. She then bent down and kissed my cheek. This made me want to cry all over again but I didn't know why.

Miss Rushmore told me to go home, I wanted to be anywhere other than home at that moment but I did as I was told. I walked slowly out of school. The sky was as blue as I had ever seen it and the white clouds were like puffs of cotton wool.

A cat jumped off the wall and walked lazily towards me, it started to twist its way around my legs. I bent down and stroked its soft grey fur. It felt like Granny's hair. I thought about Mother sitting at home on her own and I felt unkind for not wanting to be with her. I knew that she had a baby boy a long time ago but he died and now I was all she had left. She also really hated nuns and priests or anything at all to do with the church but I didn't know why.

My legs felt heavy as I turned into the lane home. I quickly wiped away a few more tears away because I didn't want to make Mother sadder. As I got nearer to the house I could see a car parked out the front. I didn't know who it belonged to; there were not many people in the village who owned a car. At least wandering about the vehicle had taken my mind off Granny. The thought of going into the bleakness of my home made my pace slower still until I could not put it off any longer. Pushing open the door I shouted:

'I'm here Mother; Miss Rushmore said I had to go home.'

I dropped my satchel onto the floor as I pushed open the front room door, expecting to see Mother sitting in the armchair looking at nothing. Instead I got the best surprise ever. Sitting on the sofa was Auntie Violet and uncle Len with my eight year old cousin Lennie sat in between them. Sitting on the floor were Hester and Daisy, the older two children of the family. All at once the gloom seemed to lift from the room. The window was open and the room smelt much nicer although the curtains were still half drawn.

Hester and Daisy jumped up and rushed over and we all hugged together. Auntie Violet got up from the couch and joined the snuggling and I felt like a weight I had been carrying for days had been lifted off my shoulders.

Auntie Violet and the rest of the family lived in Bristol. During the war Hester and Violet lived with us because it was too dangerous for them to stay at home due to all the bombs dropping. I was too young to remember but I knew that Mother was very close to them because of that. Uncle Len is my father's brother and when we didn't get a chance to visit them, they came over to Ireland to see us instead. We also wrote to each other every week.

Hester, Daisy and Lennie were like the brothers and sisters I didn't have but had always wanted. I was only eighteen months younger than Daisy but I was much smaller, more similar in size to Lennie. Lennie liked this because he always felt like the baby of the family. At fourteen, Hester was four years older than me but sometimes, I thought, she treated me like I was only about five.

Now that the house was full of people and busyness I could almost forget Granny had died. I decided to put it in a little pocket in my mind so I wouldn't feel sad all the time. Today though, it was my father and Granny's funerals. I felt nothing but relief when Mother said none of us children were going.

Hester was taking care of us all while the grown-ups went to say goodbye to my father and Granny. When the big black cars arrived I felt like running up to my bedroom but I followed Mother outside instead. She was dressed all in black and her face was still very pale. The whiteness made her eyes look very big and I could tell that she had been crying again because they were pink around the edges.

I cuddled Mother as tightly as I could and she patted my head but I knew that she wasn't really thinking about me. Hester had her arm around my shoulder as we all watched the hearses disappear out of sight followed by uncles Lens car. Hester pushed us all inside and got a pack of cards from the drawer so we could have a game of 'Snap.'

Lennie declared he wanted to play outside with his football

and Hester allowed this after she made him promise to stay near to the front of the house so she could watch him through the window. The card game was fun, at first, but suddenly the image of my father hanging came into my head.

It felt like I could hear the sound of the creaky bannister again but I knew I couldn't really. I remembered Granny's kind, watery blue eyes but then they turned cold and dead. I didn't realise I was crying until Hester and Daisy put their cards down and sat either side of me:

'I was thinking of Granny,' I told them, 'I want to remember her living face but I keep seeing her dead face,' I explained.

Hester looked thoughtful for a minute then she said:

'Why don't you try and remember the last time you and your grandma had fun together?' she suggested.

I tried to think but a lot of the time I spent with Granny was after my father had had one of his turns and I was usually upset. Then it came to me. I always thought it was really funny when Granny would get down on her knees, for no reason I could think of. She would start chanting to holy Mary, Mother of God while clinging to some beads she told me were rosary beads. I had rarely set foot in a church in my whole life and I always thought going to church was a strange thing to do. I told Hester and Daisy and they said they had also seen her do it then Daisy said:

'I remember when we visited last Christmas, I washed my hair and grandma was scrubbing it so hard with the towel to dry it I thought she would pull my head off,' she rubbed her head at the thought of it.

We talked a lot about Granny and my father too. The tears began to fall again as all three of us remembered the best times we had with Granny. About half an hour later, Lennie suddenly barged through the door, demanding a drink, breaking into our reflections. He stopped in his tracks when he saw all of us crying then stood and looked for a minute before saying:

'Only girls cry because they're cissy, boys are stronger so they never cry.'

Daisy threw a cushion at him that caught him on the side of the head. He ran back outside followed by the three of us, intent on starting a play fight with him. As we stepped out into the late afternoon, the sun was still very warm. Our shadows were long and stretchy as we play hopscotch on the pavement. I remember quite clearly that I forgot, for a while about the sadness that crept up on me when I least expected it, and enjoyed playing outside with my three cousins.

9

Three days after my father and Granny's funerals, my mother gave me some good news. She told me that when Auntie Violet and Uncle Len left, we were going with them. We were going to leave Ireland and go to live in Bristol. First of all we would live with Violet and Len then Mother would buy a place for the two of us when our house, in Ireland, had been sold.

My mother told me I would be going to the same school as Hester and Daisy and we would be living very close to them. I couldn't wait to leave the dark shadows of Ireland behind. I would miss my granny forever and would try and remember my father when he was being kind but I longed for a normal life and moving to Bristol meant I may actually get one.

First though, Mother told me her friend, Susan, had invited us to go and stay with them on her farm in Cornwall. I had always loved animals, for as long as I could remember, but I was never allowed a pet. I think Mother thought my father might hurt it when he was having one of his 'outbursts.' The thought of spending a week surrounded by all the farm creatures made me feel so excited I whooped when Mother told me.

Mother explained to me she had known Susan since before I was born. Susan lived on the farm with her husband, Edward and her children, Iris, Johnnie and Jack. She had an older daughter, Edith, who was married to a Canadian called William

Fleming and they had five children of their own.

Mother told me Johnnie was only a year or so older than me so I would have a friend to play with and Jack was a bit younger than me. I would have loved to have been part of such a big family and was really glad I would get to meet them all. Hester, Daisy and Lennie were really jealous when I told them but I promised I would write and tell them all about it. This made them feel a little happier.

The darkness that seemed to suffocate me at times was now lifting and all I could see ahead was fun and laughter. I was just ten. I said a very special thank-you to Granny's God, that night, for making me feel happy again.

10

Mother and I moved into a lovely flat in Clifton, Bristol six month after my father died. All though I adored my cousins, I was happy to be out of their overcrowded house. I loved the enormous view of Clifton Gorge and Downs and I enjoyed visiting the bustling city, of Bristol, that never seemed to sleep. The view at the front of our apartment looked out far beyond the gorge itself. It reminded me of a massive, green carpet of flowers and trees.

Luckily, our cottage in Ireland didn't take long to sell. I much preferred living in Bristol. The time passed quickly and soon I found myself sixteen years old. I enjoyed living with my mother and was relieved that the cloud of uncertainty that hung over us was gone. It was so different from my early years in Ireland, when my father could explode at any moment, for no apparent reason. I thanked God every day for sending us there.

Our home in Clifton had large windows that allowed swathes of light in which made the whole place airy and bright. I liked this so much more that the dingy cottage we used to live in Ireland. There, the small windows blocked out the sun and made the whole place feel like a cave, with the low ceilings and thick walls. The cottage reminded me of a frightening time in my young life I wanted to forget about. I rarely thought about Granny Greta or my father anymore. They no longer played a part in my new, normal life.

Mother had a friend, he was a lovely man called Desmond Masters who had become an important part of our lives. He was a tall, slim man with sandy-coloured, tousled hair that he was forever running his hands through; his gold-rimmed glasses were always perched on the end of his nose and he liked to wear brown corduroy trousers and gaudy tank tops. He was so kind and helpful to me and Mother that I'm not sure what we would have done without him.

When I was younger he would often take me and Mother to the cinema or out for a meal. I always enjoyed the happy, carefree outings. As I grew older, it was just the two of them that went out. When I turned sixteen I felt like they should have some time alone without me being a 'third wheel,' although I really missed going out with them.

It had been about six months since my birthday and an even more important day happened: I left school. Both Daisy and Hester left at the same age but they immediately began working in one of the many vast factories in the city, I went to a local typing college. Mother had to practically drag me there because I was quite sure I was not good enough to gain a place, but I did, and I loved every minute of it. We were celebrating because I was now a fully-fledged shorthand typist. I could touch type brilliantly and found shorthand the easiest thing ever.

A day or two before, I had received good news. I had found out, after a nerve-wracking interview, I had got a job in the office of Parkins Metals. It was a Saturday and I started my new job on Monday. Although I was proud of myself I was also terrified when I thought about my new job.

I was so painfully shy; the thought of meeting new people scared me. Mostly, I just wanted to hide away from everyone except Mother and Desmond but I never wanted to disappoint them, so I tried to do whatever made my mother happy. If I could have foreseen what would happen, through working at Parkins Metals, I would have begged my mother to let me work in a factory like Hester and Daisy did.

Desmond and the Rosental family were all invited. Hester, Daisy and I had become almost as close as sisters over the years. But I came to realise, deep inside, I had never felt good enough to be allowed to spend time with my bubbly, confident cousins. I was always grateful to them for giving me their time and company.

The three of us often visited the local dance hall at the weekends. Hester and Daisy were rarely short of admirers and were always being asked to dance. I preferred to spend the evening in a dark corner, hiding away while tapping my feet to the music. I was happy to sip away at my lemonade while my cousins drank their sophisticated gin and tonics. I didn't like the taste of gin.

On the occasional times someone did ask me to dance, I would always say no, simply because I didn't know how to. I would watch all the giggling people spin and gyrate around the dance-floor without, seemingly, a care in the world. It enthralled me. However, no amount of cajoling and begging from Hester and Daisy would get me onto the dance-floor so in the end they always gave up and left me to my lemonade.

Auntie Violet, uncle Len and the rest of the family arrived at seven on the dot. I heard the knock on the door from my bedroom where I was brushing my hair and I rushed into the lounge to greet them. I wanted to instantly hurry back out again when they all started to hug me and congratulate me on my job. I knew my face was now a shiny pink colour and

I was very glad when Desmond walked in and the attention switched to him.

As everyone chatted I looked at my cousins, I noticed they now both had shorter haircuts with fluffy kiss curls. Their lips were painted with bright purple-red lipstick. They wore the latest fashions, bright patterned dresses nipped in their waists to show off their long slim legs. I felt decidedly dowdy in comparison.

Hester and Daisy broke away from the adults and walked over to me. They started to tell me about the latest Elvis Presley and Jerry Lee Lewis records. They couldn't stop raving about the new 'rock and roll bands', I'd never heard any of their songs but wished I had, Mother preferred classical music so I supposed I did too.

I enjoyed listening to their giggly conversation and soon found myself laughing along with them. A small time later, we all congregated in the small dining room where we all jostled for a space at the table. The room was fairly small but nobody seemed to notice how squashed up we all were.

About an hour into the meal, a slightly tipsy Lenny junior stood up and tapped his wine glass with his fork. Gradually, we all stop eating and talking and looked up at him. With obvious pride in his voice, he announced he had decided to follow in his father's footsteps and had joined the merchant navy.

The unexpected news called for lots of pats on the back and hugs from us all, especially from his extremely delighted parents. I too, was so happy for Lennie. He had grown from a scrawny little boy into a big, strong, muscly man and I was sure that life in the navy would suit him very well.

The guests left at around eleven o'clock. The dishes stayed

unwashed in the sink as we headed off to bed, feeling exhausted but happy we had all had such an enjoyable evening. In the future I would come to realise how much I would miss these happy, carefree times. Most of all I would mourn the loss of the little close-knit family we had all become but wouldn't be ever again.

11

I was taking the small journey to Parkins Metals; the building was situated in Filton, heading out of Bristol. It felt like a million butterflies were dancing around in my stomach as I sat on the top deck of the bus taking me to my new job. As the vehicle lurched to a stop opposite Parkins Metals, I pulled myself reluctantly from my seat and walked down the steep steps. Taking a deep breath, I jumped off the bus and headed towards the small building.

Hesitantly, I pushed open the door, wishing I was anywhere in the world apart from this place right now. Inside, the first thing I saw was a narrow stairway and a closed door to the left of me. On the right was a small hatch with a sign saying 'reception' above it.

I peered into the small opening. A middle-aged lady was sitting hunched over her typewriter, so deeply engrossed in what she was doing she didn't notice me. I bit into my bottom lip as I tried to think of what to do next. It seemed rude to startle the woman or interrupt her work so I continued to stand and wait; still chewing nervously on my lip, I really hoped she would realise I was there soon.

Noisily and without warning the outside door was thrown open and two men entered, chatting loudly to each other. One was a middle aged man with a bulging stomach and grey hair, cut into a style that was meant to hide his bald head. He was smartly dressed in a suit and tie. He was accompanied by a much younger man whom, I was in no doubt, was his son.

The other man looked like a younger carbon copy of the older man. Their similarities were quite striking; they had the same mannerisms, the same stance and obviously shared the same tailor. They both stopped talking when they noticed me hovering in front of them, the older of the two then walked towards me:

'How can we help you madam?' He boomed in a voice so loud, it seemed to reverberate around the walls.

'I'm Jane Rosental, I've come to start my new job.' I said. I wanted to sound confident but I couldn't disguise the slight tremor in my voice and I inwardly cursed my shyness.

The man leant forward and offered me his outstretched hand. I held mine out and the big bear-like paw enveloped my whole hand:

'Charles Parkin, proprietor of Parkins Metals, pleased to make your acquaintance, Jane,'

As he was talked he swung around and banged loudly on the counter inside the hatch. He then proceeded to bellow at the poor lady. I cringed inside and out and wished that the ground would swallow me up as I watched the woman jump, almost out of her skin. Immediately, she rushed towards the hatch, lifted the counter and gestured for me to come in while apologising to the man at the same time. I scuttled past Charles Parkin and thanked him. Once the hatch was securely closed the woman turned and introduced herself as Miss Selby.

She had short, greying hair that fell unflatteringly around her long face. Her blue eyes looked at me kindly and I smiled back at her. There were two desks slotted into the small office, she pulled out the chair of the vacant one and motioned for me to sit. As I did this I told how sorry I was that she had been shouted at; she assured me it didn't matter and Mr Parkin's bark was much worse than his bite. I didn't believe her because she couldn't look me in the eyes as she said it.

I made sure I gave her my full attention when she began to tell me what work I was expected to do. I noticed she was not wearing a wedding ring so assumed she was unmarried. I guessed her age at around fifty but couldn't really be sure. Once Miss Selby had finished explaining, and was certain I understood what I had to do, she seemed happy to let me get on with it. After a couple of hours working at Parkins Metals I felt as if I had been working there for years.

I was surprised at how quickly the time passed in a whirl of typing letters and invoices, answering the telephone and attending to anyone who appeared at the hatch to pay a bill or order some goods. At midday, Miss Selby instructed me to take my lunch-break adding she would take hers when I got back so the office would not be left unattended.

I thanked her and asked if there was anything I could get her while I was out. She smiled, obviously pleased I had asked her, and assured me she had everything she needed. Donning my cardigan and picking up my bag I headed out of the building.

It was a beautiful May Day. The blazing sun was like a huge golden globe and was high in the cloudless sky. The scorching rays sent me searching for a spot in the shade.

I decided it was far too pleasant a day to sit inside. I found a bench underneath a large oak tree that shielded me from some of the heat. Once I had eaten the sandwiches that my mother had made, I closed my eyes and turned my face upwards towards the warmth of the sun.

I loved the light blue cotton dress I was wearing, it was my very favourite. The material was very cooling and Mother said the cut of it suited my figure and brought out the blue colour of my eyes. Hester had now cut my dark blonde hair into a stylish 'bob' that curled underneath my chin. I protested at first, exclaiming the style wouldn't look any good on me but when Daisy gave me the hand held mirror, I peered in and had to admit she was right. Daisy said it framed my face prettily.

Hester was always lamenting that I was blessed with the clearest of complexions and that my skin was like porcelain but I knew she was just being kind. All I could see when I looked at my reflection was a snub nose and full lips that made my cheeks dimple when I smiled. I wasn't exactly unhappy with how I looked. But I put most of that down to Hester and Daisy's forceful style tips and unending encouragement to make me try the new fashions and trends.

With my head resting backwards, I felt relaxed and comfortable as the sun's rays caressed my face and shoulders. Suddenly, something blocked out the light. Then the bench moved and I felt the weight of someone plonk down beside me. Instantly alarmed, I opened my eyes and felt my body stiffen, though I didn't know why, maybe it was a premonition? I wish I'd heeded it. If I had known what was to come, I would have run away as fast as my legs would carry me and never looked back.

The person next to me was sitting far to close, in my opinion, and I felt unsure and uncomfortable. I looked blankly at the smiling face of the man next to me. Realising that I had no idea who he was, he frowned fleetingly before he grinned even wider then introduced himself as Travis Parkin:

'You met me and Pops this morning, remember?'

'Oh, of course, I'm Jane Rosental, Mr Parkin, I'm very pleased to meet you,' I muttered, he smiled warmly and had the most beautiful blue eyes I had ever seen.

'Call me Travis, Janie,' He insisted, as he moved in so closely that our faces were almost touching. No one had called me Janie since my father died and I liked hearing it.

I looked into the mesmerising eyes, flecked with tiny silver specks and the seemingly ever-smiling mouth. Travis was very smartly dressed and seemed very confident in his own skin.

I knew his suit was from Louis Vuitton because I saw the label when Travis pulled back his lapel and asked me what I thought of it. His crisp white shirt was immaculately pressed and his blue tie was obviously made from silk. His raven black hair was slicked back with Brylcream. Travis had it combed back over his head where it came to a peak at the back of his neck. I remember thinking his aftershave smelt nice, a kind of a spicy aroma that wafted around us both.

Travis began to talk about the business and how far it had come in a short time. He told me he put this down to him being his father's 'right-hand-man' and how he, Travis, had dragged the business into the twentieth century. He often used his hands to express what he was saying and winked for no apparent reason. Out of the blue he said:

'Come to the flicks with me this Friday, Janie, I'll show you a good time.' He winked again as he said this and puts his hand over mine. I looked into his face and smiled shyly.

I thanked him but said I couldn't. I wasn't really sure why this obviously handsome, man-about-town wanted to take me out. I looked down at the ground shyly:

'I'm not taking no for an answer, I'll pick you up at yours on Friday,' he said, with a knowing grin plastered across his face.

'How do you know where I live,' I asked

'I'm management babe, see ya Friday.'

'Oh, alright, see you on Friday, Mr Parkin... Travis.'

As he sauntered away with his hands pushed deeply into his pockets, he glanced back at me and smiled a smile that lit up his whole face. At that point, I have to admit, I thought he was the most handsome man in the world.

12

My first week working at Parkins went much more quickly than I'd expected, I found the work varied and interesting and I enjoyed the responsibility I'd been given, it made me feel very grown-up. It was Friday before I knew it. When I told my mother about Travis's invitation she was really pleased. I guessed she liked the thought of me going on a date. She told me that it would help me come out of my shell. I felt quite all right in there but, being the type of person who went out of her way to ensure everyone around me was happy, I wanted Mother to be pleased and Travis was very handsome.

I was in my bedroom when I heard the doorbell ring, Travis was ten minutes early. As I started walking towards the front room I could hear Travis telling Mother about Parkins Metals. I thought it lovely that he was so proud of the family business.

I was wearing a cream skirt that rested just above my knees which I thought was too short but Hester and Daisy insisted that it was the latest fashion and that I looked 'fab.' When Mother had called and proudly told Auntie Violet that I was going on a date, Violet had then passed the news onto her daughters who insisted they come shopping with me to ensure I wore the right outfit. I was also wearing a matching blazer and low heeled shoes as I knew Travis was not much taller than me.

I clutched my navy coloured handbag tightly as I walked into the lounge. I blushed to the roots of my hair when Travis wolf-whistled loudly. He then walked towards me, said 'may I' and linked my hand into his arm. Mother kissed my cheek and told us to have a good time and not to be too late home:

'I won't keep her out too late, Mrs Rosental,' Travis promised as we left the apartment.

'Please, call me Lucy,' my mother gushed, obviously as taken with Travis as I was myself.

Down on the street Travis led me to a red Jaguar E Type Roadster parked a little way up from the flat. The car was like nothing I had seen before and I itched to get inside.

'What do you think of this little baby?' Travis drawled as he ran his hand over the shiny paint work of his car.

'I think it's beautiful.' I said, unable to hide my admiration.

Travis smiled at me and it felt like a thousand butterflies fluttered in my stomach. The car was a convertible and Travis climbed in and pushed the hood back. He then came around to the passenger side, opened the door and gestured for me to climb in. Once he was seated, Travis turned the key in the ignition and the car seemed to roar into life. He then expertly manoeuvred the vehicle out of its tight parking space. The engine noise grew louder as Travis sped up. A warm wind blew gently around my face, I found it oddly comforting.

As I looked around I could see that the car was getting a lot of admiring glances. I felt a little proud to be the occupant of such an interesting vehicle and smiled timidly at Travis who turned to me and grinned back. We arrived at the cinema a short time later. I stood and wait patiently as Travis took at least five minutes to secure his vehicle then I followed him into the cinema.

Travis paid for the tickets and bought a small box of

chocolates. I then followed behind him as we walked into the screening room. An usherette waved her torch at us and then guided us to where we were sitting. The smell of the well-worn seats brought back happy memories of the many times Mother, Desmond and I had come here to watch a Saturday afternoon matinee. Travis opened the box and offered me a chocolate, we then settled back to watch the film. I snuck a sideways glance at Travis; he obviously noticed because he turned and winked. I giggled and blushed once again.

I had no idea what we were watching but hoped that it will be a comedy or a romance. When the titles appeared on the screen and announced that we were watching *The Curse of the Werewolf* with Clifford Evans and Oliver Reed, I was horrified but tried to hide it. This was because I thought Travis had been kind enough to bring me here so I mustn't be ungrateful. After a while Travis seemed to notice my discomfort and apologised. He insisted we leave. I felt rude and ungrateful but Travis shushed me as we walked back to the car.

Thankfully he kept the roof of the car closed as he drove the short journey back to my flat. I waited in case Travis was going to get out and open the door for me. Instead, he leant over to me and brushed his lips against mine. The soft warmth of them stirred something deep inside; that I didn't even know existed. Travis then gently put his hand on my leg and began to slide it up my skirt. The warmth of his hand on my leg felt wonderful but as he began to push it further up my skirt I realised that I should not be allowing this.

I placed my hand on his. He pulled his hand back and kissed me once more. He then climbed out of the car and opened the door for me. I waved and he watched until I was safely inside the door. My mother had waited up and wanted to know how the evening went. I told her that it was lovely. I then yawned widely and headed off to bed.

As I lay pondering over the evening, I wondered if I should have let Travis put his hand up my skirt. Hester and Daisy were constantly talking about 'how far' they'd go with this boyfriend or that one but I just didn't feel sure. My lips still tingled deliciously when I recalled our kiss. I couldn't wait to see him again but was sure that he wouldn't ask me. I drifted off sleep and dreamt that a werewolf was trying to put his claws up my skirt. The werewolf then turned into Travis and I felt his soft lips on mine once more.

13

The following Friday, I sat at my desk and began to type an important letter for Mr Charles Parkin. I was so engrossed in my work that I didn't hear the office door opening and was only aware of Travis's presence when he began to speak. He leaned on the counter, pushed his head in through the hatch and shouted:

'Pick ya up at seven, Janie.' He then clicked his tongue, pointed towards me and winked.

Before I could answer, he was gone. The few words he had spoken seemed to light something up inside me. My heart started to pound with excitement and I immediately started planning what I was going to wear. I turned to see Miss Selby looking at me, worriedly and frowning ever so slightly. It seemed like she was going to say something but, if she was, she must have changed her mind because she looked down at her work instead.

I sat dreamily at my desk, looking forward to my next kiss from Travis. I knew my mother would be pleased that I was going on another date with Travis. She was always telling me that I needed to get out more with people the same age as me. She used to say that I was too eager to please everyone and that I should think more about pleasing myself. I was just happy if everyone around me was, life seemed easier that way.

The day seemed to drag by because all I could think about

was my date with Travis that evening. As soon as was politely possible I left the office and flew home to get ready. I remember feeling quite pleased with my reflection in the mirror. I walked out of the flat and down the stairs to meet Travis when I heard his car horn honking below. On the drive to the cinema, I again, enjoyed all the attention his flashy car received; I wondered if I'd ever own a car as nice as this but thought I probably wouldn't.

Once inside the cinema, Travis and I were standing in the foyer waiting for the film to begin when a door burst open and I heard the unmistakeable laughter of Daisy and Hester. Spotting them through the crowd, I raced over and we all began speak at once. Travis appeared at my side and I started to introduce him to Hester and Daisy. He smiled but the smile didn't seem to meet his eyes. He then merely inclined his head the tiniest bit at Daisy and Hester. They were also doing their best to smile back at Travis but they looked more like they were smirking instead.

I shuffled my feet nervously in the awkward silence, not knowing what to do or say, thankfully, right on cue, the usherette appeared and announced that the film was about to begin. I said a hasty goodbyes to my cousins as Travis bustled me towards the screen room. Once we were seated Travis turned to me and said:

'I'm surprised that you're related to those two girls: you're a lot classier than them.' He smiled and winked at me and I melted inside. I know that it was not a nice thing to say about my cousins but I loved the fact he thought that I was classy.

The film this week was much better. It was a silly, slapstick comedy that I really enjoyed it, I laughed loudly throughout. I was a little puzzled about Travis's attitude towards Hester and Daisy but thought maybe it was just a personality conflict. Travis laughed throughout the film and when he put his arm around my shoulder, I snuggled against the warmth of his body.

When the film finished and we were walking towards the car I remember feeling quite tired and wanting to get home. Travis had other ideas. He suggested that we go to the Flamingo, which was the local dance hall. I explained to him that I didn't like dancing and that I was quite tired. Travis insisted that we would have a great time, when he leaned in a kissed me, passionately, on the lips I started to falter in my decision. The kiss ignited feelings inside me that I had never felt before.

'Relax Janie, we'll give it half an hour and then if you want to go home I'll drive you, what do you say?'

He smiled reassuringly and I relented and smiled back at him. As we I sat in the car, speeding through the town, a reckless wild excitement engulfed as it had never done before. All of a sudden I didn't want to be mousey, dull Jane; I wanted to be exciting and wild. Travis parked his precious car in an isolated spot on the edge of the car park so it would not be marked by any of the other vehicles in the car park. He held my hand tightly as we walked towards the building and I loved the feeling of my hand in his.

Pushing open the heavy doors, he ushered me in. I was instantly deafened by the loud music being played by a local rock and roll band at the far end of the room. The place was jam packed with men and women gyrating around the dance floor.

We both had to shout above the noise so we could hear what we were saying; he asked me what I wanted to drink. Travis nodded when I asked for lemonade. While he was getting the drinks I watched the dancers as they jived and boogied around the room and I wandered where they got their energy from. I had to admit though that the music was very good and soon I was tapping my toes to the rhythm.

I was feeling fairly thirsty by the time Travis came back with the drinks; I think this was to do with the heat of the room and the fact that so many people were all squashed into one tiny space. As I drank my lemonade ,Travis leaned in close and pulled a small bottle of vodka from his inside of his jacket pocket. He poured a glug into his own lemonade and held it towards mine. I don't know what came over me but I immediately nodded and we giggled together as he put a generous amount in my drink.

The drink tasted a little bitter but not entirely unpleasant. After four or five drinks, I was longing to dance. I was feeling very bold and a little drunk and to my utter surprise, I turned to Travis and asked if he would like to dance with me. He grinned and nodded. His beautiful eyes seemed a brighter blue than usual and I longed to feel his soft lips on mine.

The music sounded really great and I started dancing to the beat. The vodka hit the spot and I felt like I was the best dancer in the world. I twirled around and around. Every time I stumbled or tripped Travis was on hand to catch me, he was being a proper gentleman and I was very impressed with his behaviour.

As we carried on dancing, I began to fall all over the place and found it hilarious, as did Travis. Each new song seemed to excite me even more and I whooped and clapped every time a new one started. I felt euphoric, like I was the happiest person in the whole world.

No longer shy, I chatted to my fellow dancers and complimented them on their hairstyles and clothing like they were old friends. I talked to them animatedly about my job and introduced them to my 'boyfriend' Travis, who seemed to be finding everything really funny, I didn't know what he was chortling at but I laughed along with him anyway. After an age Travis finally managed to drag me off the dance floor and back to our table. I was breathless and flushed by my exertions but also exhilarated.

Travis ordered me to 'stay put' while he fetched more drinks. I sat bolt upright and saluted him while shouting 'yes sir' then I collapsed into a fit of giggles at my own humour. I watched as the revellers whirled around in a haze of colour and noise. My ears began to ring and the music started to turn into a loud burring sound, until I could no longer make out what tune was playing. In front of my eyes the dancers began to merge into one and then became a psychedelic blob of nothingness. My throat was dry as I waited for Travis to return with the drinks.

When he came back, I told him that I felt a little strange. Travis laughed and told me not to spread it around or I'd end up in the 'funny farm'; this brought on a new spasm of loud, exaggerated laughter from me at which point Travis said we should leave. I protested loudly, saying that I was having the best time ever but Travis insisted that my mother would worry if I was too late. I reluctantly agreed and gulped back the remainder of my drink.

As I stood to leave, the floor seemed to slant to one side, pulling me down with it; thankfully Travis was on hand to catch me once again. He hooked one arm around my waist and half carried me across the room. He held my coat and bag in his other hand. Just as we reached the exit doors, they swung open and Hester and Daisy walked in with a large group of people.

I heard Travis curse under his breath but didn't know why. I screamed with joy and yelled my cousin's names. The whole group heard me, even above the din of the music. I couldn't express how wonderful it was to see them again. Hester and Daisy both look startled as I pulled them into my arms and kissed their cheeks.

As I tried to steady myself I could see Hester looking suspiciously at Travis as he glared back at her. I stepped in immediately and told them all to stop that nonsense. I tried to say that we were all friends but the words didn't seem to come out right. I heard Travis say that he was taking me home before I made fool of myself.

Hester, Daisy and Travis began talking among themselves but I couldn't make out what they were saying so I just stood there with a lop-sided grin plastered across my face. After a while I began to get annoyed, I turned to my cousins and yelled:

'So what if I've had a drink, it's not the end of the bloody world, is it?'

I pushed my face close to theirs as I finished my slurring sentence. The look on the faces Hester and Daisy was one of incredulity and they stood aside, open mouthed, as Travis started propelling me towards the door. I clumsily turned and began blowing theatrical kisses in Hester and Daisy's general direction as they stood and watched us leave.

Outside, as soon as the fresh air hit me, I felt horribly queasy. I looked on in amazement as the car-park turned into a fun fair and all the cars were spinning around in the air. I attempted to walk but I couldn't feel my feet, I guessed that I must be floating. From out of nowhere I felt Travis begin to kiss me and I kissed him back, hungrily while running my fingers through his hair and stroking his neck.

The next minute, with no recollection of how, I found myself lying on a mixture of grass and gravel. I felt the roughness of it through my dress. I became vaguely aware that someone was tugging at my pants and I thought this is very rude but at the same time I wanted to giggle at the naughtiness.

I began to feel even more nauseous and tried to swallow the sickness back into my throat. As I struggled to control the biliousness I felt something small inside me down below. I tried to pull my legs together but I couldn't. I screamed loudly as I felt something large pushing inside me. The pain was almost unbearable, as though my body was being torn apart.

I felt horribly sick and I could hear grunting noises. My body was being forced into a rocking movement. The swaying motion was making me feel even more unwell. I fought to stop myself from actually vomiting, gulping in the fresh air to quell the sickness that was trying to overwhelm me. All the time something was thrusting deeper inside me, hurting me. Thankfully and abruptly it stopped.

14

I could feel that I was moving but I wasn't sure how. There was nothing in my brain but haziness. I pushed my fists into my eyes and rubbed them hard to try and clear the fog. I was surprised to find my face wet and there were tears running down my cheeks.

I realised that I was in the back of a vehicle. I felt very sore down below and I was sure there was a kind of stickiness between my legs. I could see my handbag and coat on the seat beside me. There was a man in the front of the vehicle. He turned his head around to look at me. Squinting blearily, I could see that he had a kind face with worried eyes.

When we stopped moving the man got out of the car. It seemed as though, he was almost instantly at my side, opening the door. He leaned in and told me that I was home. I wanted to say thank you but when I opened my mouth, my lips seem to loll to one side and an indecipherable sound came out. I felt embarrassed. I really couldn't work out what was the matter with me.

I knew the man was concerned when he leant further into the car and tried to help me out. I struggled to focus on him as I felt the cold air on my face but he seemed to be swaying from side to side in front of me. I didn't realise that I was the one who was swaying.

He pulled me into a standing position then collected my

things from the back seat. I couldn't feel my legs. I hung onto the car for support. For a minute I felt like laughing but the feeling instantly vanished when I felt myself falling. I hit the cold concrete pavement but it didn't hurt. In fact, I thought it would be better all-round if I just stayed where I was.

From what seemed a very long distance away I heard a familiar voice calling my name. I knew that he was a friend but I was not capable of answering him; then I was being lifted from the ground as though I weighed no more than a feather. The taxi driver and the man talked briefly but I couldn't make out what they were saying.

I rested my head against the softness of a woollen garment. I became aware of movement and I tried to look into the face of the person holding me. To my untold relief, I realised it was Desmond and I was overwhelmed with joy. I snuggled in close into his warmth. I heard the lift doors in the building opening and closing and wondered why we are not using the stairs like we always did. A few minutes later, Desmond was banging on the door and shouting for Mother. I knew that I was home because I could smell my mother's scent.

I woke up and was lying in my bed, wearing my soft, warm winceyette nightdress, with no recollection of how I got there. I could make out the blurred image of my mother asleep in the chair by my bed. I called out her name and she awoke instantly. She knelt down beside my bed. I could see that she was very upset because tears were rolling down her cheeks and she was trying to stop them. I didn't want her to be upset and I tried to brush away her tears but my hand would not work.

She reached onto the bedside table then lifted my head up. I tried to drink some of the water that she offered me but it made me sick. Mother cleaned me up. For some inexplicable reason, I started to sob, I couldn't stop. The loud shuddering screeches seemed to be coming from someone else but I knew that it was me making the dreadful noise. I later learned that was what alcohol did to me; it made me maudlin and turned me into an overemotional mess.

Even though the curtains were drawn, when I opened my eyes, the dim light still stung them. I looked down on the floor beside me and there was an empty bowl, I didn't know why. My head was pounding and I felt like I would die from the agony. I thought I must be very ill, the flu maybe? I couldn't stop my hands from shaking.

My mouth was so dry it felt as though my tongue had been replaced by sandpaper. Closing my eyes I tried to recall the previous evening with Travis. I remembered seeing Hester and Daisy and then trying to watch the film. Then Travis was driving us to the dance hall. Following that, there was nothing, just a massive black hole in my memory.

Suddenly, I started to feel frightened for no apparent reason. It reminded me of my father, how I felt when he was having one of his fits of anxiety but why was I frightened now? A sudden image appeared in my mind, I was dancing and chatting but I had no idea who I was chatting to. The picture in my mind disappeared as quickly as it came.

Mother knocked and came in. She was looking better now and I tried to smile, I didn't want her to cry again. Was she crying before? I told her that I was ill and she nodded, I wondered how she could possibly have known that I would wake up unwell.

Mother tried to get me to eat some dry toast and sip a little of the water but I couldn't. Anything that went down my throat made me feel like I wanted to vomit up it again. I told her that I needed to sleep so she took the toast but left the water beside me.

When she had gone I tried, again, to recall my evening but there was nothing in my brain. I looked around my bedroom and saw my skirt and blouse hanging on coat hanger on the outside of my wardrobe door. Thrown into the corner of the room was my underwear. My pants were soiled with dried blood and my suspender belt was torn as was my bra. I made myself go to sleep.

It felt as though I was losing my mind. Unexplained pictures kept popping into my head only to vanish seconds later. It reminded me of the flickering cinema reels I used to watch as a child. Hester and Daisy were standing blocking my way out of the dance hall, I was laughing with them, boom, the image was gone. I remembered feeling something digging into my back. I recalled pain. I called out for Mother; she was beside me almost instantly:

'Can you run me bath please?' I asked urgently, she nodded and walked from the room.

I swung around and sat on the edge of my bed, this small movement made the room spin but I didn't care. For some reason I needed to be in the bath. Mother helped me, as though I was small child again and I wished that I was. The water was very hot and the steam frosted up the mirror. I was glad because I couldn't bear to look at myself. I started to scrub at my body until it was bright red and smarting but I still felt dirty.

I began to understand that no matter how hard I cleaned myself the filthy feeling wouldn't go away. I couldn't believe I had allowed myself to get into such a vulnerable state and make Travis think it was all right for us to have sex, I felt so ashamed of myself and utterly embarrassed when I thought about the whole incident. Mother came in and helped me into my night wear again. She guided me to the sofa and I managed to drink some of the water that she is gave me.

My mother, walked into the kitchen leaving me resting on the sofa. I could see her through kitchen door. She seemed to be trying hard to hide what she was feeling from me. I suddenly remembered Desmond bringing me home last night, my mother was very grateful. I think she had been sitting up waiting for me, I was never home late and she probably thought I had had some kind of accident.

Searching into my mind I recalled that her expression of relief at me being home was soon replaced by one of horror, because I was obviously drunk. Why did I drink vodka? The picture of my underwear, torn and stained, came into mind. I was overcome by a feeling of intense fear that I couldn't make go away, neither did I know why I was feeling that way.

I was engulfed with shame and self-loathing as I recalled myself knocking back glass after glass of vodka and lemonade, what was I thinking of? Why had I put myself to be in a position where I had no control over what was happening to me? My mother was carrying two mugs of tea when she walked back into the lounge. It seemed as though her throat lurched when she saw me and she had to fight to hold back her tears:

'How are you feeling, sweetheart?' my mother enquired as she handed me my tea.

'Quite a bit better now,' I replied. 'I thought I was going down with the flu but hopefully its only one of those twenty

-four-hour bugs.'

I said with the feigned ignorance and I couldn't look her in the eye. Mother lifted up my chin and looked at me:

'Why did you get drunk, Jane, I thought you didn't like alcohol,' the words flew from her mouth like a bullet from a gun.

I looked at her. She continued to glare at me. My eyes filled with tears as I struggled to think of an excuse for my behaviour then I felt angry that she was cross-examining me, I was an adult after all, in my mind at least.

'Mother, I'm allowed to have a drink now and then, stop looking at me accusingly, I drank too much and I got drunk, end of story,' I said, but the words seemed to be coming out of the mouth of some strange person. It didn't sound like me at all.

'Let's hope it is the "end of the story",' Mother said, 'and that there are no consequences. Do you know Desmond carried you in from the taxi because you couldn't walk?'

Another picture came into my head; I was snuggling into Desmond's chest. I felt embarrassed and ashamed. I could hardly remember what had happened. Without warning, tears spilled down my cheeks.

My mother rushed forwards and pulled me into her arms. She stroked me and whispered 'there there,' like she used to when I was a little girl. I clung onto to her and cried until I thought my heart would break. My mother continued to soothe me then I must have fallen into an exhausted sleep.

When I woke sometime later, what my mother had told me a few months previously came into my mind: that twenty-three years beforehand she had become pregnant at the age of sixteen, she was unmarried. Her parents had had my mother late in life so were quite elderly and old fashioned in their views. She explained how they could not hide the disgust; they felt at her, for bringing shame on their family.

Up to that point, my mother had been a spoiled and doted on child. Mother cried when she said feeling of shame still clung to her like a worn-out coat. In Ireland, her parents had sent her to what were known as 'the laundries.' Mother shuddered as she recalled the harsh conduct at the hands of the nuns. She still winced when she told me about inhuman treatment she had received.

Apparently the fallen women were made to work until almost giving birth. While the actual birth was taking place, they would be called vile names and be beaten with any implement to hand if they screamed out. Mother showed me her thigh and said she would never forget the pain of being beaten with a hairbrush and the wire bristles digging into her skin, she still had the scars.

She recalled the three days of agonising pain she suffered when her body felt like it was being pulled inside out as she tried to give birth. When the baby refused to arrive, the nuns finally relented and called an ambulance. The doctors performed a caesarean but my mother's son never took a breath in this world. He had suffocated to death in her womb days earlier. My mother almost died herself. My father rescued her. He hid her in England where her parents would never find her.

I knew physical scars had long since healed but the mental ones were as acute now as they had been all those years ago. My mother still suffered humiliation and pain whenever she thought about that time in her life. She told me she would move heaven and earth to ensure that I would never carry the same stigma that she had and still did; I didn't know why the conversation had come back into my mind at that very moment.

15

I woke the following day to feel the bright sun beam into the room as Mother pulled the curtains back; I was surprised at how well I was feeling. I had expected to be ill for quite a while but I felt a whole lot better. I told Mother that I would like to have lunch at Auntie Violet's house as we always did on Sundays.

This brought a smile to her face. I still felt a little queasy but the fresh air helped. The clear blue sky was calming and comforting as the rays warmed my face. We arrived at Auntie Violet's. Mother knocked on the door then pushed it open. The delicious smell of roasting beef hit our nostrils both at the same time and we turned and grinned at each other, simultaneously expressing our hunger. Once inside, Mother walked towards the kitchen and I took myself upstairs because I knew this was where Hester and Daisy were.

I knew this because I could hear the music belting out of the record player, coming from the direction of their shared bedroom. I gently pushed open the door and both girls looked up and smiled at me. I perched on the edge of one of the single beds while we waited for the record to finish. Hester then turned to me and said:

'You were in a right state on Friday evening, I thought you didn't drink?' she hissed, accusingly, as she plonked herself next to me. I blushed, I had forgotten that I had seen my cousins that evening.

'What do you mean, Hester, I wasn't drunk at the cinema?' I asked.

'I mean you were drunk at the Flamingo' she said, nodding her head.

'OK, I went to the Flamingo and had a few drinks with Travis, so what, he was a proper gentleman and I had a lovely time,' I told my two cousins as they stared intently at me as if they didn't know me anymore.

'A few drinks? As drunk as a skunk, more like,' Daisy retorted as she rolled her eyes. I began to feel annoyed, why did everyone who knew me think that it was OK to have a go at me constantly?

'Big deal, you two drink all the time, why shouldn't I let my hair down now and again?'

'This isn't like you Jane, this isn't you,' Daisy said with a puzzled look on her face.

'Maybe it is me now, maybe I'm tired of being dull as ditch-water, I'm fed up always trying to do what everyone else wants, Travis has made me realise I don't need to let anyone walk all over me.'

I could see by the look on their faces, that my cousins disapproved and weren't entirely sure I meant what I was saying.

'Did you sleep with him?' Hester questioned, out of the blue, as she stood with her arms folded.

'What do you mean?' I said, looking down to the floor to hide my guilty expression.

There was a collective sigh from both my cousins as Hester continued.

'Did you have sex with him?' Daisy demanded.

'Of course I didn't!' I hissed. 'Who do you think I am?' I had no intention of telling my cousins about my drunken incident.

Hester sat on one side of me whilst Daisy took a seat on the other side. They both put a protective arm around my now trembling shoulders,

'When we saw you, Travis was shoving your pants and nylons into your handbag, we reckon he had sex with you whether you remember or not, all we can do now is hope that there are no consequences.' She said fondly now, as she held my hand tightly.

I still stared down at the floor, unsure what to say. The two older girls both hugged me and told me that I must come to them if I was in trouble and that they would help me. I nodded, feeling very ashamed of myself, and thanked them as Daisy offered me her handkerchief for my tears.

A shout from downstairs informed us that dinner was ready and we all headed for the door. Trailing behind, I did my best to try and compose myself. I was minimally comforted by the fact that I couldn't get pregnant when I had sex for the first time. A girl had told me this at typing college and she seemed to know what she was talking about. That eased my anxiety a lot. I remembered my hungry kisses and thrusting myself at Travis. Maybe I had encouraged him and given all the wrong signals. I had to take some of the blame myself. I was drunk.

Monday arrived and I went to work, still not quite feeling fully well. I sat at my desk, I looked up when I heard the familiar growl of Travis's car and peered out of the window to see him manoeuvring it into his space. I told Mrs Selby that I needed the bathroom and left the office. I went out of the door and over to Travis. He smiled and kissed my cheek making me feel as though I had had an electric shock, I looked down at the floor:

'Sorry about Saturday night Travis: I drank too much and made a total fool of myself, I hope I didn't embarrass you,' I said with my eyes firmly fixed to the ground. Travis moved forward and put his finger under my chin then gently lifted up my head. Our faces were very close as he said:

'I had the best night of my life: you're a great girl Janie and you didn't embarrass me one bit: shall we go out again next week?' I felt weary with relief and nodded eagerly.

'On one condition, you do not allow me to drink,' I said as I grinned at him.

'No problem, sweetheart, I'll keep you on the straight and narrow.' He leant down and kissed me then headed into the office. I gave it a couple of minutes before I too went inside. Hearing Travis call me sweetheart made me feel warm all over my body. I could hardly believe that he wanted to go out with me again but was so happy.

As we continued with our Friday dates I steered clear of any alcohol. With each date our kisses and petting became more intense and I longed to give myself to Travis but without the courage that alcohol had given me, I found myself protesting if his sexual advances got more intense than I wanted. I sensed that this annoyed Travis and I always apologised. Something deep inside told me that I needed to be married to have sex. I put my one indiscretion down to excess alcohol and put it out of my head. Travis seemed to understand.

16

By now I was really enjoying my job at Parkins Metals. It had the added bonus of seeing Travis each morning; his cheeky grin would keep me smiling all day. I had been working there for three months and the time had flown by.

It was now the beginning of September and the weather was getting cooler as autumn came upon us. Miss Selby and I had become good friends and often ate our lunch together in the little office while we nattered to each other. Miss Selby had three cats, I learned. She spoke about them like the animals were her replacement children. They had human names, Larry, Gilbert and Celia and if anyone could hear her talking about them I'm sure they would have assumed that they were actually human.

Miss Selby explained to me that they were her reason for getting up in the mornings. She briefly mentioned a lover lost in the war. I sensed she was dreadfully lonely so had invited her to my home several times and she and mother got along very well.

As I walked from the bus stop to home an autumnal wind suddenly howled down the narrow lane. It chilled me to the bone and I longed to be indoors in the warmth. I unlocked the front door, hung up my bag and coat and was about to head for the kitchen, as I usually did. Today however, Mother was standing in the lounge waiting for me. I smiled at her and said that as it was Friday, we could go shopping tomorrow:

'Jane, you're pregnant, aren't you?' she fired at me, without any preamble or warning.

I stopped in my tracks. Any worry or panic I had felt with each missed period, I had pushed into the deepest corner of my mind and carried on as normal. Mother always used to put sanitary wear in the bathroom for me each month; I think she must have noticed I had not been using it.

I had suggested the shopping trip because my clothes were becoming a little too tight. I told myself I should stop eating so many cakes, but really, I rarely ate cake. Suddenly I started to shake violently. I wanted to put my hands over my ears and close my eyes. I knew that that might have worked when I was a child but it wouldn't work now:

'What do I do, Mother? I don't know what to do, how do we make it go away?' I spoke so immaturely, I sounded like a ten-year-old, but I wanted my mother to make everything all right again.

Mother was staring at me so intently that I hung my head in shame. Abruptly, she walked over to me and pushed me back towards the front door. There she handed me my coat and put on her own. Ten minutes later I found myself back on the bus sitting next to Mother.

She didn't utter one word so I kept quiet; I guessed that was what she wanted me to do. Inside I was screaming, please don't stop loving me Mother, I'll do anything but please just love me. I felt sick with worry and my mouth was dry with dread. I asked where were we were going, Mother seemed to know but she didn't answer me.

The bus came to a stop on the opposite side of Bristol to

where we lived. I followed Mother off the bus, running to keep up with because she was walking so fast. Finally, we turned a corner and a sign post said Winterfield Avenue. All the houses in the road were large and detached with wide with sweeping gravel driveways and neatly mown lawns surrounding them.

Mother pulled a crumpled bit of paper from her pocket and read it. She then opened the gate of number five and pushed me in through it. We reached a brightly painted red front door with panes of patterned glass either side. Mother tugged on a bell pull and we waited until the door was eventually opened.

A chubby, middle-aged lady wearing an old fashioned black and white servant's uniform opened the door and asked us what our business was. I almost collapsed onto the floor when Mother said that we had come to see Mr and Mrs Parkin. I gazed at her with absolute horror but she looked straight ahead as we were instructed to wait a moment. I grabbed Mother's arm and asked her what she was doing, she shrugged me off and, again ignored me.

A few minutes later the lady returned and ushered us in. We walked into a spacious foyer; the carpet was so thick that my feet felt as though they were being absorbed into it. The first thing I saw was a sweeping staircase, straight ahead of me, with white ornate bannisters that followed it around the corner and out of sight.

We stood, awkwardly waiting until we were summoned into a door to the right of the stairs. It led into an opulent and massive sitting room. There was a grand piano in one corner and lusciously thick, velvet drapes hanging on each side of the windows which looked out onto the driveway.

Bright rays of light shone around the room like laser beams.

On either side of the fire place were two large sofas. They were dark red velvet and the flocked wall paper had the same colour in the pattern. The whole room shouted of decadence and, if it were not for the circumstances, I would have loved to have explored its beauty and style.

A lady sitting on one of the sofas rose and indicated that she wanted us to sit down. Mother was nervous, I could tell because her chest was all blotchy and she was breathing through her nose. The lady sat opposite us:

'I am Violet Parkin, how can I help you?' she enquired, with a nasal twang that sounded a little false.

Violet Parkin obviously spent a lot of time and money on her appearance. Her perfectly coffered hair was stiffly lacquered into place. Her round face was heavily but stylishly made up. She wore an impeccably matched light blue pencil skirt that was complimented by a lemon coloured, loose fitting blouse and pale yellow court shoes. She was obviously overweight and the bulge around her stomach was cleverly concealed by the cut of her skirt. Mother shuffled on the sofa then looked directly into Violet Parkins eyes:

'My daughter is pregnant and your son, Travis, is the father,' she said assertively.

Violet Parkin showed no emotion as she looked my mother directly in the eye:

'How can you be sure my son has fathered this baby?' she asked, looking at me as though it was hardly a possibility.

'My daughter, Jane, is sixteen years old and has only had one boyfriend, your son, and I am in no doubt whatsoever that he is the father of this child, your grandchild,' she added with an air of authority in her voice that I had never heard before.

Mrs Parkin seemed to ponder for a moment. She didn't seem surprised that her son might have got a young girl pregnant. She then rose and tugged on a long cord beside the fire place. The servant woman entered once more and she asked her to call the club and ask the Parkin men to come home.

I sat picking at the hem on my skirt, saying nothing and gazing at the carpet. Some tea arrived but neither Mother nor I touched it. I felt strangely detached from the situation, as though I was outside gazing in through the window. Mother was insisting to Violet Parkin that Travis was the first and only boyfriend I have been out with. She also explained about my father's death and that I had been a very good girl who had never caused her a moment's worry, until now.

I heard the sound of the front door opening then recognised the bellowing voice of Mr Parkin senior. It then roared even louder, as the sitting room door was pushed abruptly open and Travis and his father Charles barged in, both obviously annoyed that their evening has been interrupted. On seeing me, Travis looked confused and Charles Parkin demanded an explanation. When Mrs Parkin had sufficiently calmed him down, by talking to him like he was a small child, she explained the situation and why we were here.

There was absolute silence in the room for what seemed like an hour but was probably only seconds. Travis looked terrified. Mrs Parkin was looking at her husband frowning and nodding ever so slightly, as though she was trying to remind him of something. He glared back at her while I wished that lightening would strike me and I would drop down dead. To say that Travis's father's next reaction was a massive shock would be a complete understatement.

The expression on his ruddy face changed almost instantly from one of anger into a beaming grin. He then walked over to Travis and slapped him on the back almost singing at him, calling him a dirty dog who had jumped the gun. Travis grinned back and shook his father's out stretched hand.

Mrs Parkin broke into their merriment and suggested that a wedding should be arranged as soon as possible. There was rapid head nodding all around then Mr Parkin announced that he would leave the arrangements in the capable hands of his darling wife. He then turned and kissed my mother on the cheek then did the same to me:

Welcome to the family…?' he stopped and looked at me.

'Jane.' I muttered,

'Welcome to the family Jane, now, we must get back to our club, there's a card game waiting for us.' Travis turned to follow him but quickly turned back and pulled me into his arms:

'Don't worry Janie, I'll make an honest woman of you.' I smiled shyly at him and looked into his eyes, I thought I saw a flicker of anger but if I did, it was gone within seconds. Travis kissed my cheek and followed his father out of the room.

Less than an hour later Mother and I were back on the bus. It had taken a very small amount of time arrange the rest of my life. Mother was obviously very pleased with herself. On the way home, she gushed that I was a lucky girl and that she was pleased that Travis was doing the right thing and 'standing by me'. A small nag inside of me thought that Travis was just doing what his parents had told him to but I dismissed that. His parents couldn't make him marry me, he must want to. I hoped he loved me but he hadn't said it yet.

For a split second, I felt like I was riding on a roller coaster hurtling around at break neck speed. I longed to scream for it to stop so that I could throw myself off but it just seemed to go faster and faster. If I could have seen into the future I would have screamed as though my life depended in it, as it certainly may one day.

Back at the flat Mother started chatting away about banal things like what we were going to have for dinner. She also remarked on what wonderful people the Parkins were. I didn't agree with her but said nothing. All I saw was a totally pretentious couple hell bent on keeping their good name. I thought, maybe I shouldn't be so judgemental; I was the fallen woman after all. Mrs Parkin had insisted that I wore her deceased mother's engagement ring although it was far too big for me. It kept twisting around on my finger until the blue sapphire stone was facing my palm.

As dinner was cooking Desmond knocked and walked in. He said hello to us both then stopped talking when he noticed the engagement ring on my finger:

'What's going on?' he asked, obviously surprised.

'Jane has got engaged to Travis,' Mother replied, trying to keep her voice normal but it actually sounded high pitched and false.

Desmond looked horrified, was that a mirror of my inner feelings?

'Is this what you want Jane, is it?' he asked urgently.

I said nothing and looked down at my feet, I thought it was but I couldn't be entirely sure, it had all happened so fast and I didn't think I knew Travis all that well:

'Jane, don't marry the man unless you want to, if you're in trouble we can help. Have you considered adoption?' Desmond begged as he rushed forward and clasped my two hands:

'It's none of your business Desmond, it's settled!' Mother shouted as she rushed forwards and put herself in between the two of us,

Desmond looked terribly hurt, so I muttered,

'I think Mother is only doing what she thinks is for the best Desmond.'

'Who for, you or her?' He shouted. I wasn't sure.

'That's enough Desmond, get out, this has got nothing to do with you!' My mother yelled as she waved her finger at him.

Desmond looked at my mother as though he didn't recognise her anymore then he turned and kissed me on the cheek. He gazed into my eyes and I felt as though he was begging me to object to Mother's plans. I looked down at the floor:

'As you wish,' he answered and left the flat.

Our evening meal went largely untouched by Mother and me. As soon as I could, I feigned a headache and went to bed.

I think Mother watched me as I left the room. I walked with my head down and it felt, I'm not sure why, as though I was carrying a heavy weight on my shoulders. My heart ached with hopelessness and I was overcome by a feeling of deep foreboding. I knew Mother thought what she was doing was for the best.

She didn't want me to suffer what she had to when she had become pregnant while unmarried. Nothing would stop her from making sure that I got married. She needed me to hold my head high and not be pointed at and talked about. Part of me agreed with her, I really didn't want to face the shame of being an unmarried mother.

She must have conveniently forgotten the state in which I

arrived home and that I was obviously far too drunk to consent to sexual intercourse. What irked me a little was that, not once, did she ask if this was what I wanted. I wasn't really sure but it would have been nice for her to ask. The only thing that mattered to my mother was 'my good name' and she was determined that I would never lose that and that and her grandchild would be not be raised with a cloud over the circumstances of its birth, at any cost.

17

Less than six weeks later, I was standing beside Travis at Bristol's main Registry office. I was wearing a pastel-pink dress that flowed outwards from the bust and hid my condition; I was also wearing a matching pink coat and pill box hat with a tiny veil covering my forehead. Mr Parkin, Desmond and Travis had pink carnations in their lapels. Travis looked very handsome in his morning suit and I felt a stirring of excitement that I was going to become his wife very shortly.

It was a small wedding party including my mother and Aunty Violet. Uncle Len and Lenny junior were at sea and, apparently, Hester and Daisy couldn't get the time off from work. I didn't believe this. I knew that both of them disliked Travis and we had fallen out over my plans to marry him. I missed their company desperately.

Once the formalities were over I showed the registrar my national identity card while Travis produced his birth certificate as proof of who we were. Mother had lost my birth certificate many years before and I always used the old wartime card as a means of identification. Mother kept saying she would get a new birth certificate but she never did.

The small, but very posh, wedding lunch was paid for by the Parkins, as was everything else. It would have been a very pleasant meal had it not been for the ever tightening ball of tension lodged in my stomach. In the middle of the afternoon

Travis and I left for a few days' honeymoon in Cornwall.

I was so very excited. I absolutely adored the countryside, having spent many wonderful holidays in Cornwall when I was growing up. Mother's friend, Susan Bromley lived on a farm in the county and we visited often, two or three times a year and it was my very favourite place.

The sun was still high in the cornflower blue sky when we arrived in Cornwall. Travis parked the car outside the Brookbank Hotel. It was a magnificent building that stood in its own well-manicured grounds on the edge of the seaside village of Portreath. A porter immediately appeared, seemingly out of nowhere, to unload our small, overnight cases while a valet took care of the car. I swept away any remnants of colourful confetti, which were still clinging to my clothes, as I followed Travis up the large stone steps through the double concrete pillars.

The interior of the hotel was as majestic as the outside, with thick pile carpets that seemed to engulf my feet as I padded silently towards the reception desk. Travis was clearly at home in the luxury surroundings but I felt strange and ill at ease. As we wait to be checked in I felt a sudden and urgent longing to be back in our cosy flat sitting on the sofa with my mother.

Travis pulled on my arm and we both followed a smartly dressed bell boy up the sweeping stair case. He placed a key into a large wooden door and gestured for us both to enter. The boy then handed Travis the key, he, in turn, placed a coin in the boy's hand and his face lit up with a brightest of smiles. Thanking Travis, the young man wished us the very best and left. I was feeling very nervous but also eagerly anticipating what was to come. I turned and smiled shyly at Travis when the bellboy left the room.

Up until that moment Travis had managed to keep up his clever façade, his mask didn't drop once. He flashed his handsome smile at everyone we met and it seemed infectious, as all around us immediately seemed to smile back. I smiled too. I remember feeling deliriously happy and proud to be with such an obviously well-liked man. That feeling disappeared as soon as our hotel door was pulled closed by the bellboy.

The minute we were alone, with no prior warning, Travis turned around and slapped my cheek. I was startled and confused, why had he done that? As I held my stinging face, he began tearing at my clothes like a depraved animal. I heard the seams of my lovingly prepared outfit tearing and saw the buttons pinging off in all directions. I begged Travis to stop and wait, to take his time, but he seemed possessed, like sort of raging monster with spit dripping out of his mouth. He started calling me vile, disgusting names, some I had never even heard of.

He hissed at me that I was a dirty whore who had trapped him into marriage and he would make sure I regretted it for the rest of my sorry life. I swear his beautiful blue eyes turned black and the wonderful smile became a twisted scowl. When I was naked, I tried to curl into a ball on the bed, I felt humiliated and ashamed of being naked in front of a total stranger. Travis laughed out loud at my obvious distress. For the next few hours, he abused my body in every way possible.

Every time I thought my ordeal was over, he would begin again. Thrusting and pushing into me, biting and pinching my skin. I bit into the bedclothes to stop myself screaming out in pain. Eventually, Travis climbed off my tortured body and went into the small bathroom. I could hear rushing water and Travis humming cheerfully to himself. I didn't move an inch; the trauma I had suffered had left me paralysed. My whole body ached and I was sick to my stomach at the things this man had made me do.

I was in absolutely no doubt that I had arrived in hell. After a while, as I lay on the bed, I gently pulled the blankets around me in an effort to retain a tiny modicum of dignity. All I could now visualise before me was a black tunnel of despair and I knew my only escape would be death. Travis re-entered the room, I remained deadly still, praying to God that he would not come near me. I heard him whistling as he dressed himself. I turned my head very slightly; he was wearing a smart pair of navy blue shorts and a pristine white shirt with leather sandals.

The relief I felt when I heard him pull the door behind him was indescribable. After a few minutes I gingerly pulled myself into a sitting position. I then walked painfully to the bathroom. The reflection staring back at me from the wall mirror was that of a total stranger. My face was as white as lint, emphasized even further by the redness of my eyes. My breasts, shoulders, stomach and thighs were covered in bruises and bites. Some of the bite injuries were oozing pus caused by Travis dragging me across the carpet by my hair.

The pain was almost unbearable, both on the inside and outside of my body. I turned on the taps and began to fill the bath. As I did so, I noticed that there was no lock on the bathroom door. I supposed that, as this is the honeymoon suite, it was presumed that none was needed. Once the bath was full with warm, soapy water I cautiously lowered myself in. The soothing effect of the fragrant smelling water soothed my skin but made my injuries sting.

After a long while, when the water was virtually cold, I climbed out of the bath and carefully wiped my injured body with a large, soft, white towel. As I did this I felt a sharp cramping pain in my stomach. I looked down as I felt trickles of blood run down the insides of both my legs. I sat on the side of the bath and watched, as the only reason for my nightmare seeped onto the floor.

In my state of extreme shock, I couldn't even cry, I just sat. Eventually, I got up and began to dress myself. I then left the hotel to try and find a shop that sold sanitary wear; obviously, I had not brought anything with me.

I walked along the narrow country lane enveloped in a blanket of misery so abysmal, I didn't think that I would ever feel happy again. I hoped the road would lead into the village. Bees buzzed and birds sang as they lazily floated in the late afternoon sky, I wished that I was one of them. Thankfully, I had headed in the right direction and found the shop I needed. I realised that I was in desperate need of a cup of tea and managed to find a tiny café right on the fringes of the crowded beach.

The golden sands were awash with colour, sight and sound. Brightly clad children ran around in their swimsuits carrying buckets and spades or inflatable balls. All had joy and goodness etched on their elfin faces. Nothing mattered to them but here and now and I yearned for my destroyed innocence. There was a mixture of smells all around ranging from freshly caught fish to the smell of chips cooking in beef dripping.

I was wearing a yellow, loose cotton dress with daisies embroidered into the hem and the same white sandals I got married in. Could it have only been a couple of hours since

I arrived? It seemed to me like a whole lifetime. It was a very warm day, I wanted to take my thin blue cardigan off but I knew that doing so will reveal the appalling injuries, inflicted on me by Travis, so I kept it on and tried to sit in the shadiest spot I could find.

Sitting in the corner of the tiny cafe, I drank my much needed tea. I was so lost my in own nightmarish world that it wasn't until I realised that someone had called my name called three times that I looked up to see who it was. Shielding my eyes with the palm of my hand I looked up and was absolutely delighted to see Edith Flemming, who was Susan's eldest daughter, standing above me wearing a smile as bright as the sunshine. I jumped up and eagerly embraced her, I was so happy to see a friendly face I almost burst into tears.

Edith sat down and told me that she had sent her two younger daughters and son onto the beach ahead of her; she went onto say that she found the children utterly exhausting so when she spotted me it was an ideal opportunity for a little break from them. Wafting her hand in front of her face to get some cool air from the stifling heat, Edith smiled as she waved her children off.

Edith was Susan Bromley's eldest daughter. She had two children the same age as me but was only seventeen years older than me. We both got along very well when Mother and I spent our holidays with them. Edith lived a few miles away from her parents' farm but was a regular visitor. She and her husband, William Flemming, had their own farm. Their two eldest children, Verity and Charlie remained at home, helping on the farm, and the whole family of five children and parents were very close.

Also in the Bromley Family was Iris. She was Susan second daughter and as soon as the government had allowed women to enlist, outside of wartime, she joined the army. Iris was a well-built almost masculine lady with curly blonde hair and beautiful blue eyes. It was obvious to everyone who knew her that the army was her life, she seemed to live and breathe it.

Iris was now twenty nine years old but had never fancied marriage or children which many people found strange. In my mind, I thought the world was made up of all sorts of people. I found Iris a was very assertive lady who had always known exactly what she wanted from life and had never veered from her chosen path. I admired her for that.

The third child of Susan and Edward Bromley was Johnny, who was a few years older than me and the most handsome man I had ever set eyes on. He still lived and worked on Carmarthen Farm with is parents. Farm work had made him muscular and working outdoors meant he has an all year tan and his skin was the colour of milky coffee. He had dark blonde hair and sparkling blue eyes just like his sister, Iris, and the same thick-set, stocky figure.

The fourth and last child was Jack, who was a couple of years younger than me. He was kind, studious boy who seemed to prefer the books to people. I could now understand that. I would have preferred to spend the rest of my life with a good book, rather than Travis.

The waitress walked over and Edith ordered some more tea. Leaning forward, she asked why I was in Cornwall. Was I on holiday and was my mother with me? I shyly held up my finger to reveal both my engagement and wedding rings, both now fitted well. I could see that Edith was utterly amazed.

All the years she had known me I had always been so shy and awkward. She had once told me that I was like a new born deer. I knew by the look on her face that she couldn't imagine how I could possibly have met someone and got married in the few short months since she'd last seen me.

Edith gazed at me; I could tell that she thought I looked nothing like a glowing eyed newly-wed. My heart shaped face was as white as porcelain and I failed to hide the terror behind my eyes, I felt almost like a shocked baby animal. Edith said nothing. She and I talked a while until we were interrupted by Edith's youngest son, a boisterous ten-year-old who was adamant that she come and look at the sea creature he had found lurking under a rock. Edith reluctantly stood up.

As she rose to leave I stood up too and leaned forward to hug her. I knew I was holding onto her a little longer than necessary, and much too tightly, but I was in desperate need of comfort. I wanted to scream at her to help me, to plead with her to take me to a place of safety, away from the sadistic creature I had married.

I watched as Edith's son, Billy, pulled her out of the cafe brimming over with excitement and pleasure. I smiled and waved to them as Edith held both hands in front of her and shook her head, but she was smiling too. She laughed as she was virtually dragged past the window and I laughed too at the comical sight.

When she was out of sight, a wave of loneliness enveloped me. It was so acute, hot tears stung the corners of my eyes. Without warning I was overcome with sadness at the loss of my child, who I would now never know. With a heart as heavy as stone, I dragged myself back to the hotel, knowing that I was only delaying the inevitable and I would have to go back sooner or later. To my overwhelming relief the hotel room was empty.

The weight on my shoulders lessened ever so slightly. I ordered a sandwich and some tea from the room service. When I had finished eating, I quickly and carefully undressed, trying not to make my injuries any worse. I gently pulled the soft silk negligee over my head that Mother and I had chosen together. The cold, smooth material was comforting on my still smarting skin. Climbing into the freshly laundered bed I was comforted by the softness of the mattress and silkiness of the sheets. Eventually, I drifted off to sleep.

I had no idea what the time was but assumed it was very late in the night as I couldn't hear any noises outside the room and it was now in total darkness. The hairs on the back of my neck prickled as I became alert and sensed the immediate presence danger. The smell of alcohol was over powering. I listened as Travis lumbered around like an injured animal but didn't dare move. In his inebriated state I could hear him struggling to undress himself.

He swore as he knocked into furniture and fell repeatedly onto the carpeted floor. I lay completely still, silently praying and begging that he would not touch me. After what seemed like a lifetime, I felt the weight of his body in the bed behind me. I shuddered as I heard him grunting like an animal as he began to paw at me. He pinched my bruised breasts and tried to lift my nightdress up. The overwhelming stench of beer on his breath was making me feel sick. I couldn't move.

Suddenly his clammy hands stopped jabbing at my body and Travis began to urge. I heard him vomiting over the side of the bed. Eventually he lay back on the bed and began to snore like a large animal. My relief was so great I felt breathless. Many hours later, I fell into a disturbed sleep with my mind endlessly reliving the horrors of the day.

When I woke the next morning I was very stiff and sore. All yesterday's events came flooding back into my mind; I felt an avalanche of pain and humiliation tearing through my body and I wanted to scream and shout and smash up anything that got in my way. I could hear Travis being sick again in the bathroom and it turned my stomach. I got up as quickly as my injuries would allow. Grasping my clothes, I threw them on as quickly as I could.

After half an hour, Travis emerged, fully dressed and looking terrible. He walked from the room and I followed him without saying a word. The bellboy was putting the luggage into the boot of the car as we stepped outside. Travis again, pressed a coin into the boy's hand, he looked at Travis as if he were some type of God. He then opened the car door for me and wished me a long and happy marriage. I couldn't muster a smile, not even for the sake for politeness.

I was relieved to be heading home but I also felt numb and empty. I looked forward will to seeing Mother and Desmond. Of course, I would never be able to tell Mother what happened between me and Travis. Mother was originally from a Catholic family and she had said on many occasions that marriage is for life.

All throughout my childhood I had been told that I must love my father, even if he hurt or frightened me. I assume Mother would say I must love Travis as he was my husband. This, however, was something I could never do. I would stay with him because that is what Mother would expect me to do and because he was my husband, but I would never love him.

As the car spun through the country lanes, I looked across at Travis. I thought that now was as good a time as ever so I told him that I had lost the baby. Travis screeched the car to a halt and stared at me with an incredulous expression on his face. I watched as his expression seemed to change from amazement to intense anger. Fear surged through my body as though a lightning bolt was striking me. Travis shouted a tirade of vile obscenities then, while looking me directly in the eyes, he leant over and punched my stomach so violently that I couldn't breathe for a second:

'You are my possession, to do with, as I wish, from now on: you tricked me into marriage Janie, I won't forgive you for that: I'm too young to be tied down, especially to someone like you,' he said, as he pushed his face into mine.

He then yanked the car into gear and proceeded with the journey home. The speed and carelessness at which he was driving was terrifying. With each bend that he manically twisted around, I was sure the car would spin out of control and crash into the hedgerows. It didn't matter to me; I didn't care if I died. I made no sound and showed no emotion. I knew that was what he wanted, I realised he liked seeing me afraid.

It was October 1962, in the wider world, the Americans and the Cubans were hell bent on starting world war three so the chances of anyone surviving that were relatively small. Death, I decided, would be a joyous release, whoever or whatever it was that killed me; I would welcome it with open arms.

We arrived at our new flat as the late afternoon sun beat brightly down from a cloudless sky. The apartment was bought by the Parkins. A flight of concrete steps led up to the top floor of my new home. It was small but I could have made cosy and homely, if I was allowed to. Travis's parents had had the place professionally decorated but Mother and I had bought some cheap little ornaments in an effort to put our mark on the place. I waited while Travis unlocked the door then I followed him up the steps.

I had not been given a key of my own. Throughout the journey, not a word was uttered after I had told Travis about the miscarriage. He was now looking around the flat. A Vase of fresh flowers had been placed on the table along with a bottle of champagne and two glasses.

This would have been a lovely gesture if the circumstances had been different. Travis strode forward and, with his fist, he knocked the vase sideways, across the small lounge, causing the water and flowers to splatter across the sofa and side board. He then smashed the two glasses and ground them into the carpet. I stood still and watched as he uncorked the bottle and began to drink from it.

As he continued to ignore me, I started to walk quietly towards the bedroom to unpack our few items of clothing. What had happened to the Travis I had been dating for the past three months? I now knew his whole persona was some kind act he had been putting on. Now that we were married, the pretence had gone. The kindly outer shell of the man I had married had smashed to pieces and now only the monster beneath remained.

There was a sprinkling of confetti on the bed and I smiled as I saw my old teddy bear. It has presumably been put on the bed by my mother. I picked it up and hugged it to me. I often used to bury my head into the soft toy when I was a child. It was a comfort to me and I used it to try and drown out the noises of Mother being hurt by my father.

The smell of the toy brought these memories to the forefront of my mind but strangely, I still felt glad my mother had left it. I didn't hear Travis enter the room and squealed as he ripped the toy from my arms. Travis then tore the head off and hurled it across the room; he then turned towards me and pushed me onto the bed. I lay as still as a corpse as he ripped my clothes off and forced himself on me. It felt as if I had been lifted out of my body and was staring down from the ceiling above, looking at the poor creature below being stripped of her dignity with every punch, bite and slap.

18

Travis told that I was to have no visitors while he was at work. The money he gave me was barely enough to buy food but it didn't matter, Mother had taught me how to be thrifty. I now had a key but was under strict instructions that I must not be out for more than an hour a day, this was to shop for food and whatever else Travis needed. As I had always been the type of person who wanted to placate others, at first, I obeyed Travis's wishes.

Three or four weeks into the marriage, I staged a mini rebellion, in my mind. I decided I didn't want to be cooped up in the tiny flat all day with no one talk to and, anyway, how would Travis find out?

One day, in late September, I was sitting outside a Lyons Corner house with a cup of tea when I saw someone waving at me from across the street. At first I was terrified that it may be someone that Travis knew but, as the person approached, I could see it was Miss Selby, who I had worked with at Parkin's Metals. It had been a while since we last saw each other so she sat down and joined me. She asked how everything was going; I looked down, caught unawares by her question. She reached forward and put her hand over mine:

'Did your mother tell you I came to see her before you got married?' she asked.

I shook my head and looked at her questioningly.

'I told Lucy not to let you marry Travis Parkin,' she said. 'In fact I begged her to stop the marriage going ahead.'

She clutched my hand more tightly, looked down at the ground, then went on:

'Two years ago, Travis was arrested for sexually assaulting a fifteen-year-old girl: it was in some of the local papers but Travis used his mother's maiden name, Smythe, so no one connected Travis Smythe with Travis Parkin. He picked up the young girl in his flash car as she walked home from school. He plied her with alcohol and raped her in a car park. When he was done with her he put her in a taxi and sent her home.'

She stopped talking for a while. I looked in horror as Miss Selby took out her handkerchief and blew her nose. She began again:

'When she got home her parents were so shocked at the state she was in, they called an ambulance, the poor girl took weeks to recover, and she was all torn up inside and out, I don't know what really happened, but it was said that Charles Parkin paid for a very expensive lawyer to represent his son. He got away by the skin of his teeth, first offence and so on. I know, from then on, Charles Parkin rarely let Travis out of his sight.' She was visibly distraught when she finished talking and tears fell, unstopped, from her eyes.

I thought back to the time when Mother dragged me to the Parkin's house and the look that Violet Parkin had given her husband. Now I knew why, their sadistic, rapist son had stuck again and this quirk of his personality needed to be covered in a cloak of respect:

'Mother knew this, before I married him?' I asked her.

Miss Selby dried her eyes and gazed at me:

‘She told me to mind my own business and not to come around bothering her again, next thing I know you already married, I’m sorry Jane, I should have told you but I didn’t want to interfere.’

‘It’s OK, Miss Selby, it’s not your fault but I really should be getting home,’ I said, as I reached down for my shopping bag.

Miss Selby embraced me tightly before we separated and I hoped we would meet up again sometime. As I walked back to the apartment the first stirrings of hatred fizzed up, towards my mother. She was supposed to love me but she had pushed me into the arms of a maniac. What type of love was that?

19

Every Sunday we had lunch with Travis's parents and tea with Mother on Saturday evenings. I detested both of these events. At lunch with the Parkins the atmosphere was always stilted and awkward. Travis and his parents spoke among themselves but I was rarely included in the conversation. After lunch Travis and his father would go and play a round of golf.

I was left sitting in the plush lounge on my own while Mrs Parkin played bridge with her friends in the parlour. I was never invited neither did I want to be, I felt that all her friends looked down on me and despised me as though I was some pathetic creature to be pitied.

Tea at Mother's flat was just as awkward. Travis's attempts at being charming just made him seem smarmy and ignorant. Desmond and Mother had now become a couple and Desmond was often present at these get-togethers. Both Travis and I could sense the loathing Desmond felt for my new husband. Mother spent the whole time chatting away about nothing and constantly offering more tea. It was relief when it was over.

We had been married for just under two months as we drove back to the flat after one such outing. I was as subservient as I could be, trying to keep the peace as always. I never forgot Mother fighting with my father years before. More often than not, as time when on, Mother stopped fighting back and whatever happened was over quicker. That was the way I played it with Travis.

He seems to prefer it if I cried out in pain or showed any distress so I just shut my mind and let him do whatever it was he felt he had to do. As he parked the car outside the flat I told Travis that I was pregnant again. I did this outside in case he got angry and felt the need to hit me. He was always on his best behaviour in public. Although he turned to look at me made no comment or showed any other signs of acknowledgement.

20

I was now six months pregnant and looked like a tiny whale. It took me a while to work out if I was happy to be bringing a new life into the world; I knew I'd forgotten what it felt like to feel unafraid. My body was always on high alert, taut and afraid of any approaching abuse Travis would inflict on me. I had developed a twitch in my left eye and a terrible stammer whenever Travis spoke to me; this seemed to infuriate him. A lot of my sentences would go unfinished because Travis lashed out at me when I couldn't get the words out.

Daisy and Hester visited once but they were offended when I told them to leave before Travis came home so they stopped coming. Aunty Violet was not at all fazed about Travis but when I told her he would sulk if he knew she had been to the flat, she stopped visiting too. The isolation and loneliness I felt was almost as painful as the beatings.

Sometimes I stood at the window of the flat for hours on end, staring down at the world below. I watched everyone going about their business and they seemed happy with their lives. The couple that lived in the flat below didn't work. Each morning the husband went to the shop along the street to collect his morning newspaper.

He always wore ill-fitting trousers, held up by braces with a string vest which was always peppered with different coloured stains. Without fail, he always had a roll-up cigarette stuck out of the corner of his mouth. His wife's hair was forever in curlers and she never appeared to wear anything different from her brown striped overall but they seemed pleasant enough.

They always looked up at me when they walked by. They smiled and waved when they saw me standing at the window. I always waved back; I liked to think they were my friends but in reality I knew nothing about them. It was three thirty in the afternoon. Travis always insisted that his meal was on the table at quarter past five sharp. I had already prepared it, it was liver, onions and mashed potato; it just needed to be cooked.

The sound of the doorbell ringing made me almost jump out of my skin. I had no idea who could be calling on me. It could have been the post man or bread man but they usually came earlier in the day. I lumber carefully down the steps, pulling my cardigan around me for warmth. It was mid-February and bitterly cold but Travis had instructed me not to put the portable heater on until he arrived home.

I pulled the door open and gasped with joy. Standing there was my cousin, Lenny, looking extremely handsome in his navy uniform. I was so delighted to see him that I squealed then threw my arms around him. Lenny beamed as he followed me back up the steps hoisting his kit bag over his shoulder.

We sat down in the lounge he explained that he was on his way back to his ship and his mother suggested he popped in. I loved auntie Violet for that, did she know that I was starved of human company? I quickly boiled the kettle and made a pot of tea. As I poured us each one, Lenny shivered and asked as to why it was so cold in the flat. I lied that my pregnancy was making me overly warm. Lenny didn't seem convinced and insisted on switching the plastic coal effect heater on.

We both sat cupping our drinks in our hands and talked about childhood memories and how much things had changed. We then move onto more current issues. Both of us agreed about the massive relief we felt once the Cuban missile crisis had ended and expressed our astonishment of the men behind it. No one wanted another war but it had come so close.

I was having a wonderful time chatting to Lenny; I still couldn't believe how much he had changed since he had joined up. The whole time he was here I had half an eye on the clock. I knew Travis would not be pleased if he came home to find a visitor in his home.

At twenty to five Lenny stood and announced that he had better be going otherwise he would miss his train. I tried to disguise my relief but it felt almost palpable. Lenny would be long gone by the time Travis came home. I watched as my cousin pulled on his great coat and chattered away; amazed that he has not noticed my tension. But then, I had become a master at hiding my emotions since I married Travis.

Such was my anxiety it seemed to me that Lenny was moving in slow motion but he wasn't. At last, he leant down and picked up his kitbag then turned to give me a final embrace. Travis had crept in so quietly that I had not heard him, I only saw him when Lenny released me from his loving bear hug.

Immediately I could sense Travis's anger. Lenny must also have noticed how frosty the atmosphere had become despite the heat from the fire. He moved forward and put his out his hand to shake Travis's. Travis swatted it out of the way like a cumbersome fly. Lenny countenance immediately changed. He frowned and his bushy eyebrows almost became one, he looked at Travis and growled:

'What's your problem, mate?'

'I'm not your bloody mate and I don't appreciate my bloody wife whoring around while I'm at work!' Travis snarled, as he glared at Lenny.

Lenny moved towards Travis. He was a head and half taller than the weedy, skinny coward of a man. I looked at Travis's face as he weighed up the situation. He knew he was no match for a man of Lenny's size. He immediately burst into fake laughter and declared:

'Only joking mate, I know who you are, aren't you Jane's cousin Lenny, living life on the high seas?'

Lenny turned and looked, first to me then back at Travis. He nodded at the man standing in front of him. It was blatantly obvious that Lenny disliked Travis with a fierce intensity but he still managed to give him a curt nod. Lenny then got all his stuff together. He gave me a final hug then I walked him down the steps and closed the door behind him.

I felt a desperate, almost insane longing to run after him and scream for help, but I did not. Beads of sweat trickled down the back of my neck as I dragged myself up the steps to the flat. Travis was standing in the middle of the room, he turned and stared at me at me with an expression I could only describe as a deep loathing.

Then it started; first he began shouting loudly at me for having the heater on when he had expressly forbade it. He then kicked it to pieces. Yanking me by my hair he pulled me to my knees then unzipped his flies and tried to push my mouth down onto him. He screeched vile obscenities at me when I refused to do what he wanted.

The more I protested and begged Travis to calm down, the

more I seemed to ignite his anger. Travis twisted me around and kicked my stomach, I curled into a ball to try and protect my unborn child. Travis leant down and started to drag me by the neck, towards the bedroom.

It felt like he was going to choke me to death, his face was dark purple and spittle spewed and bubbled at the corners of his mouth. He hurled me onto the bed, making my billowing maternity dress rise upwards, revealing my swollen stomach. I put my hands on my aching throat as Travis bent down and pulled at my underwear.

Abruptly, Travis stopped in his tracks and looked at me, cowering and quaking, with a look of utter disgust. He began to scream at me, telling me how abhorrent and revolting I was. I shuffled back towards the corner of the bed and pushed myself as far into the corner as I could get. Without warning, Travis lunged forwards and began to haul me from the room, again by my hair.

I was crying loudly and trying to hold onto my hair to stop the burning pain all over my head, caused by his vicious tugging. Travis sounded like a demented maniac. He demanded over and over again that I leave the flat. I shouted that I would go but begged him to allow me to get my coat and shoes; it was a freezing cold evening with temperatures dipping below zero outside. I was sure my baby would not survive if I didn't have, at least, a coat on to keep me warm.

I turned and looked into my husband's enraged face. Spit was still drivelling out of his mouth which was now twisted with hatred. I realised, terrifyingly, that I was now fighting for my life. Travis began to punch and kick me, sparing no thought for our unborn child. He was pulling and pushing me towards the stairway to try and get me out of the building.

I clung onto the handrails as I pleaded with him leave me alone. Travis turned and picked up a vase containing winter wild flowers that I had picked that morning. He then smashed it into my skull with such force I felt like it had caved my head in. The blow stunned me and the next minute the concrete stairs seemed to come up and smash me in the face. I rolled down the cold, hard steps, desperately trying to protect my stomach from the unforgiving surface.

I heard my wrist bone snap and the base of my back crunched painfully as it hit each stair. Then I was still, I lay, twisted and broken at the bottom of the stairwell. I felt as though there was no life left in me, Travis had won and he could do what he liked as far as I was concerned, I had run out of fight. A few minutes later I could see a distorted vision of Travis appearing at the top of the steps. I could see the light reflected from the steel blade of the large bread knife he was holding.

My sight was partially obscured by blood pouring from my head wounds and all I could do was watch as he slowly and menacingly walked towards me. I was so badly hurt and in far too much pain to move so I just braced myself for what was to come. All the fear had now left my broken body and I lay feeling the warm blood trickle down my cheeks and as it mingled with my tears.

For a fleeting moment, in my mind I saw a picture of Michael, my long-dead adoptive father. He was wearing his army uniform but his face looked peaceful and untroubled. He smiled reassuringly at me and held out his hands. I tried to reach for them; I so wanted to feel the comfort of his touch. Then I heard Travis's heavy breathing close to me then I felt his breath on my face. I tried to open my eyes but it hurt too much. I knew that, anytime soon, I would feel the cold steel of the knife stab into my flesh.

Through my haziness I thought I heard the noise of glass smashing. I wasn't sure. I thought I must have been dreaming but then I felt tiny shards of glass falling on my body. My arms were too heavy for me to lift up and protect myself from the glass. Through blurred vision, I watched as a hand reached through the broken window and unlocked the door. As it was being pushed open, it started to squash my legs against the wall. I cried out.

Travis raised his head, obviously startled by the noise. I continued to watch as an almighty arm appeared around the door and a large fist smashed into Travis's face lifting him clean off his feet. I vaguely wandered who my knight in shining armour was and tried to shift myself out of the way of the door but I couldn't. It was gently pushed open as Travis scurried back up the stairs like a rat fleeing from a cat.

I turned and looked up into the worried face of my downstairs neighbour. One of his braces had fallen off his shoulder but his vest was clean, for once. There was no cigarette hanging from the corner of his lips. His thin, greasy, grey hair which was normally uncombed was now greased neatly onto his head as his face hung over mine. He stroked my cheek:

'Oh my little lass,' he muttered, 'I should a' stepped in earlier: I've heard 'im batterin' you many a time but didn't like to butt in.' He then turned towards the doorway and yelled:

'Doreen, run to the phone box on the corner and get an ambulance, get the police as well while you're there,' he added

Doreen appeared behind her husband and on seeing me she

pressed her hands into her shocked face:

'Oh Stan, shouldn't I stay with her while you go, she looks awful?'

'No, I'd better stay in case that nut job comes down to finish her off.'

Doreen nodded and rushed away. I lay still as I realised that almost every part of my body ached. I was, inexplicably, numb when I thought Travis was going to kill me but now, I was wracked with pain. Stan, my heroic neighbour, reached into his pocket and pulled out his grubby handkerchief. He then began to wipe the blood away from my eyes. I looked up into the gentle man's concerned face and shakily reached for his hand to hold. Stan immediately wrapped mine in his large rough hand and there he stayed until the help arrived.

I could not move anything without pain so I stayed motionless. Ironically, I thought, that after all this time, I now knew my neighbours names, Stan and Doreen. I was glad because their daily smiles and greetings had helped me more than they would ever know. It had taken the edge off my suffocating loneliness and now they had become my hero's.

I screamed out in agony as the ambulance men lifted me onto the stretcher as gently as they could. Lying in the vehicle I could see Stan and Doreen standing, arms wrapped tightly around each other. They were, obviously, very distressed but dependent on one another. I tried to wave to them. As the doors closed I drifted out of consciousness and the violent, throbbing ache ceased.

21

My mother was at work when the police arrived and, like the rest of the staff, had no idea what was going on as all present watched them as they walked into the office manager. My mother told me that an unexplained feeling of foreboding washed over her, she had no idea why. But it made the hairs on the back of her neck stand on end. She put her head down and carried on with my her work, all the time something was niggling in her head, until she felt a tap on her shoulder: A colleague explained that she was wanted in the office.

The foreboding feeling grew, immediately her heart started to pound and Mother somehow knew that she was going to hear bad news. Stepping nervously into the small office she turned to see two concerned looking constables gazing in her direction. She said that she thought they looked ridiculously young but maybe that was because she was getting old. A seat was offered and she nervously accepted it then listened anxiously to what the older of the two policemen was saying:

'There's no easy way of putting this madam so I'll come straight out with it. Jane your daughter has been very seriously injured: she in Clifton General Hospital fighting for her life but, I'm sorry, she may not survive.'

Mother couldn't really process what the man was saying, such was her shock, she gabbled:

'Jane can't be dying, I saw her on Sunday and she was

absolutely fine… or was she?'

She thought back, had she tried to pretend that everything was all right but deep down she knew it wasn't. Mother remembered I was so jittery and stuttered when I spoke. She knew should have asked her if I was all right, but she didn't. She started speaking again:

'I think you're mistaken, Jane was fine the last time I saw her, are you sure it's my Jane – Jane Parkin?' she asked.

'We're in no doubt Mrs Rosental, we need to get you to the hospital: is there anyone we can call for you?'

She felt sick and a little giddy, someone pressed a glass of water into her hand and she sipped at it. Desmond was away on a course so she asked them to call Violet. She spoke to the policeman once more:

'What happened, has she had some kind of accident?' She queried as she hurriedly picked up her coat and bag:

'No mam, someone tried to murder her, we believe it was her husband, Travis Parkin, we have him in custody, and we really must hurry madam.'

She followed the two men to the car outside, locked in a dreadful feeling of numb bewilderment, and climbed in the back. As the vehicle sped into motion the noisy whirr of the siren startled her:

'Is the baby OK?' she whispered, 'Jane's six months pregnant, you see.'

'The doctors will talk to you at the hospital: our priority is to get you there as fast as we can,' she was told.

The journey was the most terrifying one that she had ever endured. As she sat in the blue and white panda car the siren seemed to screech even louder, ringing in her ears. The traffic passed in a blur. There was so much going through her mind. She wouldn't contemplate the idea that I might die. She cried when she told me that she begged God throughout the whole journey to let me live and pleaded with Him not to take me away from her.

She decided that if I died she would too; there was a constant nagging voice in her head telling her that she knew there was something wrong with my marriage but she chose to ignore it. Now it looked as though her ignorance would cost me my life.

They arrived at the hospital and she hurried out of the car and raced inside. She had always hated hospitals with every fibre of her being but she was so very grateful to this one for trying to save me. One of the policemen went over to the reception and spoke, a few minutes later a doctor appeared. She thanked the man then followed the doctor into his untidy office. The doctor introduced himself as Mr Kenneth Fields then slowly began to explain the situation to my mother:

'Your daughter Jane is gravely ill and, in my opinion, her injuries are too severe, she will not survive," he explained in a monotone voice.

Mother began to shake and sob uncontrollably. The doctor asked her if there was anyone he could call. She spluttered that Auntie Violet was on her way. She began to feel as though she was floating; the ground came up to meet her. She then felt a strong pair of hands, grasp her trembling shoulders.

A nurse pushed her back into her chair; she talked soothingly, telling her to remain calm for my sake as I may need her at some point. She heard this and shook the fogginess from her brain then inhaled some deep, calming breaths. She interpreted that the nurse was saying that I would need me so I couldn't be dying. At that moment, Auntie Violet rushed in and immediately took control of the situation and my mother. Once both Violet and she were seated the doctor began to explain:

'There's no easy way to tell anyone this, especially a parent, but there's no other way. Your daughter, Jane has been systematically tortured over the past months. Her entire torso, chest legs and buttocks are pockmarked with bruises, bites, scratches and cigarette burns, even the soles of her feet have scars from previous burns on them. She has an old wrist fracture that will have to be re-broken and set. She has been hit over the head by an object that fractured her skull and the fall down the staircase as left her with a broken pelvis, ankle and elbow.'

The doctor finished his speech and sat looking at the two women with extreme sadness as well as anger in his bright blue eyes.

My mother told me later that she felt as though she had been struck by a large sledgehammer. The blood was rushing into her head and swilling around it loudly. She could not comprehend that something so horrific had happened to me, her only child, who wouldn't harm a fly. She couldn't understand, she saw me on a weekly basis and I seemed to have everything that I could want. I had my husband, a lovely new home and a baby on the way.

Thinking about the baby made her jump up and if ask the doctor if the child was all right. The man gently explained that they had performed a caesarean operation to get the baby out. Sadly, the small boy was already dead when he was taken from my womb, the victim of many bone fractures himself. She recalled looking at the man as though he was some kind of alien life form. He seemed to be saying that not only had I been beaten but so had my unborn son. The floating feeling returned and there was nothing she could do to stop being overcome by the welcoming blackness.

When she opened her eyes she found herself lying on a bed with Violet standing over her, holding her hand. Violet insisted that she must pull herself together if she was going to be there when I woke up; Violet impressed upon her that the whole family would all have to try and help me get through this terrible thing that had happened to me. With immense difficulty, she pulled herself into a sitting position and waited for the dizziness to pass. Mother told me that she couldn't get the image of a tiny, dead and battered baby out of her head.

A nurse came into the room and told Violet and Mother that she would take them to my bed. I was in a private room at the end of the ward. I lay deadly still with my complexion as white as the sheets I lay on. There was a large cage under the covers keeping the weight of the blankets off my injuries. My face was a mass of cuts and bruises and my hair has been shaved in places to allow the medical staff to stitch my wounds. There was also a large padded bandage covering the back of my head.

Both of my wrists were plastered and I was being helped to breath with oxygen. Mother tottered on the verge of collapse but fought the urge to scream and yell at the top of her voice and demand to know why this has happened to me. Two chairs were placed beside the bed. Violet and my mother sat down on either side of my bed. Both of them took in turns to speak gently and encourage me to fight. They told me they loved me very much and that they would keep me safe from harm when I was well again. I heard nothing, happily oblivious in the warmth of my pain free world.

As they did this my fragile body began to convulse and various alarms rang out. They heard footsteps racing down the corridor. A member of staff pushed them out of the room. They stood outside watching through a large window. A doctor punched my chest with such force that my mother's mouth fell open in horror. The medical staff then began to take in turns to pump on my heart with such ferocity they thought they would break me.

Tears fell silently down her face. She could not begin to imagine what I had been going through at the hands of Travis. Hester and Daisy arrived sometime later. Neither of them had any idea how long mother and Violet had been at the hospital, all concept of time had disappeared. They told them that I had now been stabilised. Hester and Daisy ordered them to go home and get some rest. When they both started to protest my cousins promised they would sit with me until they got back:

'Neither of you would be any use to her without food or sleep,' Hester whispered as her eyes brimmed over with tears.

'We'll make sure she's never on her own, we promise,' Daisy told my mother and aunt.

As she finished talking the tears tumbled down her face and all four of them held on tightly to each other until they had all regained a certain amount of composure in order that they would be capable of taking care of me when I needed them.

My mother and Violet reluctantly agreed. Mother bent down and gently kissed my face, still unable to come to terms with the state of my terribly broken body then walked out of the small, sterile room and promised she would be back soon.

22

Hester and Daisy had both hidden their shock from their mother and aunt very well. As they sat down, each holding one of my hands, tears rolled unashamedly down their cheeks. They were speechless. There didn't seem to be an inch of my battered body that was not injured.

They had been told that my baby had been born without taking a breath in this life. Both of them felt weighted down with guilt. They had stopped visiting me because they couldn't stand Travis; they despised the way the contemptible man looked down on them when he arrived home to find them in the flat.

When I said nothing to my husband about the way he treated them, they felt let down and annoyed with me, now they knew why I kept silent and were very ashamed of themselves. They both realised that they had left me at the mercy of a mad man. Hester and Daisy held hands and prayed to God to let me live and they promised that they would take better care of me if He would please answer their prayers. Daisy leaned towards me and stroked my face, I felt nothing. She leant close and whispered, I must have heard her:

'Please Jane, please live: we're so very sorry for leaving you but we won't do it again, please live and then we can take care of you, we can have some great times, you me and Hester.' Her voice cracked with emotion as she wiped her eyes on her sleeve. Hester took over:

'You bet Jane, we've got so many plans for the three us: so please don't die Jane, we're never going to leave you again, we promise.'

Both girls cried silently. They told me, later, they thought that I looked like a small innocent child as I lay colourless and still in the big bed. But after what I'd been though they didn't think I would ever know innocence again.

Violet and my mother emerged from the ward into the corridor. As they walked exhaustedly along the seemingly endless passage a couple, who had been sitting on two of the chairs lining the walls, nervously approached them. They apologised for bothering them but wanted to know how I was:

'The doctors couldn't tell us a thing, see, because we're not relatives,' they explained and introduced themselves as Stanley and Doreen Lyle.

Mother stared at the couple and wandered how they knew me. Stanley explained that they lived in the flat below mine and had broken in to stop Travis beating me again. Stan sniffed as he told my mother:

'Heard it so many times,'im batterin 'er, shoulda done something sooner but we didn't want to get in between a husband a wife: she's such tiny little thing: she used to stand at the window like a little lost child.'

Tears rolled down his weather worn face and Mother watched as Doreen wiped them away with her sleeve. Violet thanked them for everything they had done and told them the truth, which was that no one knew if I would survive. Doreen immediately began to cry and said that she wished that they had intervened earlier:

'I'll never forgive myself, as long I live, that poor sweet girl,' she sobbed.

Violet reached for the Doreen's hands and held them in her own. She explained that all who knew me were feeling the same type of guilt and shame but that wouldn't help me to get better so they must all be strong. Doreen and Stanley nodded tearfully and then went onto the say that the police had arrested Travis:

'That's a bloody good job, otherwise I'd have gone round there and stabbed the bastard myself,' Auntie Violet spat.

They all then headed homewards, praying that there would be some chinks of light in dark times ahead.

23

At times I thought I sensed a presence around me, at other times I felt desperately alone. I revelled in the total oblivion that surrounded me and had no wish to leave it. The warmth seemed to protect me. It made me feel safe. Accustomed, as I was now, to the sanitary smell and the shadows of people passing by, I wanted to stay in this limbo state forever where I could feel no pain.

Several times I saw my father in my imagination and we spoke a lot. He kept saying sorry for all the bad things he'd done. He tried to explain that sometimes his mind tricked him into thinking he was somewhere else. We talked a lot about his imprisonment in a Burmese prisoner of war camp.

I feel wretched for him as I listened to his harrowing tales about the guards who would put a sword straight through a man's body if a prisoner so much as looked at them in the wrong way. I wanted to tell him that I knew his fear because Travis was my very own Japanese guard. I had lived his fear.

I listened as he told me that all the prisoners ate any insects they could find to supplement their meagre diet of rice. They toiled relentlessly in scorching temperatures and as time went by they welcomed death, I knew that feeling too. My father explained that every day one or more of his fellow inmates would die of disease, starvation, exhaustion or at the hands of their captors. It was a hellish life and he thought that when he got back to Britain he would forget, but the nightmare followed him home and haunted his dreams.

I told him that it was all right and that he could rest easy now. My father also told me that it is not my time yet but that we would meet again sometime. One morning, it seemed as though my father and I were holding onto one another tightly. As we did this we spoke of our love for each other and I didn't want to let him go.

Then slowly my father walked away from me towards the brightest most beautiful light I had ever seen. I felt as though I was being propelled towards the brightness and I longed to follow him. I wanted to go with him, towards the peacefulness, away from the fear.

Out of nowhere I heard a faint, hollow sound swishing around my head. I strained to listen. I thought I hear Mother's voice desperately pleading with me not to go but to please stay because she didn't want to live without me. I thought I felt the presence of a demon but I couldn't see anything. I didn't want to live with Mother and the demon, or were they the same person? I was going to stay in my cocoon with my father, I was sure he would be back.

Mother sat holding my hand as she had been doing for a long time, she told when I had recovered, all the time willing me to live. It had been seven weeks since my arrival in hospital and there had been little change in my condition.

Mother told me that she seemed to spend her entire life trying not to harbour any thoughts of hatred and damnation against another human being. This time though, she could not. She wanted to put a knife through the heart of Travis Parkin and watch as he bled to death; the intensity of her emotion frightened and disturbed her. Desmond had told my mother he had been reliably informed that Travis was out on bail. His parents had, once again, run to his rescue by throwing their money at some expensive lawyer.

Such was the intensity of Mother's anger she felt like punching someone or something very hard and without stopping. She hadn't felt such murderous feelings of aggression since the nuns let her son die. She thought she had buried all those feelings along with him, now they were working their way to the surface again.

My hospital room has become a second home to her and the rest of the family; they all made sure someone was sitting at my bedside, always, to make sure that I was never alone. Mother looked down at me and thought I looked a picture of peacefulness and serenity. The bruises on my face had all but disappeared and the stitches and bandaging had been removed. She gently stroked my downy hair each day and spoke to me as much as she could so I would know she was with me.

One day, as she sat beside my bed, she was sure she saw me move, ever so slightly. She leaned closer down to my face and stroked my warm cheek, telling me she loved me very much. My mother thought she heard me mumble something but it was incoherent. She moved her head closer to mine and was sure she heard me mutter quietly that 'we must love my father'.

She didn't really understand why I was saying this, after so many years, but she didn't care, this was the first time I had stirred since I arrived. She pressed the buzzer above my bed. My mother then kissed my face again so I would know that she was there. Slowly, I opened my eyes and looked into hers. The joy she felt was like nothing she had ever felt before. As the nurses rushed into the room my mother looked up and mouthed a silent thank you to God; she had not spoken to Him for many years but now it seemed the right thing to do.

24

It was another four weeks before I was well enough to leave the hospital. Violet and my mother had to help me dress because I still felt as weak as a new born lamb. Violet wheeled me out of the ward in a wheelchair and I thanked every nurse and doctor that I saw for saving my life. There were tears of joy from many of the staff as they watched me leave, knowing what an ordeal I had lived through and how close I had been to death.

Desmond was waiting outside in the car. He bent and lifted me up then gently put me in the back seat of his car. Tenderly, he tucked a tartan blanket around my legs and kissed my cheek. I gripped his hand and thanked him for taking care of my mother. Desmond smiled and insisted it was a task he enjoyed. On the way home, Desmond drove past my marital home. My heart began to beat so wildly I struggled for breath. I pulled the blanket up around my chest. I looked at my mother. I knew she couldn't bear my suffering but neither can she stop it.

I felt like I was in some kind of limbo land, alive but not really living. I knew my mother saw my expression when we passed my old home but I also knew she wouldn't understand. I closed my eyes and breathed deeply as we drove by, when I opened them again, the vision of the flat was gone, along with my old life.

Desmond helped my mother to settle me on the sofa in the

flat then he left us alone together. Previously, as he had carried me up in the lift, my mind travelled back to the last time he had done that. That was the beginning of my nightmare, hopefully now was the end. Involuntarily, I placed my hand on my stomach and felt a deep yearning for the son I'd never meet and had never even held.

The familiarity of the flat warmed me a little. I wanted to hide away here forever. My treatment at the hands of Travis Parkin had left me feeling grubby and soiled. No matter how many baths I took, the feeling never quite left me, like a lingering nasty stench. I had secretly named my son Michael. Everyone at the hospital had told me not to think about him, as though he had never existed. I knew that I would never forget him.

Deep inside my heart, I thought that I should have done more to protect him. I let him down and for that, I would never forgive myself. Throughout the next few days I was inundated with visitors. Violet, Daisy and Hester all visited and I enjoyed sitting and chatting with them. Normality returned my sanity to me. I no longer stuttered or trembled. Stanley and Doreen also visited; shy at first but true friends by the time they left after a few hours.

Sometimes and without warning, overwhelming tiredness would hit me like a steam train and, oblivious to any visitors still in attendance, I would just drop into a deep sleep. After one of these naps, I awoke feeling much stronger. I swung my legs off the sofa and, very tentatively stood up unaided, it was a great feeling. I began to walk, very slowly, using the walls for support.

At the open kitchen doorway I saw my mother and Desmond embracing and kissing each other hungrily. The look of love in their eyes was so intense that it caught in my throat. I swallowed deeply, feeling as though I was intruding upon a very private moment then I smiled as I said:

'Don't mind me, carry on you lovebirds.'

'Jane darling, what are you doing walking on your own, you should have called me,' my mother exclaimed:

'I can see you're busy.' I said, grinning.

Suddenly I felt my body sway a little. My mother gasped and both she and Desmond immediately rushed over to help. I was grateful for her their intervention. I thanked them both and told them they made a lovely couple; I felt a tinge of regret that I may never feel the way they did because of what had happened to me.

Desmond was cooking a meal for us all that evening. I joked with Mother that had trained him very well. She laughed, as she laid the table with her best cutlery and table cloth. It was good to see her happy. As I sat on the sofa, reading a magazine, the delicious aroma of grilled steak seeped into my nostrils and I felt ravenous.

A while later, we all sat contentedly around the table, enjoying familiarity and each other's company. We drank a toast, with wine, to my very good health and a future ahead of me. I couldn't help but wonder what I would do when I was fully fit.

Once the meal was over, Desmond began gathering up the plates and took them into the kitchen. He returned a few minutes later and, instead of returning to his seat, he walked over to Mother. She sipped at her wine with a puzzled expression on her face. Desmond dropped onto one knee and reached into his trouser pocket. He then opened the blue velvet box that he had taken out and held a gold ring with a small diamond in the centre aloft. He looked into my mother's eyes and asks her if she would do the honour of becoming his wife.

I watched as my mother sat speechless then a single tear rolled down her cheek. Both Desmond and I watched in nervous silence until, at last, she managed to squeak a 'yes'. The tension was now broken, Desmond slipped the ring onto Mother's finger. He then rushed back to the kitchen and returned with three glasses and a bottle of bottle of expensive looking champagne.

Desmond unscrewed the cork and let it fly into the air as we looked cheerfully on. Once the glasses were filled, Desmond explained us that he had fallen in love with my mother, the moment he had set eyes on her, eight years ago, but had never broached the subject until he felt she was ready.

He turned to me and said he has always looked upon me as a daughter and he loved me very much. His beautiful words brought tears to my eyes and it was a wonderful, loving moment as the three of us embraced and, cautiously, began looking forward to a new life together.

In an instant, the bubble of happiness was shattered. A loud pounding on the door and the unmistakable sound of Travis's voice screaming:

'Open the bloody door, I'll smash it down if you don't, I'm taking that bitch of a wife of mine home, and she belongs to me!'

I couldn't stop it; my body began to tremble as blind terror raced through my veins. I let my champagne glass slip from hand and heard it smash on the floor.

I sat bolt upright as I gazed, transfixed, at the door. The banging and cursing continued and Desmond stood up and marched to the door. My mother begged him not to open it. She screamed at him that she couldn't bear the thought of him being hurt. She carried on pleading with him not to open the door but Desmond proceeded to undo the latch. He did so purposefully, regardless of Mother's terrified pleading.

Fearlessly he continued, seeming not to hear anything except the pounding on the door. He pulled it open and was pleased to see the expression of surprise on Travis's face. He had obviously expected mother and I to be alone. Travis hurriedly disguised his shock at seeing Desmond and pulled himself up to his full, puny height and raised his fists in a fighting stance.

Desmond merely stood and looked down at the feeble man, who was at least foot shorter than him and was dancing around like a demented fool. He looked farcical and I wanted laugh, but I knew that I was on the verge of hysteria so swallowed down my humour. My merciless torturer was in my home, there were only a few feet between us and I was paralysed with terror.

Travis carried on jumping around then started to demand his wife back. Desmond stood still and, with his steely eyes, looking down at Travis he told him to leave immediately. All the time Travis was hopping around, Desmond never took his eyes off him. When Travis continued to try and get to me, Desmond calmly removed his glasses and placed them in the top pocket of his shirt and again told Travis to leave.

My mother was breathing deeply as I stood frozen with fear. When Travis ignored Desmond for the second time, Desmond hit Travis straight between the eyes with his right fist. Travis looked confused for a moment then toppled backwards. Desmond had knocked him out cold. Coolly, Desmond then replaced his glasses and walked towards us both and held us until our quaking calmed.

He told us not to be afraid and to wait while he went to the phone box across the road to call the police; he promised us that Travis would be 'out' for at least another ten minutes.

Desmond left, inexplicably I felt the need to venture carefully nearer to Travis. I looked down at the man who had put me through so much misery and all I could feel for him was pity tinged with a deep hatred. His snakeskin leather winkle picker shoes looked ridiculously stupid, sticking up in the air. I remembered that he was very proud of his expensive footwear and would spend at least half an hour polishing them each evening.

A small drop of blood fell from the split on the bridge of his nose and trickled over his eye; I hoped he was in pain and was suffering. I felt a small movement beside me. Mother slipped past me. She was holding the stem of my broken glass in her hand. She bent down and dug the sharp jagged glass into Travis face then dragged it down the whole side of his cheek, from his eye to his chin, like a can opener digging into a tin, it tore into his skin.

At that moment Desmond returned. Looking at my mother bent over Travis, he rushed over and pulled her away, she looked blankly ahead and said: 'He's coming round.'

Desmond took the sharp piece of glass from Mother's hand, wrapped it in newspaper and threw it in the bin. He then led her to the couch. Pouring two large measures of brandy, he handed one to me and the other to Mother. He then fetched a tea towel from the kitchen and held it over Travis's bleeding wound.

I remember feeling utterly astonished that kind and gentle

Desmond had floored Travis with a single punch. I was in awe of his coolness at the situation that developed. Seeing my expression, Desmond explained that he trained as an operative in the Second World War and had been dropped into France several times on secret missions and was more than capable of taking care of himself. I began to think that I hardly know Desmond at all.

The police arrived just as Travis was regaining consciousness. Desmond was ready to for them. He explained that Travis had charged at us with a knife and that we had to defend ourselves as best we could. Travis was helped to his feet. As he started to regain full awareness, he began to struggle with the policemen, trying disparately to stop them handcuffing him.

Blood ran from his face wound. He swore continuously, threatening every kind of torture under the sun if he was not instantly released. Travis ranted that his father knew people in high places and he would make sure that both men would lose their job if they did not release him. Neither of the PCs took the blindest bit of notice. As Travis struggled a knife fell out of his pocket. I recognised it as the penknife that Desmond always carried but had no idea how it got into Travis's pocket. As Desmond bent down and picked it up, Travis screeched:

'That's not my knife; I've never seen it before in my life, useless lousy plods!'

Desmond handed over the knife to one of the policemen, as he was doing so Travis caught sight of his face in the mirror, hanging on the wall. He stopped in his tracks when he saw the skin flapping around his cheek:

'What the hell, what's happened to my face?' he squealed.

He looked firstly at me then at my mother. She was looking

at Travis with a smug expression. Travis opened his mouth in astonishment then fell to the ground in a dead faint. His wound was temporarily tended to and an ambulance was called. As he was lifted onto the stretcher, he came around once more. I listened as they carried him out of the flat, waiting for raging, shrieking voice to fade into the night.

As he closed the door behind them, Desmond turned to my mother:

'That was a very foolish thing to do Lucy, the man's unhinged.'

'He deserved it and I'm glad he's hurt!' my mother screamed. 'He almost killed Jane and her baby is dead because of him: I hope he rots in hell!'

Desmond pulled her into his arms and held her as she began to sob. I walked over and stroked her back, unsure what to do:

'Listen,' Desmond said in a soothing voice, 'I think it would be a good idea if you two went to stay with Susan, in Cornwall, for a while. The fresh air will do you both good and: who knows, it might blow away some of the cobwebs, help you to think more clearly: what do you think?' He held his hand under Mother's chin, talking to her as though she was a small child.

My mother sighed and nodded as a fresh pool of tears formed in her eyes. Desmond said he would drive us both down tomorrow. In the meantime, he ran Mother a bath and helped her into it.

I sat down; my body was still trembling uncontrollably. Desmond walked in and immediately bent down and held me. He talked, comforting and reassuring, telling me that everything was all right and that he would take care of me and Mother. I clung onto him. I couldn't see anything ever being all right again. Something inside my mother seemed to have broken. The expression on her face as she slit Travis's skin unnerved me but I wasn't sure why.

I went to bed feeling thoroughly exhausted but my mind would not let me sleep. The following morning turned out to be a typical rainy April day. Desmond hauled our cases into his car. It was fairly early on a Sunday morning and there were few people out and about. As we drove though Clifton I saw a young woman pushing a baby in a large pram. The poor girl looked sleep deprived and at the end of her tether but I would have given anything to swap places with her.

It sounded daft, even when I thought it in my head, but I felt that my empty arms should be carrying something and I yearned to hold my two dead babies. If only I could have held my son and said goodbye, maybe that would have helped but he was just spirited away. All I woke to was an empty womb and an even emptier life.

The past year and been one of horror and pain but I had come out of it alive and for that I was grateful. I still couldn't get rid of a nagging feeling that I hadn't seen the last of Travis. It made the hair back of my neck stand on end. I concluded this was a natural feeling due to the trauma Travis had put me through, I was sure it would pass with time. As we travelled away from the city, I began to feel calmer and the motion of the car lulled me to sleep.

25

I was shaken awake by the uneven road as were driving through the gates of Carmarthen farm. It was now Sunday lunchtime, meaning that the whole of the Bromley family would be present. I braced myself; I honestly didn't feel up to meeting a large number of people but knew there was nothing I could do about it. Desmond kindly helped me out of the back seat of the car and then he and Mother began to unload the cases.

As they did this Susan Bromley appeared. She walked purposefully over to me and asked me if I would like to go directly to my room. She must have realised that I was still feeling very weak and unwell after the ordeal I had suffered. I was very grateful for this thoughtful, kind woman, who seemed to know how I felt, and I nodded thankfully.

I could hear loud conversation coming from the large kitchen as Susan led me along the passage and upstairs to the room I had always stayed in. Susan closed the window while explaining that she had opened it to air the room then she sat down on the bed beside me. Grasping my hands, Susan asked me if there was anything that I needed to talk to her about. For some inexplicable reason, I threw myself into Susan's arms and held onto her as though my life depended on it.

She was of the same small stature as me but she seemed so much more confident and capable. I sniffed back some tears and said I would dearly love to chat but was I very tired.

Instantly, Susan stood up and lifted my legs off the floor and onto the bed. She then pulled the thick curtains across the window to block out the daylight and walked back over to me.

She held my hand and told me to sleep for as long as I needed. Susan then promised faithfully that I would be safe here and that she would take the best care of me, she then leant over and gently kissed my cheek.

The way she spoke and the warmth of the kiss instantly made me feel protected. I wished that Mother was more like Susan. Sometimes I felt like I was the parent and she was the child. Now, I desperately needed someone to care for me and it seemed as though Mother was unable to do that. Here I felt safe; I quickly dropped into an easy, unhindered sleep.

Back downstairs Susan welcomed Lucy and Desmond into the house and insisted that Desmond have some lunch before he left. Carmarthen Farm had changed a lot over the last twenty years. What had once been a three bed cottage was now extended to a six bed house. Two small cottages had also been built in the grounds for the farm workers.

Much more land had been acquired over the years and the farm was a thriving industry. Once in the kitchen Susan introduced Desmond to everyone. Her eldest daughter and her husband William were present with their five children, Verity and Charlie who were both nineteen years of age, the same age as me. Also present were Edie and Lisa who were thirteen and eleven years old respectively and ten-year-old Billy.

Susan's second daughter Iris was a member of the armed forces and was not at home. But Susan's two sons, twenty two year old Johnny and fifteen year old Jack were part of the assembled gathering. Desmond told me later that he struggled to remember all the names but tried to do so even as Susan introduced him to the rest of the people in the room. There was her husband Edward and their housekeeper Ethel, also present was Ethel's son Cyril who was a professor of geography in Truro.

Mother said the meal was a jolly one and Desmond was sad to leave when it was over but he had to work the following morning. My mother had taken two weeks off; she went out to see him off and tearfully clung on to him imploring him to take care of himself. Desmond, as always, reassured her that he was more than capable of taking care of himself and Travis, if he started hanging around.

He also asked Mother to say goodbye to me as he didn't want to disturb me. I watched from the window as they kissed passionately. Mother stood and watched Desmond go until the only thing she could see was dust from his car then headed back into Carmarthen farm.

The whole two weeks Mother stayed at the farm, she spent trying to take care of me. She told me that I needed get my strength back so I could get over what had happened. To me, it seemed like I had landed in paradise. I awoke each morning to birdsong which seemed to sooth my battered soul. Carmarthen Farm was, truly, my sanctuary and although the physical scars remained the mental ones began to, very slowly diminish.

When the time came for Mother to leave I asked if I could stay. Mother was against the idea. I explained to her that I needed time to heal and that Carmarthen Farm was the best place for me to do that. After some cajoling, and a little help from Aunty Susan, Mother tearfully agreed. Uncle Edward drove her to the station and as the car disappeared into the distance I found myself feeling more peaceful than ever. Why the departure of Mother made me feel like that, I couldn't really explain.

I had been at the farm for seven weeks. The month of June had arrived in haze of heat and hay making. I began to regain some of my full physical strength. Tentatively, I began doing small jobs around the farm. Like a tiny bird, afraid to venture too far from its nest, I didn't go too far. The farm was my comfort blanket, hiding me away from a world that frightened me.

I learned how to find eggs from the many hens that wandered around the yard. Susan showed me how sterilise the milking parlour. I also helped to keep the yard tidy and assisted Ethel in the kitchen whenever she needed me. I got on so well with everyone. I really wished that I belonged to a larger family, the sheer number of people around made me feel safe.

I had been at the farm for six months when my Mother announced that she and Desmond were getting married. I was so very happy for both of them. Together with Susan and Edith, we all travelled to Bristol to witness the wedding. Being back in Bristol gave me mixed feelings. It was pleasant being home but I did not feel entirely safe. Travis had received a one year prison sentence two months ago, but I couldn't shake off the feeling that he'd be back for me. I was very relieved when we were on the train heading home, as I now thought of Carmarthen Farm.

September in Treruth, Cornwall, was uncomfortably hot. Any small task made me sweat profusely but it was no use complaining, we all just got on with it. On a particularly hot day, I made my way to the milking parlour because it was the coolest place on the farm. Johnny was in there finishing up the milking. He smiled broadly when I walked in and told me how beautiful I was, now that I had colour in my cheeks and had gained some weight.

I blushed to the roots of my hair at the compliment. Johnny was over six feet tall and farm labouring had turned him in to a muscle-covered Adonis. His skin was the beautifully tanned by the summer sun and his curly blonde hair fell in tendrils around his handsome face, his bright blue eyes shone like stars in the night sky.

Johnny laughed, as I put my hands on my face, and said he had meant to make me blush which made me redden even more. For some reason I was overcome by a fit of the giggles; maybe it was the normality of the situation, two friends teasing one other. Johnny moved closer to me and pushed a lose strand of hair away from my sweaty face. He looked down at me and his countenance changed, with his voice now stern, he said:

'If I ever meet that stinking husband of yours, I'll tear his bloody limbs off one by one.'

I gazed up into his soulful eyes and thought, Johnny would keep me safe.

Neither of us heard Susan enter but we were both startled by the tone of her voice as she barked orders at us:

'Jane, get back to the kitchen and give Ethel a hand, she's rushed off her feet in there!'

I had never heard Susan talk like that before, she sounded really angry and I was puzzled because I didn't know why. I scuttled away as quickly as I could and hurried back to the house.

When I was out of sight Susan turned to her son, gazing up at him, she sighed:

'Johnny, I don't ask much of you do I?' she said, as she stared straight into his eyes:

'No, Mum, you don't at all, what's this about?' he asked. Susan looked close to tears as she continued:

'Keep away from Jane, she's not for you,' she finished lamely, sounding as though she was ashamed to say the words:

Johnny laughed, an awkward, bewildered laugh:

'Come on, Ma, it was just a bit of harmless flirting, we were hardly walking up the aisle,' he laughed as he finished his sentence but stopped when he saw the expression on his mother's face:

'Please Johnny, promise that nothing will happen between you and Jane,' Susan pleaded, her eyes uncharacteristically filling with tears:

'It's OK, Mum, I promise, nothing will happen don't worry.'

Susan told me how she stroked his cheek and thanked him, and then headed back to the farmhouse. She was sure Johnny would do as she had asked but thought it a shame. He once told me I reminded him of a tiny little bird, that needed his protection and he would have been only too happy to give it. His father, Edward, had always said that women had their funny ways and, in this instance, Johnny totally agreed. Even his mother could be a little odd at times.

26

I walked into the kitchen the next morning and was relieved when Susan turned around and gave me a beaming smile. I thought she would be a little off with me after the incident in the barn with Johnny the day before but she seemed fine now. The large farm kitchen was always spotlessly clean and very cosy. It was the heart of the family home and I was very glad to be here among people I felt safe with.

I smiled back at Susan; glad that any ill feeling had been forgotten and began to lay the plates out on the long, well-scrubbed wooden table. When everything was done Susan asked me to sit down for a minute. She looked a little nervous as she told me about a job at the post office; Cissy had popped in yesterday and thought I might fancy a change. I was immediately interested.

Although I loved helping around the farm I missed using my brain. I had no intention of ever returning to Bristol to work. The more I thought of it the more I liked the idea of trying for the job of post mistress; Susan told me that it was a well-paid job for the right person. I asked Susan if she thought I should apply and she said that I definitely should if I liked the sound of it. I told her that I did and, for the first time in a long while, I found myself happily looking forward to trying something new.

Susan advised me to not waste any time and to ring the post

office right away. I returned to the kitchen, unable to hide my delight. I informed Susan that I had been told to come in for an interview the following day. All of a sudden I felt nervous about leaving the safety of the farm. Susan instantly noticed my frown; she leaned towards me and said:

'Anyone who has been through what you have, Jane dear, is likely to be anxious about setting out into the big wide world again, it's only natural, but you're a young girl Jane and you have your whole life in front of you, thank God, so kick any nerves you have up the backside and go and do whatever makes you happy.'

The thought of kicking my nerves up the backside made me laugh and I thanked Susan as I hurried up to my room to see if I could find something suitable to wear.

The following day both Susan and Edith helped me prepare for my interview. It was a beautiful July day. The birds were singing tunefully as they soared lazily above in the cloudless blue sky. The distant hum of farm machinery whirred in the distance. I loved being at the farm but all I could think about was the interview. I hadn't realised how much I had missed using my mind every day.

I felt that the time on the farm had helped me to heal and now I was ready to become a functioning, bill-paying part of the human race; the feeling gave me a little thrill. The outfit Edith and Susan had chosen consisted of a powder blue pencil skirt with a small slit at the back, a plain white blouse and smart white low heeled shoes with pointed toes. I had intended to catch the bus into the village but Johnny insisted on driving me, in the old farm van, to make sure I got to the interview in good time.

This offer caused Susan to shiver involuntarily as she watched her two children walk towards the vehicle and she wandered if she should have heeded Cissy's advice and confided in her son.

As the van trundled toward the village I began to feel very tense and afraid. Johnny must have noticed my anxiety. He teased that he thought all postmistresses were old maids with grey hair dragged back in a bun and glasses resting on the tips of their noses. His words made me giggle and eased my nerves straight-away. I told Johnny that all the postal workers must have been young once.

Johnny shook his head and informed me, in an exaggerated fashion, that he whole heartedly disagreed. He said that he was quite sure thought that they were all kept in jars of vinegar until they were suitably wrinkled and ready for the job. The thought of a shelf of pickled postmistresses made me laugh even more and soon the both of us were soon holding our stomachs as we rocked with side-splitting laughter.

Without noticing the time going by, we quickly arrived outside the village post office. It was a tiny little shop with a bright red post box built into the wall. I felt lighter and much less nervous than I had been when we first left the farm. I climbed out of the van then leaned in the window and thanked Johnny. Then, taking a deep breath, I headed up the steps and into the shop. The bell jangled noisily as I entered. Mrs Birch, the present post mistress, rushed forward to welcome me.

As the place was empty of customers Mrs Birch ushered me through a door into the back of the shop. This led to a cosy little sitting room with an unlit fire in the grate. Mrs Birch began to explain to me about her forthcoming retirement. She went onto say that her son was coming to see to the retail side of the business but was not interested in learning the postal side, hence the need to advertise the job.

The little old lady, who was very stereotypical of the way Johnny had described aging post mistresses, leaned forward and held my hands in her own. Looking straight into my face with sharp, hazel coloured eyes she began to explain the responsibility of running the post office. She went on to talk about the very strict laws that governed it; every day the postal service were in charge of the queen's mail, they also took care of other people's hard earned money.

Mrs Birch was obviously very passionate about her job. She reiterated that it was a big obligation and not one to be taken lightly. I listened intently to what she was saying. I wondered if I was actually up to the job; what if I messed up? Travis had done a good job of making me doubt myself, which was a good reason to try harder to impress the lady so she should hopefully offer me the job.

I told Mrs Birch that the job sounded just what I was looking for, I explained that I hadn't any experience but that I was eager to learn and would take the role very seriously if I was lucky enough to get the job. The old lady pondered a moment then, announced that the job was mine. I could hardly believe my ears.

I felt as though I was walking on air as I left the building. I couldn't remember the last time I was so pleased and proud of myself. I began to walk out of the village back to the farm. I became aware that someone was calling out to me and turned to see Cissy, Susan's friend, standing in the doorway of her grocery shop waving. I walked over to her. Cissy asked how it went with the job interview. I grinned as I told her my good news.

Cissy seemed really happy for me; it made me feel glad that I would be working in the village. Cissy then told me that she was thinking of renting a room in her home for a bit of extra income, she asked if I would be interested. It had not crossed my mind to move out of Carmarthen Farm. As I thought about it, I realised that it would make a lot more sense if I lived in the village.

Walking to from the farm this time of year was no problem but I didn't know if I would fancy it in the depths of winter. Mrs Birch told me that I would have very early starts and I wasn't happy about walking along the farm lane in the dark.

I told Cissy I thought that it would be a good idea but that I needed to talk to Susan first. Cissy nodded in agreement but asked me if I would like to look at the room anyway, just to make sure it was what I wanted. Before I knew it, I found myself following her through the well-stocked shop and into a small backroom that seemed to act as an unofficial staff room.

I then followed Cissy through another doorway leading into a thin passageway and up a narrow flight of stairs. Once on the landing Cissy opened a door to the left of us then ushered me in. Once inside the room I gasped with pleasure.

The room seemed huge compared to all the other rooms I had slept in. In the middle was a large double bed covered in a beautiful patchwork quilted blanket. There was a large bay window overlooking the village square and at that moment, the sun shone and a cascade of warmth and light illuminated the room. There was also a large chest of drawers with a wash basin and jug on it. Everything about the room was beautifully quaint.

The curtains matched the cover and pillowcases and the whole room was decorated with light floral wall paper. It really was a lovely room. I told Cissy that I would telephone her as soon as I had spoken to Susan. Tears of joy welled up in my eyes as I walked home. I had managed to get myself a job and also a room to rent. This was the first step towards my independence; it was frightening and exciting at the same time.

As I walked up the narrow lane towards the farm I felt as though everything in my world was falling into place. I was thankful that I had escaped from Travis with my life. Mother had told me that Travis had been sentenced to three years in prison. I felt safer that knowing he was behind bars but also angry at the length of his sentence, I felt he should have got longer.

Now I was recovering I could not comprehend why I had allowed myself to be abused so badly. I tried not to harbour any bitter feelings towards Mother. It was a difficult subject; I really couldn't work out why she had coerced me into marriage with a man I hardly knew, all for the sake of 'her good name'. It made no sense to me, but I felt that it was not something I could talk to Mother about without upsetting her. After consideration, I thought it best to let everything rest and look forward to the future and leave the past where it belonged.

The sky was now a coloured cacophony of orange with pink streaked across it. It was a stunning sight. The hedgerows were alive with wild life. Dotted about were lovely shades of blue, red and yellow flowers scattered along the whole lane and I felt very lucky to be alive and in this beautiful countryside.

Only a few days later, my belongings were all packed into a small case and I began my new life in Cissy's home. I was surprised and moved at the depths of Susan's sadness when I left. I hugged her tightly and assured that I would visit often. As it was the weekend, the whole family were on hand to help me move my few possessions.

I had never felt so close to anyone in my entire life; these wonderful people felt like the extended family I had never had and I was truly grateful for their love and support. At Cissy's I arranged my stuff in my new room and gazed out of the large window into the square below.

It was a busy Saturday morning with lots going on below. Ivan Pellow, Cissy's husband, was loading up his van with grocery orders ready to deliver to his customers. Two women chatted animatedly as they stood outside the white painted butcher shop next to the grocers. The town hall had doubled as the library for the day and there was a stream of people constantly going in and out.

I decided there and then that I absolutely loved my new home. Padding down the stairs, I asked Cissy if there was anything I could do to help. Cissy stood behind the shop counter rocking baby Linda in her arms. She explained that she was a bit fractious because she was teething. I offered to take the tiny baby out for some fresh air.

Cissy thanked me wholeheartedly and with obvious relief she handed me the child. She then led me around the back to where the pram was. She put a bottle of milk in the basket below and informed me that Linda would want feeding in about half hour.

As Cissy began to tell me to put extra bedding on if it grew cold, I stopped her and promised that I would take great care of her daughter. Cissy laughed and thanked me again exclaiming that she had turned into a mother hen without even noticing it.

I pushed the baby out along the back lane and into the large village square. I looked down on the gurgling little girl and realised that Linda was the same age as my son would have been had he lived. A blanket of sadness monetarily enveloped me but I shook it off, determined not to dwell I things that I could not change.

I walked along a small tree lined lane until I came to the village church. It was a magnificent building with its tall spire and stained glass windows. Just then, Linda stopped gurgling and been to scream at full pelt. I hastily looked around and spotted a seat amongst the colourfully decorated grave stones. Heading for it, I grabbed the bottle from underneath and pulled Linda from the pram.

The moment the milk was in her mouth, Linda's screaming stopped, much to my relief, I actually felt her raucous screams could awaken the dead. As I continued feeding the now contented baby, a small figure shuffled towards us. The woman sat down next to me on the bench and took in a deep breath of fresh air. I said hello and, after a few minutes of silence, the lady turned and smiled at me. She then lifted her head and announced that there was no better place to be in the world than in Cornwall; I enthusiastically agreed.

She then introduced herself as Betty Miners and told me that her late husband used to be the vicar of this very parish. We chatted a little more then, to my surprise, Betty Miners repeated her whole conversation again; I listened again as I realised that the poor old lady's mind was wandering. I sat patiently and answered the same questions she had asked me before, all over again.

As we sat, I saw a movement in the corner of my eye. I turned to see a man approaching; I knew that he was a vicar because of his gown and collar. His gentle face was full of concern. He apologised for his aunt, Betty Miners, and explained that she had wandered off while he was doing some chores. I assured him that the lady had been no trouble at all and that we had enjoyed a pleasant conversation.

The man smiled warmly and thanked me; he then bent down towards his aunt and led her away talking to her as though she was a small child. I watched as they went towards the church and briefly wandered if that was all there was to life. Did a person come into this world helpless and vulnerable and then leave it in the same way? If I could have seen into the future, I would have thanked Betty Miners there and then for saving my life.

I decided not to follow that line of thought and began to wind Linda, who had gulped down her milk as though she hadn't been fed in a month. The little girl finally burped loudly and vomited on my shoulder. I laid her back into her pram, wiped the stain from my clothes and meandered back towards the square. The whole atmosphere of Treruth was one of friendliness and belonging and I realised that I was content to spend the rest of my life in the safety of this tight-knit community.

As evening approached I headed back to the shop and parked the pram in the back yard. Linda was now sound asleep so I secured the gate and went indoors. I found Cissy also sound asleep in the makeshift staffroom with her feet up and snoring loudly. Quietly I put the kettle on and, on hearing the shop bell clang, I headed towards the counter.

An elderly woman was waiting to be served, she asked if I

was new and I nodded. She told me she wanted some flour and bread of which both I found easily. The cost of the items was displayed in front of them, so I took the money and rang it into the wooden till.

I turned my head, as I heard the house door opening, to see Cissy standing there with her hair jutting out in all directions, yawning loudly and rubbing her eyes. Once she had woken herself up more, she thanked me, overly, for my help with Linda and in the shop.

Cissy went onto explain that she had not really wanted children but Ivan had talked her into having 'just one'. Of course, she loved little Linda but she found raising a child exhausting and vowed that Linda was her first and last. Just as she finished her sentence a loud howling could be heard from the back of the house, we both grimaced as Linda's raucous screeching grew in volume.

As Cissy started to go and see to her daughter, I stopped her and offered to take care of Linda whilst Cissy served in the shop. Cissy thanked me all over again and happily began to restock the shop. I realised that although Cissy would take care of her little girl, her maternal feelings were lacking. I thought maybe Linda would help to soothe the constant ache I felt at the loss of my own child.

27

Lucy, my adoptive mother, wrote and told me that she had never felt so safe and happy in her entire life. Desmond was the soul-mate she had always wanted to meet. She had loved Michael but in a childish, immature type of way. Mother came to the conclusion that it was more through thankfulness than love for rescuing her from the nunnery in Ireland.

She may have been imprisoned, with the nuns, her entire life had Michael not stepped in and took to Bristol to stay with Violet and Len in the tiny terraced house, where they still lived. When she was a child my mother had lived a cushioned life, smothered by her over-protective parents. Her own mother was forty-two when she was born and Mother became the focal part of both her parents' lives.

When she became pregnant, her comfortable existence instantly vanished and her once loving parents dumped her one of the notorious laundries that were and still are common place in Ireland for unmarried mothers to be.

For many women, who were condemned to those dreadful places, it was the only home they would ever know. Then and now, only a male member of the woman's family were permitted to free them. If no one did so, they were left to life of drudgery working for the nuns for just food and board.

Some of the women would rise through the ranks. The ones that had been there the longest became as evil as their captors; they would treat the new comers as barbarically as the sisters did. My mother had given birth to a baby boy who had died because the heartless nuns had failed to get medical help throughout the labour. Not a day went by when she did not think about her son.

Mother now smiled with joy as she felt the butterflies fluttering in her tiny stomach signalling the start of a new life inside her. She was forty-two, the same age as her mother when she had given birth to her first child; she promised herself that the child she was carrying would be loved forever, no matter what mistakes he or she made.

28

I helped Cissy prepare the dinner for the family, which included Cissy's brother Alan. He worked as a mechanic at the local garage and had always lived with Cissy. I discovered that they had lost many family members during the war so stuck together and were very close. Ivan, Cissy's husband popped his head around the door and announced that he was closing the shop. He also said that he could see Alan doing the same at the garage across the square.

As I began to spoon the food onto the plates Alan came in through the scullery at the back. He commented on the lovely smell of the food as he always did. I been living here for a month and felt very comfortable with the whole family.

I turned to thank him for the compliment. We both looked at each other at the same time. Momentarily our eyes met and remained locked together for a few seconds longer than necessary. I remember feeling like I had goose bumps but I didn't know why. Presently, we all sat around the table. Cissy said some prayers and I looked up to see Alan smiling at me across the table and I grinned back at him, suddenly feeling shy.

Thankfully Linda was asleep which allowed Cissy to enjoy a meal using both hands, instead of one, while balancing her daughter on her knee and feeding her at the same time. No sooner had Cissy finished her last mouthful when Linda's crying rang out, sounding like an air raid warning. Cissy rose tiredly and Ivan gobbled down his meal and followed her shortly afterwards.

Alan smiled and told me how Ivan had talked Cissy into having baby Linda and now felt extremely guilty about all the extra work the baby made for her. Alan explained that he knew they both loved their daughter but had not realised just how much care a new baby demanded. Together with the sleepless nights and running the business together the poor devils were completely exhausted.

He went onto say that he wasn't much help as he worked long hours at the garage, being the only fully qualified mechanic. He told me that loved his job and enjoyed fixing cars but felt guilty that he couldn't help out more at home. As we chatted, we cleared the table and washed and wiped all the tea dishes. When we were all done Alan asked me if I fancied a drink in the pub across the way and, to my own surprise, I decided that I did.

It was a fairly warm evening as we strolled across the village square. I had a cardigan around my shoulders in case the weather became cooler as the evening went on. The large oak tree seemed to be standing guard over the village and, in particular, the heavy wooden bench underneath. Although the timber had been replaced the original iron frame remained and I wondered what the bench would say, if it could talk, and how many people had sat there and watched life go by.

Alan looked sideways at me as we meandered across the road. He later told me that he thought my dark blond hair fell down my back like a golden curtain; it was tied back with a blue ribbon that matched the colour of my cotton summer dress. I wore white sandals with no heels and carried a small black handbag. The trees bristled quietly as a small breeze whipped through its branches causing my cardigan to fall from my shoulders.

Both Alan and I bent down together to retrieve it but Alan got there first. We both remained, for a moment, in the crouching position, gazing into each other's eyes, as though this was the first time we had met. Alan then placed the garment back around me my but not before he noticed the terrible scars on my shoulders, neck and upper arms. He told me that he felt bitterly angry about all the pain I must have suffered and wished he had been there to protect me from that fiend of a husband. Cissy had told him a little about what had happened when I was married to Travis.

The Three Lambs ale house had a small pub garden at the back where Alan and I headed for, with Alan carrying the drinks. It was deserted as it was still quite early. We both sat down to enjoy a glass of refreshing lemonade. Both of us were glad that there was no one about, although neither of us really knew why. Alan began to talk. He had a habit of pushing his hands through his thick black hair when he discussed anything that troubled him and his hazel brown eyes shone with unshed tears when he spoke about his childhood.

We talked about our families. Alan told me that he was three years old when seven members of his direct family and more than twenty of his relatives had been killed in the London blitz. He remembered clinging onto Cissy, his sister, fearful that she may too disappear and told how she, too, clung onto him. He described arriving in Treruth from the bustling city of London and being afraid of the lack of noise and people but he soon grew to love the countryside.

The vicar's wife, Betty Miners, had taken care of them; she had fed and comforted them both until they found somewhere to live; Alan said he would never forget how grateful he was to that lovely woman, caring women. She found them a home at Carmarthen Farm. Alan laughed as explained that he felt he had been dropped into another world. He had never seen a pig or a cow in his entire life and it took some getting used to.

As he spoke, I watched as his strong arm muscles tensed and loosened, they were so big they seemed to be fighting to escape from the short sleeved cotton shirt he was wearing. I guessed that he must be over six feet tall. As I listened to story, about his life, I thought how about how awful it must have been living through a war.

I thought Alan's bronzed skin and dark hair made him very handsome. I noticed that his dark eyebrows turned down into a frown when he became animated or sad. I felt sorry that someone so young had suffered such a terrible loss, but that was life and there was nothing anyone could do about it.

Alan told me that he and Johnny were closer than brothers and I laughed as he told me how they bickered on many occasions, just like real siblings. He explained that he lived the last years of the war with Ethel Haversham and her son Cyril when Cissy moved to Bristol to be a bus driver. I listened as he explained that many people had entered his life, who were not blood relatives but he regarded them all as family and was forever thankful that he still lived among them.

We finished our drinks and decided to go for a walk as it was still a very pleasant evening, weather wise. As we strolled along a boulder-strewn path Alan took my hand in his huge bear-like paw and smiled down at me. With me being so small and Alan so large, we looked a little like the couple in the fairy tale, Beauty and the Beast.

The scent of the many flowers in the hedgerows smelt like nothing I had smelt before. We walked a complete circuit then found ourselves back by the bench in the square. We both sat, now obviously comfortable in each other company, and I told Alan all about my life, about my mother and father, Travis and Desmond, and just about anything that I wanted him to know about.

Alan's features clouded over when I described my treatment at the hands of Travis and his eyes welled up with tears when I told him how I longed to hold my dead children. Talking as I was, seemed to be unburdening me, I'd never spoken so intimately to anyone in my entire life. It was refreshing and upsetting at the same time.

Alan held both my hands as I spoke and when I had finished he told me that he wanted to make sure that no one would hurt me again. He said that the moment he set on eyes on me he wanted to protect me, for the rest of his life. Strangely, due to the fact that I barely knew the man, I liked the idea of being safe, it made me feel warm inside.

I had known this man for just a few weeks but felt at completely at home in his company. I smiled and said that I would like that very much; we walked hand in hand back to the shop and both laughed at the surprised expressions on the faces of Cissy and Ivan. When we walked in, Ivan was marching up and down the living room with Linda screeching as he jiggled her in his arms, desperately trying to get her to sleep.

I walked over to him and took the screaming bundle; Linda instantly stopped crying and gazed up at me curiously. Ivan sighed resignedly so I explained the reason that Linda has stopped crying, when I held her, was because she could feel his tenseness. I was calm and unflustered and Linda could sense my serenity. I told Ivan and Cissy to get some rest while and I took care of the baby for a few hours. With utmost gratitude they thanked me and headed wearily to their beds.

The next few months were what I could only describe as the healing months of my life. The close knit village all knew about Travis and they all seemed to look out for me, without really saying anything about it. I happily began to take on more responsibilities in my role as post mistress and I really enjoyed the job. I had my own keys to let myself in and out and the customers seemed to like me.

I was truly astonished when Alan presented me with a sparkling sapphire engagement ring on my birthday. I was so overwhelmed that I burst into tears. When I had finally composed myself I explained to Alan, that, oddly I had never felt part of a family before, but now I did. I told him that I felt loved and needed him more than I had ever needed anyone before; this made the soppy devil shed a few tears before he quickly swiped them away. That evening we all drank a toast to our future.

29

In July 1963, Lucy, my adoptive mother, gave birth to a tiny baby boy whom she named Mikey. She and Desmond brought their son down to Cornwall to visit me and the Bromley family. Although I thought the little boy was perfect in every way, I was puzzled to find that I probably had more feelings for baby Linda than my half-brother. I didn't worry too much though and decided that my feelings towards my step- brother would grow over time.

Alan and I spend many wonderful hours together doing not much at all. We loved to walk around the beautiful Cornish countryside, wandering down the country lanes in the warm summer evenings. We tried to guess the names of the many birds that flew above us. We picked blackberries to make jam and spent hours trying to find out the names of the vast amount of woodland plants that grew in the area. Lots of girls my age might have found that dull but I loved the feeling of normality, our excursions brought me, and didn't think I'd ever get tired of it.

We arrived home one evening to find Cissy and Ivan had bought a television set. Lots people owned them nowadays but this was the first one that I'd seen. We were all totally transfixed as we sat and watched the black and white figures on the tiny screen. Most often, Alan and I would sit on the small comfortable sofa in the parlour; I would listen to the wireless while Alan read the daily paper.

The comfortable nature of our relationship meant we were completely at home with the silence. I felt happily cocooned and wanted nothing more than to spend the rest of my life with Alan. It could have been an idyllic life if only the dark clouds hadn't began to gather as trouble loomed ahead.

One blissful, warm, balmy day I sat on the bench under the oak tree. I had my eyes closed enjoying the warming feeling of the sun on my face. I was making the most of my dinner hour; I opened my eyes when I heard Cissy shout from across the square. I waved as I watched her wheeling her daughter down the lane towards Carmarthen Farm in a pushchair. Linda had now grown out of the needy, new born stage and slept through the night, making life a lot easier for her once frazzled parents.

The square was almost deserted as I shut my eyes once more and turned my face towards the sun once again. Suddenly, even though there was no wind, the leaves in the oak tree rustled then a shadow fell across my face blocking the heat. I opened my eyes and froze in terror.

At first, I thought that I was dreaming as I looked up to see the face of Travis stood above me, twisted with hatred and bitterness. But when he began to spit his bile, I knew that this was no dream but a living nightmare. I realised that the square was now empty of life. I looked, frantically, around as Travis clamped his hand around my wrist.

I began to fight with every part of my body. I was about to scream when Travis fastened his hand over my mouth. With his other hand still tightly clutching my wrist he dragged me, effortlessly, towards his hastily parked car.

I think it surprised Travis to realise that I was putting up some type of fight. He had always regarded me and my mother as the worst type of simpering, useless females. Although Travis was a small weasel-like man he was still much stronger than me. He shoved me down into his car with little effort. He then quickly jumped into the driver seat and sped his way out of the village.

As the car hurtled along the narrow country lane, I made an attempt to open the door. I knew that I would rather be killed rolling under the cars wheels than at the hands of my psychopathic husband. This earned me a punch in the face then Travis leant over and slammed the door close. I was stunned by the blow and felt hot, sticky blood trickling from my nose. I tried to shake the imaginary mist away and regain my senses.

As I looked above into the bright, blue cloudless sky I was sure that I could see the smiling face of Michael Rosental and I waved to him. Seeing him brought me a feeling of calm; he didn't wave back, he just shook his head sadly until his image disappeared altogether. Travis saw me waving and told me I was a stupid bitch to be waving at fresh air.

I turned and looked at the demented face of Travis, as he told me what he was going to do to me before he cut my throat. When I was dead, he was going to throw my body of the Cornish cliff tops to be eaten by the sharks and I would never be seen again. He carried on shouting his vitriol as spittle drivelled down his chin. His face was twisted in a mask of hate as he screamed that I had ruined his life:

'I would still be in that damn hell-hole of prison you bloody sent me too if my father hadn't paid a good lawyer money to get me out!' He shook with undisguised rage as he ranted on:

'I've got no bloody home or job, nothing at all and it's your fault!' He screamed as he said this, his voice much louder than it usually was.

I refused to react and continued to stare straight ahead as he fumed and raved, like a man possessed. This must have enraged him even further because he turned and punched me in the stomach with a ferocious blow.

As the car careered madly around the country lane, I knew that I was going to die; death itself didn't frighten me, just the thought of what Travis would do before he killed me. I felt physically sick at what I was about to endure at the hands of this crazed lunatic. I hoped that he would stop near enough to the cliff edge so that I could jump off before he had a chance to touch me; killing myself would be preferable to the suffering that he was so desperate to mete out to me.

We were now approaching a cross roads. I saw a tractor lurch to a halt, like a large hippo stopping for a drink. Travis effed and blinded, while waving his fist at the bemused tractor driver. I felt a stirring of optimism but the tractor began to continue with its slow, clumsy journey. I looked above in the hope that I would see the image of Michael again but the sky now only showed the fast appearing granite coloured clouds that were now scudding across it like deliverers of doom.

Strangely, it was at this moment that I felt a sense of peace. I was happy that death, at least, would bring me freedom. I would no longer have to be frightened or have to fight anymore: I could just enjoy the ethereal tranquillity that dying would bring.

Mother's face briefly flitted into my mind and I felt sorry for the sadness I knew she would feel. I hoped that her new son would help to soothe her pain. I closed my eyes and begged

God to bring my end as quickly as possible but my prayer was interrupted by the loud cursing of Travis.

I opened my eyes and was almost faint with relief. I could see that the tractor had merely driven forward to manoeuvre itself into a different position and was now reversing down the lane towards us, blocking Travis's way. As the vehicle drew closer and stopped, I saw Johnny climbing down from the cab. His curly, unruly hair had now been cut short and was pushed back from his face. He flexed his muscles and every inch of his brawny body looked taut and ready for battle.

Travis leant forward into the car and pulled out a large kitchen knife from the glove-box then, impatiently, swung his legs out of the car. Johnny didn't flinch, not even when he saw the weapon that Travis was waving wildly in the air. As Travis unleashed a hate-filled tirade at Johnny, I heard the screech of brakes. Twisting around to look behind me, I saw the grey van which Alan drove around in but that actually belonged to the garage.

The door flew open and Alan jumped out. Every inch of his body looked angry and seemed set to explode with rage. Travis now realised that he was caught in a trap and looked wildly around for a place of escape. It would have been comical if I wasn't so terrified. Travis was like a mouse being approached by two giant elephants.

Alan and Johnny advanced towards Travis from either side. I could see Travis trembling, I was glad that he was now afraid:

'If any of you bloody morons lay a finger on me, my father will have you locked up and they'll throw away the bloody key!' His voice faltered as he finished speaking.

Travis reached into the inside pocket of his jacket and pulled out a small stiletto- bladed knife. As the two men advanced further, Travis started waving both weapons wildly around. Johnnie leaned forward and flicked the two knives out of his hands, as though they were irritable insects. Alan then lifted Travis off the ground by his hair as he squawked and squealed like a baby bird. The two men then began to punch and kick Travis as he lay on the floor flailing and sobbing, begging them to stop.

This seemed to stoke up Alan and Johnny's anger even more and the blows continued until Travis stopped moving. Alan then walked over to Travis's treasured sports car and lifted me gently out of it. He proceeded to carry me over to the van and started the engine. Johnny moved the tractor onto a grass verge to allow us to pass. Alan parked the van and walked back; he and Johnny picked Travis up and dumped him into his sports car. Alan returned to the van as Johnny began to drive the sports car away. We followed him to a very remote spot, used mostly by ramblers. I watched as Johnny and Alan stripped Travis of all of his clothes and hurled them over them cliff top.

Alan then reversed the van a small distance away so that it was hidden by a thatch of brambles and undergrowth. I then observed, from my hiding place, as they put the now naked body of Travis into the driving seat of his own car. Johnny and Alan then rested his head on the steering wheel causing the car horn to beep loudly. Both men then ran and hid behind a high mound of grass and foliage.

They watched as two walkers, obviously hearing the noise of the horn, advanced towards the car and peered into. The man and woman gasped when they saw the bloodied, naked body. Once they knew that Travis had been discovered, Johnny and

Alan crawled through the grassland back to the van. They both clambered in. It was a massive squeeze in a two seater, with the two burly men, so Johnny pulled me gently onto his lap as Alan cranked the vehicle into gear, hit the accelerator and sped away.

Alan jokily warned Johnny to keep his hands off 'his girl' while Johnny spoke in the same voice telling him to keep his eyes on the road. Once they reached the parked tractor, Johnny and Alan both climbed out of the van. I watched as they chatted a while then they both shook hands. Then Johnny went one way in the tractor whilst Alan and I headed back to Treruth. All throughout the journey Alan kept apologising for letting me down. He stroked my shoulder and lap as he told everything was over now and Travis wouldn't dare show his face again.

I said nothing but didn't agree at all, I knew Travis far better than Alan did. I knew that he is like was cat hunting a rodent and he would not give up until he had tortured and killed his prey. I asked Alan how the found me. He explained that Betty Miners had seen me being dragged away by Travis. She ran and told the Ivan and Cissy but, at first, they didn't believe her because of the state of her mind. It wasn't until she mentioned a red Jaguar E Type car that they realised she was telling the truth. Ivan rushed over to the garage to alert Alan who then phoned Johnny.

They both concluded that Travis would take the coast roads back to Bristol to stay out of sight and luckily they had been right. They had planned for Johnny to block his way with the tractor. They were both going to threaten him and send him away with a flea in his ear but when they met him, they knew this wouldn't be enough to keep him away. He needed a much harder warning than a verbal one. When they had spoken earlier, he and Johnny had decided that they would both act as each other alibis.

They were quite sure I could now sleep safely in my bed. I wished that I could share their enthusiasm but, sadly, I could not. I was absolutely certain, in my mind, Travis would never let me get away with 'ruining his life' and dread prickled around my body.

That evening as Cissy and Alan fussed around me, I asked them to stop which they both did abruptly. I only managed to pick at my meal as I tried to think about what to do for the best. As we sat in the living room, drinking our cups of tea, Cissy asked what was bothering me. Taking a deep breath, I explained that I was sure Travis would be back and he would be angrier than ever.

All were thoughtful for a while. Suddenly, Alan jumped up and then hurried from the room. He went into the front of the shop and came back with the daily newspaper. He speedily turned the pages until he came across what he was looking for. He spread the tabloid over the small coffee table and pointed. I leant forward to see what he was so animated and excited about and gazed at the advert on the page.

I peered at the print. The government were encouraging families to immigrate to Australia to start a new life. The article stated that at least one of the family members needed to have a valid trade. Also, if the family could come up with five hundred pounds then the government would match that to help cover the costs of moving overseas. It was called the nest egg fund.

For the first time in many months I saw a make-believe gate opening ahead of me. I felt hope, for the first time, of a future free from fear. I could hardly comprehend that I had a means of escape. I envisaged the imaginary chain that had been holding me melt away and I rushed over to Alan and threw myself into her arms, even Travis the maniac would not follow me to Australia.

As I stood in Alan's warm embrace a thought occurred to me and the chain tightened again. How would we find five hundred pounds? I turned and voiced the question to Alan. He smiled widely as explained that he had three hundred and forty pounds, which he had saved over the years, and he would borrow the rest from the bank. Cissy then piped up that he would do no such thing and that she would give us the rest of the money, if it meant that her brother was happy and safe.

I was again overjoyed and filled with gratitude for the wonderful, kind-hearted people. As tears of happiness fell unashamedly from my smiling eyes, the make-believe shackles broke then vanished into thin air.

Alan and I immediately began to set the wheels in motion for our move to another country. I was beyond excited; I felt so very happy to be moving to a place where no one knew me. I could start afresh and maybe re-invent myself as someone mysterious and exciting. First and foremost though, we both had to submit our birth certificates to the authorities to prove we were who we said they were.

I read every snippet of information I could find about life in Australia and the more I read the more impatient I became to leave. As we were claiming assisted passage we were required to stay in Australia for the minimum of two years. Everything I read seemed to indicate there were better living conditions and employment opportunities across the sea; I could hardly contain my enthusiasm and I ached to board the ship and head to my new home.

At the weekend Alan and I both strolled happily along the lane to Carmarthen Farm, we were going to tell Susan, Edward and the rest of the family about our plans. I hummed happily as we walked down the narrow country lane. Both Alan and I were eager to share our news with the Bromley family. When we arrived at the farm I was delighted to see Iris, who was home on leave. I had always admired Iris's independent spirit and the unwavering decision she made regarding the path she wanted to take in life.

I embraced her warmly and expressed, as I had done many times before, how wonderfully smart Iris looked in her army uniform. Iris, in tune, extolled army life and reiterated that her decision to enrol was the best she had ever made.

When all the family at the farm were together in the over warm kitchen, caused by the Aga being continuously lit even in the middle of summer, Alan and I nervously made our announcement. At first there was an astonished silence then Iris was the first to pipe up and congratulate us on our wonderful news. One by one Johnny, Edward, Ethel and the rest of the family all joined in with the congratulations.

Only Susan stood back, not uttering a word. She told me sometime later that all she could think about was that she would never see me again and that thought devastated her. She remembered that she quickly composed herself before anyone noticed her desolation and embraced both Alan and I sincerely. Susan wanted to make sure that I had made the right decision and I, steadfastly, assured I had. Susan could see that I was very keenly anticipating my new life and put aside her own sorrow for the sake of my happiness. My next words, however, shook her to the bone.

I explained that I had telephoned my mother to ask her send my birth certificate to me as we wouldn't even be considered for the programme without it. Curiously, Mother had insisted on delivering it by hand and would be down at the weekend. I noticed that Susan's pallor had turned to a pale grey and she made the excuse that she needed the toilet.

It seemed as though Edward had noticed his wife's distress but he did not go after and comfort her as I thought he would have done. I remember feeling troubled by his attitude and worried about Susan but no one else in the room seemed to sense anything amiss so I said nothing and began to talk excitedly about my life in Australia.

Susan told me of her terror as she stood motionless in the large bathroom. In the centre of the room was a large, iron, claw footed bath with a matching sink and toilet at the far wall. She looked around this room that was so familiar to her and began to retch. She was absolutely sure that everything she had ever worked for would now be taken.

She was positive that Edward would never forgive and he would almost certainly throw her out of the home they had shared for so many years. She had worried about how Johnny and the rest of her children would take the news, would they hate her and banish her from their lives?

For the first time in many years Susan felt totally out of control. Her throat felt like it was closing tight and she could no longer breathe. She felt over-heated and nauseous and the bathroom began to sway in front of her. Blackness engulfed her for a small amount of time before she opened her eyes and saw, to her great relief, Edward looking into her face with a concerned but distressed expression.

Susan told me she recalled that she was trembling uncontrollably and grasped Edward's hands for reassurance that she was not going insane. She could not understand what was happening to her, she had no idea that the inner anxiety that she had managed to keep the lid on for so many years was now escaping, in a physical way, and was making her body to twitch and shiver involuntarily.

Edward eventually picked up his distraught wife and carried her though the narrow passage to their bedroom, out of the way of prying eyes. As he laid her gently on the bed he was overcome with compassion at his beloved Susan's plight. He could see that the thought of her family discovering her indiscretion was crippling her. Edward lay down on the bed beside Susan and held her tightly until the trembling had subsided. Susan turned to him, her face wet with old and new tears.

She gently whispered that she had something to tell and that he would hate her for it and she wouldn't blame him. Edward pulled out his large white handkerchief from his pocket and began to dab at his wife's face, at the same time as telling her that he already knew. Susan was totally shocked and immediately began to gabble incoherently; she then began to fire questions at Edward.

He silenced her and explained that he'd only found out a couple of months ago when he had heard her and Cissy talking. He went on to say that he was devastated and felt very badly treated but had put a lot of thought into the matter. The war, he continued, was a dangerous and uncertain time and lots of people acted out of character due to a mixture of loneliness and fear and, to Susan's overwhelming relief, he announced that he forgave her.

This brought a fresh wave of tears from Susan but this time Edward was a little sterner. He told her to pull herself together and dry her tears. Their children must be told before Lucy arrived with the damning birth certificate. Susan nodded but still clung onto Edward in a way that was alien to both her and him, she had always been the strongest personality out of the two of them.

Edward held her for a moment longer and told her that he would be right beside her if any of the children decided to turn against her. They would stand together and both try and explain what it was like living through the hellish nightmare of a country at war. He also said that their children loved her very much and he was quite sure they would forgive her. He said it a lot more conviction than he felt it, he just hoped they would understand.

Susan told me she had never loved Edward more than she did at that moment. Less than ten minutes ago she had seen her safe, comfortable world collapsing in front of her; now Edward had forgiven her and for that she would be eternally grateful. Telling her children about her deceit would be one of the hardest things that she had to do, but tell them she must and the sooner the better. Susan made a superhuman effort to compose herself but in truth, she felt physically weak and drained.

Susan's eyes were awash with admiration when Edward looked her directly at her and told her that she was a tough woman who had suffered a lot in her life. He said that this set back would make them stronger as a family, of that he was sure. With those words ringing in her ears Susan went downstairs and apologised to me for her absence blaming a bilious attack.

I embraced and told her that she was looking a little peaky and that I hoped she would feel better by the weekend when my mother and Desmond arrived. I remember Susan nodded and attempted a smile but she doubted very much that she would feel better when Lucy arrived.

30

It was a slightly cloudy Saturday morning when Alan and I, once again, made the journey to Carmarthen Farm. The day before Alan had deposited the five hundred pounds in our joint post office account. I could hardly contain my excitement; it made everything seem more real now we'd actually got the money sorted.

The whole time we meandered up the winding lane, I jabbered on about our new life. Alan seemed to love listening to me talk about our future together. As we approached the farm we spotted Desmond's car, now a more sensible family car than the one Desmond had previously.

I rapped on the door then entered through the passage into the warm fug of the kitchen. I was slightly taken aback when I saw Edward and Johnny standing in the kitchen, they were usually working on the farm at this time of day. Susan turned around as we entered the room and I noticed that she looked no better than she did a couple of days ago; in fact her complexion was whitish and she appeared deeply uncomfortable.

Unusually, Susan asked us to come into the living room. I was puzzled but did as she was asked. Ordinarily, we all sat in the large, homely kitchen. Alan and I entered the living room to see my mother and Desmond already waiting in there; Desmond was holding little Mikey. As soon as I walked in the room he walked over and warmly embraced me. I became aware something was going on when I saw Edith, Susan's eldest daughter, and Iris perched nervously on one of the armchairs. I turned towards my baby brother and tickled his soft chin.

When the door was shut behind us all, Susan asked everyone to sit. I was beginning to feel suffocated by the unexplained atmosphere. Feeling uneasy, I grabbed Alan's hand. Mother stood and approached me then she held her hand and gave me my birth certificate. I decided whatever illness Susan had caught, Mother was now also suffering from it, her skin was as white as porcelain and her eyes watery and red rimmed.

I looked around the room, everyone here seemed to be anticipating something but I had no idea what. Johnny looked intently at me but Edith wouldn't even look in my direction.

I reached for the birth certificate and thanked my mother then began to introduce Alan to her and Desmond. I stopped mid-sentence as my Mother pointed to the document. Unfolding the piece of paper, I swallowed nervously. I had never seen it before and began to read. At first, I didn't really absorb the importance of what was written; I read it over again, feeling the eyes of all those in the whole room upon me. It felt like, at that precise moment, time stood still as I read and re-read what was written on the birth certificate.

Apparently, I was born on the same day as Edith's eldest two children, Verity and Charlie but we had always celebrated my birthday a few days later. The words that seemed to spring out at me were:

Jane Fairly born April 5, 1943

Mother: Susan Bromley – munitions factory worker

Father: James Matthew Fairly – airman in the United States Airforce

For a short time my world seemed to stop as I tried to make sense of the words. I looked up at Mother; she was staring at me, intently, with tears falling down her cheeks. Desmond placed a protective arm around her trembling shoulders. I then turned to Susan who was standing, as if frozen to the spot, her expression a mask of shame. I began to speak quietly, only just above a whisper:

'Are you saying that my whole life is a lie?' I asked my mother, hoping that this was some kind of nightmare:

'We thought it for the best, at the time.' Mother explained but it sounded pathetic even as she said it:

'You thought it was best for whom?' I screamed, 'I don't know who the hell I am!'

My initial disbelief was now replaced by a ferocious emotion of anger and distrust. I walked over to Susan and leaned in very close into her face:

'You bloody gave me away to save your bloody good name, you left me with a psychotic father and a pitiful mother, I've never ever felt safe, not for the whole of my life and then she bloody forced me to marry a monster!' I spat at Susan as I jabbed my finger towards my so-called mother.

I don't know why, or what came over me, but I couldn't stop myself, I then raised my hand slowly and slapped Susan across the face. She gasped then clasped her hand to her now smarting cheek as the sound of the blow reverberated around the room. Still feeling a mixture of rage and bewilderment, I grabbed my handbag and birth certificate and headed towards the door. I thought for a moment then swung round and glared at Susan:

'What about him, James Fairly, does he know about me?' I asked.

Susan nodded; I just shook my head, still unable to grasp the enormity of what I had found out. I walked towards the door:

'Where are you going love?' Enquired Alan as he ran his fingers, worriedly, through his thick dark hair,'

'Anywhere, as far away as I can get, this is so insane, I need time to think.'

'What about Travis?'

'He's hardly going to bother me for a while after what you two thugs did him, it makes you just the same as him, did that cross your minds?' I spat, unable to control the anger bubbling inside me.

Both Alan and Johnny looked shamefacedly at the floor as all the eyes in the room turned on them:

'I need to be on my own to try to work out why I've been deceived for the whole of my life, so don't anyone dare follow me!'

I stormed out of the room and slammed the front door loudly behind me and began to walk purposefully back down the narrow lane. I couldn't comprehend how my whole identity had vanished in the last ten minutes. I wasn't Jane Rosental and my parents weren't my parents. It was too much to take in.

31

After I left, Susan told me that the room was silent for a while, as everyone in it struggled to find something comforting to say. Edward later told me that he was immersed in his own thoughts. This was the first time he had heard the name of the father of Susan's baby. His memory travelled back to many years earlier when he had just returned from a hellish fighting mission in Burma. Susan was at work so he had gone to the pub with Ivan Pellow. He could still remember how delicious a pint of English bitter had tasted after the months he been away.

Ivan had introduced Jimmy Fairly to him and he remembered him distinctly. The man had seemed ill at ease with him and couldn't finish his drink quickly enough, before making an excuse and leaving. At the time Edward had thought him odd and rude but had soon forgotten about it; he never met the man again. Edward turned and looked at Susan. She stood with her hand to her cheek looking like a lost little girl, his heart instantly went out to the woman he had loved for so many years.

Edward's mind went back to 1943. He recalled how, during the war he had spent some illicit nights with a lady called Doris. They had both got a lot of comfort from each other as they both missed their spouses enormously. Suppose he had gotten her pregnant and he had a child he knew nothing about? Edward quickly put this thought out of his head and rushed over to Susan and pulled her into his arms. He felt Susan's body tremble as he drew her closer to him and she began sobbing quietly.

Johnny, Edith and Iris joined them and put their arms around their mother until her tears stopped. At that point, Edward knew that they would get through this and that their children had forgiven Susan. Life would go on as is always had done, and for that he was very glad. Susan told me that she felt the luckiest woman alive to be blessed by such a wonderful family but she couldn't get the sight of my shocked expression out of her head. If she could have turned the clock back and prevented all the pain she had caused, she would have done.

32

My rage slowly ebbed away as I tramped down the uneven track. It was quickly replaced by an inner turmoil, so severe, it took my breath away. I was frightened, I felt like a stranger in my own body, almost as though I didn't belong to it. I wanted to run to my mother for comfort, but she wasn't my mother, she was nothing to me, just a stranger who brought me up.

I reached Cissy's house quicker than I had ever done previously and walked in through the back door. I was very relieved to find place empty. I could hear Ivan's voice coming from the front of the shop, chatting loudly, as he served his customers. I crept up to my room and sat on the edge of my bed.

Even though I was knocked sideways, by what I'd been told, little jigsaws of my life began to slot together. I remembered my father dying and being thankful rather than sad, when I was a child. This had made me not like myself because Mother had always explained that my father was ill and I didn't think I should be glad he was dead.

But the unbelievable thing was, Lucy wasn't my mother and Michael had never been my father. I took the birth certificate out of my bag and looked at it. I felt as though I was in some kind of surreal universe where everything I'd ever stood on had floated away leaving me flailing and struggling to balance.

I had no idea what I was going to do but I knew I couldn't

stay in Treruth. In my mind, everyone in the village probably knew my true identity and had conspired all these years to keep it from me; I wandered if Iris and Jack knew and concluded that they probably did, everyone but me probably knew.

Out of nowhere, a thought popped into my head. Hadn't I always wanted to go to London? Didn't everyone say that the streets were paved with gold? I had very little money so was about to dismiss the idea when I remembered the money in the joint post office account. That was how I would escape the turmoil that was swirling around me like autumn leaves in a gale.

Quickly, I packed as much as I could fit into my large suitcase. Turning around, I took one last look at the room that I loved and had wanted to call home. Tugging it off my finger, I sadly put my engagement ring on the bedside table. Checking that the coast was still clear, I walked out the back way and across the square to the post office.

Using my own set of keys, I opened the door and slipped behind the counter. I then unlocked the ancient wooden drawer and counted out what money was in it. There was four hundred and twenty pounds and some change deposited in the drawer, which would have to do. I put the pile of cash into my bag.

Being predominately honest, I filled out the necessary paperwork and stamped the post office book so Alan would know I had taken the money from the account. I gazed around the little post office that I had come to think of as my own private domain before hastily walking out of the door. I made sure that it was securely locked before posting my keys back through the letterbox. I then headed for the bus stop outside of the village square as it was less obvious than the main bus stop, meaning that there was a smaller chance of me being seen by any of the villagers.

I stood well back, as I waited for the bus, partially concealed by the tall, grassy hedgerow until I heard the familiar sound of the ancient old vehicle and looked up to see it trundling towards me; with seconds to spare I stuck my hand out, the bus driver slammed the brakes on, bringing the vehicle to a creaking halt. I apologised to the elderly driver for startling him, he just grunted and restarted the bus.

I had a quick look around the vehicle was relieved to see there was no one familiar on the bus who might have wanted to know where I was going. The conductor appeared and I paid him my fare then I was left alone to think about everything that happened in the last few hours. The Cornish countryside passed by in haze of summer colour, bright red poppies and blue cornflowers sprouted out of the thick hedges accompanied by brambles, stinging nettles and yellow gorse bushes.

I looked ahead at the portly bus driver and couldn't imagine the petite Cissy driving a bus, like she had in the war. Cissy had sat down one evening and told me how learnt to drive a bus because she wanted to do something to help with the war effort. I wandered how she could possibly see out of the cab window let alone manoeuvre the clumsy vehicle through the narrow lanes.

In no time at all I arrived at the train station and clambered off the bus. I was slightly encumbered by my bulky case but made my way to the platform and staggered towards one of the ticket booths. The ticket seller told me there was not a train due to go to London until for o'clock in the morning. This stalled me, as it wasn't part of my hastily made plan. I dithered a little, unsure of what to do. It was just after four in the afternoon so there would be a very long wait for the next train.

After some thought I made the decision that I would leave my case in a locker at the station and walk into town to find something to read while I was waiting and a sleeping bag. I intended to bed down in the waiting room until my train was due. Once my luggage was secure, I bought my ticket and took the short walk towards the town. As I approached I realised that it was now late in the day, on a Saturday, and most of the shops were closed. So much seemed to have happened in the space of a few short hours that I had simply forgotten what time of day it was.

I searched the narrow streets and was lucky enough to find a small bookshop still open and was able to buy two hardback books. At least that meant that I had something to keep me occupied so I wouldn't get bored whilst waiting for the train.

33

Unbeknown to me, Iris had followed me, at a distance. She explained that she could see how distressed I was. She felt very sorry for the devastation I must have felt when I heard the shocking news. Hiding in the shadows, she first spotted me heading to Cissy's house then emerging, a short time later, with a large suitcase. She then watched as I went into the post office then, momentarily, lost sight of me when she took her eyes off me for as short while.

Iris told me how she shook her head and cursed the low attention span, that had plagued her all her life, and began to walk around the village searching for me. It was an extremely warm day and Iris was sweating in her thick military uniform; even though she felt uncomfortable she was so proud to be a member of the armed forces that she never tired of wearing it. She adjusted her peaked hat, on top of her blonde curly hair and this kept the sun off her already pink face. She looked around but had no idea where I could have gone.

As the village bus drove by Iris suddenly had a thought. She knew that I was going to leave because of the suitcase I was carrying but she needed to find out where I was going. Iris turned and quickly tried to follow the bus but being on foot she raced around the corner only to see the tail end of the bus disappearing down the narrow, dusty lane.

Meanwhile, I managed to find a run-down café a couple of

yards from the station where I bought a stale cheese sandwich and an apple. Normally I would have been appalled by the quality of the food but, at that moment, I was so ravenous I enjoyed every morsel. I had retrieved my case and was now ensconced in the smelly waiting room, reading my way through one of the books. It was called Vanity Fair; I had read it before but enjoyed it so I didn't mind reading it again.

As I leafed through the pages, a memory popped into my head from many years ago. Susan had shown me a vast collection of books and told me to read as many as I liked. I could still remember the musty smell and the joy on Susan's face as she pointed out her favourite reads. Lucy had never been much of a reader so I must have inherited my love of books from Susan.

I looked out of the small, grimy window, it was now early evening and the sun was disappearing and the shadows were getting longer. I heard the scrape of the wooden door opening and folded over the page of my book. Looking up I saw Iris stood framed in the doorway. I couldn't hide my annoyance as Iris turned and shut the door. She walked over and plonked herself, heavily, down next to me on the hard, unforgiving bench. She grasped my hand tightly and looked directly into my eyes:

'I'm not here to stop you,' Iris said soothingly, 'I just wanted to make sure you were all right, it must have been a terrible wrench, finding out you were adopted.'

I sighed and relaxed a little then twisted around and hugged Iris tightly. I began to try and explain how I felt. Iris listened intently as I began, haltingly:

'I feel utterly lost and adrift, as though my whole life has been a complete lie, I can still hardly believe it, to think that after all these years nothing about me is real, I need some time to come to terms with everything and time to try and find myself, I don't even know who I really am.'

Iris nodded and listened. As tears began to trickle down my face Iris passed me a handkerchief and told me to carry on. I continued:

'All my life I've felt that some pieces of my existence didn't seem to fit but now they are falling into place like pieces of a jigsaw puzzle. Since I was a little girl it had frightened me that I felt very little love for Lucy and Michael but, because they were my parents, I felt it wrong to feel that way about them. All I actually ever felt for Michael was a mixture of pity and fear.'

I blew my nose once more and paused a while, trying to regain my crumbling composure then went onto say:

'I tried so very hard to love Lucy but found her difficult to understand, at best, and irritating at the very least. When she coerced me into marrying Travis I felt as though I hardly knew the woman, now I know why, she's not even related to me.' I finished talking then dissolved into a fresh bout of crying.

Iris waited until I inhaled a few deep breaths and regained control of my emotions, once more, then asked me what my immediate plans were. I told her that I had none but was heading to London for a fresh start. Iris promised to keep my whereabouts secret, on condition that I promise to write to her at her barracks as soon as I was settled. I agreed and Iris scribbled her address down on a piece of paper.

We stood and hugged, once more, Iris then rose to leave. As she walked out of the waiting room I shouted that I'd always wanted a sister and Iris turned to look back and replied, with grin across her face, that now I had two.

With the waiting room door firmly shut behind her Iris headed back to Treruth. I gazed at my watch and was surprised to see that I had been chatting to Iris for more than two hours. I think I hoped that unburdening myself would make me feel better in some way but it hadn't.

I laid my case on the bench then rested my head on it; pulling my legs up on to the hard surface I put my hand under my face. I tried to get some sleep but eventually gave up, only finding myself waking up in the dark gloom of the night.

I pulled myself stiffly into a sitting position and rubbed my aching back and legs. The room was in complete darkness except for a small shaft of light coming in through the tiny window. It was coming from one of the brightly lit lamp posts on the station. My watch told me that it was quarter past three and my stomach lurched with a combination of excitement and anticipation. A short time later I heard the distant rumble of the night train. I stretched pulled myself off the bench and walked onto the platform.

For a second I felt a dagger of fear run through me. I was running away from everything I had ever known. Shaking myself mentally, I quickly dismissed this and struggled onwards with my baggage. The distant rumbling grew into a thunderous roar as the vehicle approached. I thought it looked like a raging dragon with wide fire-filled eyes and nostrils.

It was fairly empty and I found myself a seat in a carriage that was virtually empty. The train began to move. As I got further away from the only family I'd ever known, it wasn't only the miles making me feel distant and alone. The rocking movement of the train sent me into a restless sleep.

I was jolted awake by the screeching of the train whistle and quickly shook the sleep from my tired eyes. I gazed out the window and looked out at an enormous station. I was amazed at all the different types of people milling around or working on the platform. There were African, Pakistan, Chinese and Jamaicans, mostly dressed in their own traditional, colourful clothing. Some ladies wearing colourful flowing saris and others had their identity almost entirely concealed apart from a small slit for their eyes.

I thought my eyes were going to pop out of my head as I looked at the multicultural people in front of me. I rose from my seat and wrestled my luggage from the train. I had never before seen so many people in one place in my entire life. I was utterly amazed. Now I had arrived, I realised that I had not thought further than actually getting to London. I made my way to a doorway with a large exit sign flashing above it and struggled to push open the large double doors, awkwardly manoeuvring my heavy case.

I finally exited the building and stepped out onto an even busier street. I would have thought that in a city filled with so many people no one would be lonely but, at that moment, I felt the loneliest I had ever felt in my entire life. It was as if the world was still turning but it had left me behind.

34

Susan explained to me many years later, that although she tried several times to halt the constant flow of tears, she couldn't. In her mind, all she could see the hatred in my eyes that was so similar to Edith's when she and Edward had sat down and told the family about me. Edith had not held back and let flow a torrent of obscenities about how terrible she was for sleeping with another man while her father was fighting in a war. Johnny had, at first, an incredulous expression on his face.

Susan knew he had long held her in such high esteem that he couldn't think that she would ever do anything wrong. She also knew that he was ashamed of her and it felt like a dagger was being rammed into heart. Iris just sat, seeming to slowly absorb the bombshell her parents and just dropped whilst Jack seemed unaffected but eager to leave the strained atmosphere of the kitchen.

The dreaded revelation were not going well, Edward walked over to Susan and put his arm around her trembling shoulders. He needed his children to understand:

'You probably think that the war was no excuse to be unfaithful, and that's true, but you have to live through a war to understand what it was like. One minute we're a normal family getting by, living our lives: suddenly boom, everything's gone. I'm sent away for years on end: you girls were sent to live here and your mother was left alone in Bristol.'

Edward moved away from Susan and nearer to his children, 'The family home was destroyed and your mother was living in a room in a house. The constant threat of death from the air raids and the long, relentless working hours made life hard: many people, I know, found solace from the relentless fear and graft by falling into someone's arms and Susan was one of them. I'm not saying what she did was right, I'm just saying that they were different times and, as a family, we should all stick together: get through this and look forward to a peaceful future.'

Edward swallowed as he waited for a response.

Susan had looked at her children's faces one by one and knew they now saw her in a different light. I had run off and Susan was sure she had lost me for good, although the rest of her sons and daughters were present, she could not be sure that she had not lost them as well.

35

I stood in a kind of bemused daze, with no idea what to do next. Farther along the road, I saw a row of parked cars to the left of the station door with a sign saying 'taxi rank' above them. I walked towards the nearest vehicle, at the front of the line and knocked on the window. A coloured man stepped out of his taxi; he wore a grin that was so infectiously large, I could help but smile with him. He asked how he could help and I explained that I needed a place to stay for a couple of nights.

As he leant down to pick up my suitcase his long, Rastafarian dreadlocks fell around his face. He put my bag into the boot of his car then opened the back door and gestured for me to get in. As he was doing this he explained that he knew of a comfortable bed and breakfast in the centre of London that was moderately priced and very clean.

I looked out of the window as he drove, I thought the streets of London were supposed to be paved with gold but they weren't. They were just the grubby, grey colour. I thanked him and a short time later he came to a halt outside a large house.

Opening the back door for me to get out, the taxi driver retrieved my luggage and carried it up the few steps to the entrance. He then knocked loudly on the front door. It was quickly opened by a large lady, who I was sure was a related to the man, wearing an enormous flowery apron wrapped around her whole body and her face was showing the same joyous expression as my driver:

'Oh Solomon, have you brought me another waif and stray.' She asked, as she smiled widely at me.

'This young lady needs a place to stay so here we are.' He answered.

As I turned to pay the fare he told me the lady was his sister and that she ran the best lodging house in London. I thanked him kindly and followed my new land lady into the house. She led me to a door at the back and to the right of the house. I walked into the room and was pleasantly surprised at the size and layout.

It wasn't dissimilar to my room at Cissy's and I felt a small pang of homesickness. The name of my landlady was Mrs Rollins. She told me how much the rent would be and when it was due. I thanked her and paid a week in advance.

As I sat in the strangely familiar room, a new emotion overwhelmed me. A paralysing fear crept all over my body. I felt as if I belonged nowhere and that no one in the world cared about me. I imagined the kitchen at Carmarthen Farm and felt a dreadful longing to be there. I wanted to hear Susan's confident voice calming me, telling me everything was fine. But the betrayal by everyone I knew and loved had hit hard, I knew that the only person I could rely was myself.

36

Iris told me that she explained this when she arrived back to Carmarthen Farm. Everyone was waiting for her; they all knew that she had gone after me. Iris told them all I was safe but needed time on my own to come to terms with what I had been told. She also said that she and I would keep in touch. She told Susan not to worry, and that she would keep an eye on me and make sure that I was all right.

Iris looked at her mother and she felt such sadness for the woman, who loved them all so much, that she couldn't stop herself from rushing to her and pulling her into her arms. All throughout her childhood, Susan had been a strong and self-assured woman, who would go to any lengths to protect her off spring but now she clung onto Iris like a small child, in need of comfort herself. When Susan had calmed herself, Iris made a pot of tea and poured a good glug of brandy into Susan's cup in an effort to try and lift her out of misery.

As she drank Susan began to talk. Both Edith and Johnny sat at the table while the rest of the family stood. They all listened intently as Susan tried to explain why she did what she did. Susan explained to them all about her horrendous childhood, how she'd always been looked upon as some type of wild creature for everyone to pity.

She went onto to tell them about the terror she suffered on a daily basis at the hands of an angry, drunken father and how her mother had abandoned her when she was a small child. Consequently, she could not abandon any of her own children, not even one that was the result of an affair.

Susan continued to say that the mother who had left her came to help her by offering to adopt me and bring her up as her own. She believed it was her way of recompensing Susan for abandoning her. At first the arrangement worked wonderfully well. It meant that Susan could visit her daughter and watch her grow. Sadly, when I was three months old, Susan's mother was killed when a bomb exploded in her house. Her mother had died shielding me from the blast.

Lucy had been a friend and confidante when Susan had become pregnant so when her mother died she took me to Lucy in Ireland so that she and her husband, Michael, could raise me as their own.

It was when Lucy and I moved to Bristol that Susan began to invite us down to the farm, primarily to ensure that I had not suffered any lasting effects from Michael's illness. She hoped that she could coax me out of my shell because I was so timid and unsure. Susan knew what she had done was wrong and was very sorry. She should have told the family the truth about me from the start but she was afraid of losing everything and everyone.

Susan told me how scared she was. She sighed deeply as, with difficulty, she explained to her family that the feeling of being pitied and pathetic had never left her. She didn't want me to feel pitied in any way so continued inviting me to the farm to ensure I was nurtured and loved in every way. Susan bit her lip as she told them all that she realised that she was doing a very selfish deed in flaunting me under the noses of her unknowing family.

A small amount of time lapsed, probably less than a minute but in Susan's tormented mind, it felt like a life time and was so consuming she feared that she would collapse. After a while, in unison, the four grown up children each stood and walked over to the hunched figure of their mother and they jointly embraced her as their tears mingled with hers. Edward fought to control his emotions but a giant lump formed in his throat as he heard his children tell Susan that they forgave her. Later on that evening, when she was alone, Susan fell to her knees and silently thanked God.

37

I had been in London for only four days when I managed to find myself a job. I had visited the labour exchange on the advice of Mrs Hollins and had been given an interview for a job in a typing pool. My exemplary secretarial skills meant that I was offered the position within the hour and now, here I was, on my way to start my new job.

The previous day I had been out shopping and had bought a pale pink dress, the type that Hester and Daisy used to wear, with a matching jacket with large buttons in the same material. I wore low heeled white court shoes and a white patterned head scarf. I took a few deep breathes as I walked along the busy street heading for the tube station. Mrs Hollins had insisted that this was the quickest and cheapest means of transport.

I was pleased to find that she was absolutely correct, the tubes ran constantly and my stop was just across the road from the building where I would be working. I was still trying to accustom myself to the many different faces and smells but was beginning to enjoy the frantic hustle bustle of city life. I decided that it gave me a lot less time to think, which had to be a good thing.

I took the lift to the floor I was working on and walked through the double doors with an air of confidence that was completely false. Several girls turned around and looked at me, some held tea of cups or smoked while others just turned to stare. I smiled shyly as I walked towards the nearest group of woman.

I explained about my job and was pleasantly surprised to find that they were a friendly bunch of women who were happy to help me find my feet. The room had rows of desks with typewriters and paperwork on them. I was led to a desk near to the front of the room.

As I sat down, a screeching siren sounded which was obviously the cue that the working day was about to begin. All around quickly put out their cigarettes and finished their tea before sitting down. The room was now transformed from a gossiping melee of women to an orderly office where the only noise was the clacking of the typewriters and the dinging sound as they started a new line.

A supervisor arrived and explained to me what I was required to do. I was glad to realise that I easily understood. As I was looking through the paperwork, the double doors at the end of the room were flung open and the noise of high heels, clicking on the parquet flooring, could be heard above the sound of typing noises. Before I had the chance to turn around and see the source of the noise, a tall, tanned girl plonked down on the chair next to me.

She immediately began taking off her out door clothes and quickly set about her work. The supervisor turned and reprimanded the girl about her lateness and she in turn apologised sweetly, blaming the buses. She then made a comical face at the woman as soon as her back was turned.

I laughed then carried on with my work. I was so absorbed, in what I was doing, that when the bell for the tea break rang out, I nearly jumped out of my seat. As the workers began to pile out of the office, the late-comer turned and introduced herself to me. She told me that her name was Mary Magar and that she was always 'bloody late', no matter what time she left home.

I thought the young woman was strikingly beautiful with long, slender legs and beautifully manicured finger nails. Her clothes were classy and looked very expensive. I said that I was pleased to meet Mary and that my name was Jane Fairly, it rolled off my tongue and sounded so much better than Jane Rosental. That mousey girl was now a part of the past and, with my new name, I found a new me.

We hit it off straightaway. Mary linked my arm with hers as she directed me to the large canteen which was now a hive of activity. Each and every employee in the building seemed to be jostling their way to the counter to grab a cuppa before the hooter sounded for them to return to work. We got ourselves a drink and sat at the end of a packed table. We began to talk and, in no time at all, it seemed as though I'd know Mary Magar all my life.

38

Lucy, my adoptive mother, walked down the front steps of her flat with a shopping bag in one hand and baby Mikey under her other arm. It was a warm September day and the air seemed to be so heavy that she found it hard to breathe. At forty-three years old she was now pregnant again. Mikey was only eight months old and Lucy told me that she had no idea how she was going to cope with two small babies.

The pregnancy was a 'happy accident' as Desmond, her husband, had called it but Lucy felt far from happy. She felt exhausted and listless as she put Mikey in the back seat of her car, a nippy Austin Seven that Desmond insisted she have. Lucy looked up and gazed around her, she couldn't shake off the feeling that she had felt for a few weeks that someone was watching her; she wanted to think it was me, but she knew in her heart that was unlikely and I was, probably, not coming back.

Unintentionally, she knew she had hurt me far too badly by keeping the truth from me. That was something that she would have to live with for the rest of her life. The way I had looked at her as I left Carmarthen Farm made Lucy very certain of this. Lucy shielded her eyes with her hand as she continued to scan the area in front of her but there was nothing unusual about the scene so she struggled into her car and began to drive to her doctor's appointment.

She had discussed her fears of being watched with her doctor and had been reassured her that it was probably her pregnancy, causing her mind to work overtime. She, desperately, wanted to believe that was true but she wasn't entirely convinced.

Travis watched as the small car carrying Lucy Masters and her baby drove out of his sight. He could hardly contain his hatred as he stood watching her lumbering into her car. He would wait for the right moment. He didn't care how long it took but he was going to make certain that the woman would pay for everything she had done to him. In his mind, I had disappeared off the face of the earth so any punishment would have to be dealt out to his ex-mother-in-law.

He sighed angrily as he thought about the way his life had turned out as fingered the jagged scar down one side of his face. Travis's mother and father had come to visit him in hospital after Johnny and Alan had beaten him up. Instead of the sympathy, he felt he deserved from his parents, they berated him for trying to see me.

Travis had tried to tell them he was still secretly in love with me and that was the reason he came looking for me. Neither of his parents was stupid enough to believe that. His father banged on about how much money he had wasted on solicitors to keep him out of prison only for him to go and do the very thing he had warned him not to.

When Travis was released from hospital he returned home only to find that his father had reclaimed his beloved sports car and replaced it with a tiny Standard Motor car. When he had begun to protest, his father screamed at him that he didn't deserve anything and was lucky to have a car at all. His mother, who always took his side in the past, stood resolutely beside her husband nodding in agreement.

In a further blow, his father informed him that he was being sent to Wales to work in a friend's company, in an effort to keep him out of harm's way. The rage and injustice Travis felt was so immense he wanted to beat his father to death, pummel his fist into his face until there was nothing left but pulp. Travis knew that his father could match him physically so he did what he normally did, he argued, begged and pleaded but this time, to no avail.

Now he was working in small, grimy office as general dogs-body on a pitiful wage driving a pathetic vehicle. In his warped mind, he blamed this all on Lucy who had pushed for his disastrous marriage to me and scarred him for life. Someone needed to pay for ruining his life and, in his warped mind; he decided it may as well be Lucy. Travis snubbed out his cigarette and ambled back to his car. He swore to himself he wouldn't rest until he had killed Lucy Masters and her squawking child. Travis would bide his time until the opportunity rose and then he would pounce.

39

I simply loved working in the office with the other girls. We were all roughly the same age and our break times were spent talking about Elvis Presley, Jerry and the Pacemakers or any one of the other new bands that seemed to dominate our lives. I felt a genuine sense of belonging and normality in my life. A few months ago, I had moved into the spare bedroom in Mary's flat. I remembered fondly how I gasped with pleasure when Mary showed me around.

It was the most wonderful apartment I had ever seen. The carpets were plush and thick and in the corner of the lounge was a little cupboard that housed a television set. Every bit of the flat was opulent with expensive furnishings and it even had a washing machine. I wondered how Mary could afford such a place on the wages we were both earning.

Very soon after I had moved in, I discovered exactly how Mary could afford the rent on such an, obviously, expensive apartment. When I first moved in, Mary made it clear that I had to make herself scarce on each Friday evenings as she was entertaining friends. Feeling a little puzzled and pushed out, I stood across the road from the flat on one particular Friday, hiding behind a massive oak tree whose roots had broken through the pavement.

I waited then watched curiously as James Sinclair, our boss, arrived and let himself into the flat, as if it was his own home.

I then stood and waited until I saw Mary close her bedroom curtains. As I waited, in my concealed spot, the penny dropped and I realised that Mr Sinclair and Mary were obviously having an affair. I then realised, it must be him who was subsidising the rent.

I knew that he was married because his wife had come into the office a couple of time. She was a snooty little madam who obviously thought herself a cut above the typists. She never spoke as she walked through the room, just stuck her nose in the air like we were all some kind of bad smell.

Later on that night, as I lay in my comfy bed staring up at the ceiling, I couldn't work out whether I disapproved of Mary or not. As the night went on, I came to the conclusion that it was none of my business how my friend conducted her life. Over the past six months the pair of us had become as close as sisters but both of us still had our own secrets, I finally dropped into a deep sleep. I stayed in my room the following morning until I was sure that I had heard Mary's visitor leave.

Mary was sitting on the large sofa with her feet tucked underneath her. She was wearing a frilly white negligee with a matching dressing gown. I walked in the room carrying two cups of coffee. When Mary saw her me she stood up and twirled around, her beautiful face alight with joy. I told her that her lingerie was stunning. She laughed and we both plonked back down on the large sofa together. I turned and looked Mary in the eyes then asked her if she was happy to be sleeping with her boss.

Mary smiled and told me that she was delighted. We both agreed that although he was more than twenty years older than the both of us James Sinclair was a handsome man. I was curious and couldn't help asking Mary whether she felt guilty about sleeping with a married man. Mary explained that she was doing nothing wrong, she was, after all, a single girl and that any guilt should fall at her lover's door.

I thought about it and although I agreed, I also knew that it was always the 'other woman' who got the blame if anything went wrong. We talked for a long time about our lives. Mary said that she thought beauty could be a hindrance or a help, depends how it was used.

Mary also said that we were both beautiful in different ways. She was tall and willowy with honey coloured skin and sparkling hazel eyes. Her hair hung, like a shimmering black cloak, down her back. I had now grown my dark blonde hair long and loved the way it curled around my heart-shaped face.

Mary had persuaded me to dye my hair a few shades lighter. She said that I now looked like a young version of the Doris Day. For the first time I could remember, I was enjoying life on my own terms. Mary and I became closer by the day. We both enjoyed the simple pleasures in life, like shopping for clothes together and dancing our evenings away in one of the many dance halls dotted around the city.

Eventually, I too, began to realise that men were attracted to me and began to view men through the same eyes as Mary. Most of the men that we dated were much older and almost certainly married. We had more shoes, coats and perfume than anyone could ever imagine. Life was being good to us both, for once, and we were enjoying every second.

40

Life continued as normal at Carmarthen farm. Susan told me that she was increasingly glad that the amount of work it took to run a large farm kept her from thinking about me. Although I had promised Iris that I would keep in touch, I had broken that promise and no one knew where I was. Knowing she had no place in one of her children's lives, upset Susan immensely and she hoped wherever I was I was happy.

At least she knew that I was alive and must be earning some type of living as Cissy had informed her that I was transferring money orders, via the post office, to Alan to repay the money I had taken. Cissy could not conceal her dislike of me for what I had done to Alan. The poor lad was still heartbroken at losing me and the light seemed to have gone from his eyes altogether.

Susan could understand Cissy's bitterness but she wished that her friend would keep it to herself; she was, after all, insulting her daughter. Now, Cissy was once again, sitting at the table wringing her hands as she lamented to Susan how worried she was about Alan. Susan advised that only time would heal and that it had only been six months since I had left. She went onto say that Alan was lovely man and would eventually meet someone else.

Cissy spat that she hoped he would meet someone the entire opposite of bloody Jane Rosental. Susan sighed as she poured them both, a much needed, cup of tea.

The following morning the shrill ringing of the telephone rang out through the house. Susan rushed to answer it and was surprised to hear the voice of Desmond, Lucy's husband. After a couple of moments of idle chit chat he, haltingly, asked Susan if would be prepared to come and stay with them for a few weeks when it was nearer to Lucy's due date.

He went on to confide that he was worried about his wife as she was finding her pregnancy gruelling both mentally and physically. Susan told him that she would be glad to; she explained that she was sure Ethel would be able to cover her work load.

To the surprise of all at Carmarthen Farm, Ethel's thirty-two year old son, Cyril, had embarked on a whirlwind romance with a work colleague and had married a lady he had only known for a few months. This was a complete shock to Ethel as she was sure that he was a confirmed bachelor. The poor woman was even more upset when Cyril and his wife left for a new life in New Zealand.

Susan explained to Desmond that Ethel missed her son very much and was always glad to be at Carmarthen Farm, rather in her cottage all alone. Lucy's due date was in eight weeks' time so Susan and Desmond made plans for Susan to stay for between one and two weeks, or however long she was needed.

Desmond sounded much less panicky as he thanked Susan and replaced the receiver. Susan was feeling quite excited, she hadn't been away from the farm since Lucy's wedding. She would love to see Bristol again and spend time walking around her old haunts and the added bonus would be spending time with Lucy and her family. She hummed happily as she made her way to the milking shed to sort whatever work that needed to be done in there.

41

I was lying comfortably in bed with Rob snoring quietly beside me. Rob Salmon was a lovely, kind, gentle man who was well built with soft hands and a teasing smile. I thought it was a shame that he was married but then, all the best men seemed to be.

I slipped out of my warm bed and pulled a silk kimono style dressing gown around my naked body. I then lit a cigarette and walked towards the window to look down on the street below. It was quiet and peaceful, as it was a Sunday morning. I listened to the sweet sound of birdsong, now that it was not obscured by, the usual, never ending noise of the flow of traffic on week days.

I was so lost in my thoughts that I didn't hear Rob sidle behind me. He wrapped his arms around my waist. I turned to face and offered him a puff of my cigarette which he gladly accepted, as he wife had banned him from smoking at home, something he was not at all pleased about. As he inhaled deeply the two of us were disturbed by an urgent banging on the front door. I walked out of the room to answer, just in time to see Mary heading in that direction so I left it to her to see who our early morning visitor was.

As I headed back to at the window I heard some loud screaming and shouting. I peered down at the road below but couldn't begin to think where the din was coming from. I turned to look at Rob who was frowning and looking a little afraid. I was about to ask him what was wrong when the screeching voice sounded nearer, it seemed to be coming from the lounge area of the flat.

Suddenly and without warning the bedroom door flew open and a middle aged woman barrelled in, obviously enraged. I looked at the panic on Rob's face and quickly realised that this must be his wife. I reckoned she was probably around forty years old. She was a plump, shapeless lady with finely coffered hair and beautifully manicured finger nails. Her chubby cheeks were livid red as she hurled herself towards me.

Rob instantly sprung in front of the woman and tried to wrestle her to the bed. I felt the ludicrous need to giggle as I watched the stark naked Rob grapple with his portly wife. As her hairstyle began to suffer in the farcical fight, Rob's wife broke free and she began to charge towards me like a raging bull.

I stepped back and braced myself for a battering just as Mary flew into the room. She caught the flailing figure in a strangle hold. From what Mary was yelling, it seemed that the woman had shoved passed her and locked her out. Rob had now put some clothes on and was stood like a rabbit caught in a car headlight.

Mary was yelling at the still struggling woman that she was gunning for the wrong person. She yelled that I was single and her husband was the married one and the cheat. As Rob moved forward to talk to his wife, she wriggled free from Mary's grasp. Both of us looked on in amazement, as the enraged Mrs Salmon pulled her fist back and smashed it into Rob's surprised face.

Everyone in the room heard the cracking sound as his nose was shattered and blood began to spurt out and pour over his mouth and chin. Quickly taking control of the situation, Mary gathered up Rob's things and began pushing the warring couple towards the door. Once she had pushed them both outside she hurled his possessions after him and slammed the door.

Mary headed back indoors slapping her hands together, as though she was congratulating herself for a job well done. She then turned to see me standing in the doorway. The next second, we had both dissolved into breathless, uncontrollable laughter that neither of us could stop.

42

Susan later told how me how she was packing for her visit to Lucy and looking forward to a few weeks of change in her life. It was crisp November morning and the autumn leaves were still strewn around the hedgerows and farm yard. The leaves blew around creating a natural brown, yellow and orange carpet. The chill in the air made Susan aware that winter was around the corner. Once she had finished what she was doing she began to make a sandwich for herself when the door opened and Ethel stepped into the warm kitchen.

Susan explained that's she and Ethel had become good friends over the years. Susan's heart went out to Ethel as she knew she was missing Cyril very much. Before he had got married, he only came home at weekends but these were the times Ethel lived for. Susan tried hard to ensure that Ethel was invited to the farm on a regular basis, so she was not lonely.

As her friend came further into the kitchen Susan noticed that Ethel was holding a blue airmail letter and envelope. Before she could ask what it was about, Ethel gushed that Cyril was going to become a father then promptly burst into tears.

Once she had composed herself she explained that she was overjoyed for Cyril but devastated that it was unlikely that she would ever meet her grandchild. The cost of air fares were beyond Ethel's limited means. Susan completely understood, there was nothing she loved better than being surrounded by her children and grandchildren. Susan comforted Ethel as best she could and Ethel was soon apologising for her outburst. Susan told her not to be silly. She then had to leave so she wouldn't miss her train.

Edward drove her to the station in the small van that they normally used for deliveries. It was an ancient rust heap with gears that crunched every time they were changed but Edward refused to get rid of it. He was adamant that the trusty vehicle was a much valued part of the family. Susan thought he was mad but said nothing.

Once they had arrived at the station Edward carried Susan's case onto the train and placed it on the luggage rack above. They then said their good byes and Edward quickly jumped off the train as the whistle rang out, warning them of its departure. They both laughed at the idea that Edward almost left with Susan. She waved until the Edward was out of sight and then sat back in her seat. Susan felt extremely contented and blessed with her life. She knew that she would feel forever grateful that Edward and the rest of the family had forgiven her.

The heartache she suffered due to my continued absence was constantly around her, but there was little she could do about that so she pushed it out of her head and heart. In no time at all she had reached Bristol. As she alighted from the train she realised that she had already forgotten how different the city was since her last visit. She told me that she wondered if I had moved back to Bristol and wished we could meet up.

Quite quickly, she spotted Desmond waving feverishly as he tried to wriggle his way through the throng of bodies. Finally, he reached her and immediately pulled her into a massive bear-like hug. He then took her luggage and walked her towards his car where he loaded everything in the boot. Once Susan was comfortably sat in the passenger seat next to him, he began the short drive home.

When they arrived in Clifton, Susan related to me that she immediately noticed how much less hectic it was on the outskirts of Bristol as compared to the centre of the city. As Desmond retrieved her luggage Susan turned and looked at the large expanse of greenery that was the Clifton Downs.

Tears pricked at the corners of her eyes as she remembered herself and Jimmy Fairly pushing me, as a baby, in my pram as the sun's rays warmed their backs in the summer of 1943. The Downs were almost empty now as it was getting late; it seemed, to Susan, a lot chillier here than it was at Carmarthen Farm. Susan shivered as she recalled that her father had taken his own by jumping into Clifton gorge.

Her father was a terrible man who had struggled to with alcoholism and failed. One day he had beaten Betty Miners, the vicar's wife from Treruth and Margery, his lady friend almost to death. That was why he had ended his life and Susan thanked God every day that he did it.

She had lived in fear of him for years. Her childhood had been terrifying as she fought to keep out of his way with the help of the villagers and her lovely next door neighbour. She smiled as Desmond roused her from her thoughts with a comforting arm around her shoulder and led her indoors to the warmth of his home.

Lucy and Desmond had moved into Desmond's flat as his was the bigger of the two. As Susan walked through the door she could instantly tell that a single man had once lived here. The decor was dull browns and drab greens but she could also see the efforts of a woman's touch in the shape of a few ornaments and photographs that were scattered around the place. She noticed a beautiful one of Lucy, holding me in her arms, on the sideboard. Susan guessed that I looked to be around five years old and she was suddenly sad that she had missed so much of my childhood and then lost me when I became an adult.

She shook away her gloomy thoughts and smiled as Lucy lumbered into the room. She was very large and Susan asked if she was sure there was only one baby in there and Lucy assured her that there was. Desmond stated that he must return to work and left the two women, with cups of tea, chattering away. As soon as the door had closed on him Lucy expressed her immense relief that he was gone.

She smiled widely as she explained that he fussed over her like a mother hen and sometimes it could be suffocating, Lucy knew Desmond meant well but she was extremely glad that Susan had arrived.

43

Susan had been at Lucy's for three days when Lucy doubled over in pain. She wrote, in great detail, and told me how she grabbed baby Mikey from Lucy's arms and placed him in the playpen, in the corner, with a rusk biscuit to keep him happy. At ten months old he could sit unaided and attempted to cruel but he was always hankering after any attention he could get so Susan hoped the food would take his mind of his mother. She then helped Lucy to the sofa.

They both had a birth plan drawn up, in readiness. As soon as Lucy's labour began they were to call Violet to come and collect Mikey. The case was already packed for the hospital and as soon as she had spoken to Violet, Susan phoned for an ambulance to take Lucy to hospital. Once all the preparations were made, all they could do was wait; Susan gripped Lucy's hand as each contraction tore through her body turning her face purple and making her cry out in pain.

This, in turn, caused Mikey to become alarmed and tears ran down his cheeks, as he screamed the place down. Susan picked the little boy up to comfort him then found as many toys around the house as she could and placed them in the playpen with him, in an effort to keep him entertained. She wondered why the ambulance was taking so long.

Susan then helped, the now sobbing, Lucy to the bedroom so that her son would not have to listen to his mother's discomfort.

Immediately they entered the bedroom Lucy's waters broke bringing on a long painful tightening which made Lucy to kneel on the floor and bite into the eiderdown, in effort to stifle her screaming.

Susan looked urgently out of the window to see if there was any sign of the ambulance but all she could see was a snarl up of rush hour traffic, gridlocked outside the window. She turned abruptly as Lucy begged for help. Susan was now becoming alarmed. She had had her last baby sixteen years ago and had not been present at any of her daughter, Edith's deliveries as William, her husband, had booked her into a private nursing home for each one. She was terrified that something would happen to Lucy or the baby if she was unable to assist her.

At the moment Lucy began to remove her undergarments. The poor woman's face was contorted with pain and her whole body was sweating as she began to try to push her child into the world. Susan could hear Mikey crying from the lounge but there was nothing she could do about it, Lucy needed her.

All at once Lucy began to panic and scream that she couldn't bear any more pain. At the at point Susan saw the baby's head crowning and promised Lucy that it was nearly over and ordered her to push with all her might. Ten minutes later, with Lucy swearing and using language that made even Susan blush, the tiny baby slithered from her womb into Susan's arms. The child was a dark purple, almost blue, colour and was still and silent.

Mikey was now screeching at fever pitch as he realised he was not getting the attention he wanted. Lucy lay on the bed panting and sobbing as the afterbirth also appeared. Suddenly the all noise stopped and an eerie silence hung in the room.

Susan gazed at Lucy's new born child. It seemed to her that time stood still and she could hear the steady ticking of the bedroom clock. It seemed like she was frozen like that for hours, but it could only have been seconds.

As if someone had a flicked a switch in her, Susan picked up the child by the ankles and slapped its bottom. On the third attempt a high pitched mewing sounded from the child, quietly at first, the erupted into a loud, screeching cry. The relief she felt almost overwhelmed her as she handed Lucy her new born daughter. Tears were now falling down Susan's cheeks as she watched the bonding moment as Lucy stroked the tiny girl's soft skin, now a healthier pink colour.

Regaining her practical side, Susan race to the airing cupboard for a towel and returned to swaddle the infant, to keep her warm. The tiny face gazed up at her, her light blue curious eyes made Susan melt with love for the tiny, vulnerable being. She then returned the baby to Lucy and went into the lounge to check on Mikey. The tiny boy had cried himself to sleep. At that point the door burst open and Violet hurried in, closely followed by two ambulance men. Susan laughed and told them that they had missed all the fun.

44

Mine and Mary's cosy lives were interrupted when James Sinclair suffered an attack of guilt and ended his relationship with Mary. This meant that we had to leave our plush flat and move to a smaller, much less posh, one with no washing machine and an outside loo. It was quite depressing, as it was a basement flat with very little natural light and appeared cave-like and was damp in places.

We made the best we could of the place by decorating it with colourful cushions and little ornaments. Both of us were glad we had each other as it would have been even more disheartening if we had to live in the dingy place alone.

Mary left her job at the typing pool as it became awkward every time she came into contact with James Sinclair. She managed get a job in a large department store. She was an assistant to Miss Langdon, in the haberdashery department. Although it wasn't the most thrilling job it was quite varied and she enjoyed it. She confided in me that she had been sending money to her mother every week, since she had moved to London, in the hope she would spend it on the necessaries for her brothers.

As this job paid a little less, she had to lower the amount she sent but hoped it would still be enough to feed the boys. Mary and I had also started a relationship with two brothers whom we met in the pub one evening. They were both older than us but we enjoyed their company and loved the many presents we received from the two besotted men.

45

Lucy wrote and told me when she came home from the hospital, she was still exhausted but happy that the ordeal of birth was over. Desmond had picked his wife and new daughter up from the hospital whilst Susan had stayed home with Mikey. When the rest of his family arrived at the flat, the little boy couldn't take his eyes off his new sister. It was almost as if he was afraid to touch her, as though he thought she was made of porcelain.

Susan made the tea while Lucy carried their sleeping daughter into the bedroom and placed her in her cot. Lucy and Desmond had decided to name her Gertie in honour of the wonderful Gerta who had offered her and I sanctuary when Michael was unwell. Lucy was quite sure that Gerta had saved her life, on many occasions, and missed the kind old lady every day.

When Susan was in the kitchen, Desmond entered, closing the door quietly behind him. He drew level with her and said in a hushed voice that he thought Lucy needed someone to help her out with the children. The doctors had told him that she was suffering from 'nerves' and he had no idea what that meant. The doctors had sent her home with a prescription for Valium, in the hope that it would calm her a little.

Susan immediately offered to stay on for a few extra days when Desmond interrupted; he went onto explain that he wanted someone to come in on regular basis, on weekdays while he was at work. The cogs started whirling in Susan's brain as she thought of her friend Joyce. Susan had known her for many years and knew she would be perfect for the job. They had met up a few days ago while Susan was out with little Mikey and she knew Joyce was looking for employment. This could be the perfect solution. She told Desmond about her and he was keen to meet her.

At that moment Lucy walked into the kitchen, looking tired and frightened but no one knew why. She turned to Susan and asked if she would be Gertie's Godmother. Susan was overjoyed and filled with pride and gratitude at being given the honour. She hugged Lucy and promised to help her as much as she could.

Joyce came to meet Desmond, Lucy and the children the very next day and it was clear, to all present, that the position would suit Joyce very well. Both Desmond and Lucy instantly took to Joyce's sunny personality and the little Mikey made the final decision by clambering up onto her lap, sticking his thumb in his mouth and promptly falling asleep.

46

Two years later

Susan walked into the warm fug of her kitchen clutching the post which she had retrieved from the box at the end of the lane, she told me that enjoyed collecting the mail, sometimes it was the only time she got to herself all day. She handed the letters to Edward as she began to make some breakfast for her family and the rest of the farm workers. They now had an extra four farmhands, toiling on the ever expanding farm.

Edward leafed through the mail and picked up an envelope that didn't resemble the normal household bills that came, nor was it Iris's handwriting. He tore it open curiously and began to read. He was delighted to see that it was an invitation to a reunion of English, American, Polish and Canadian military personnel who fought in world war two. His mind travelled back to 1944.

Although the war was terrifying, the camaraderie between all the fighting forces, brought together with the common purpose to defeat the enemy, would never leave him. He smiled at the idea of pulling on his uniform again, he would always be proud that he served his country. He showed the letter to Susan who was thrilled; she hugged him warmly then left the kitchen with the egg basket to raid the chicken coup.

47

It was a Saturday evening and for the first time, in a long while, Mary and I had nothing planned. I had noticed that my lovely friend had seemed a little down in the mouth for a while and I wanted to try and cheer her up. As I walked home from work the previous day, I had seen a notice about a reunion for service men that was to be held at the Royal British Legion. I suggested going to Mary who seemed reluctant at first then changed her mind quite abruptly.

We both enjoyed getting glammed up in our sexiest outfits. We certainly seemed to turn all eyes on us as we walked, arm in arm, towards the reunion. We discussed that, probably, the men would almost be definitely old but that we may be lucky enough to find a wealthy boyfriend. We both really liked the sound of that and Mary seemed happier than she had been for days.

The place was decked out marvellously with flags from many different countries including America, Poland and France. Mary noted angrily that there were no Nepalese flags. It constantly irked her that the role the Ghurkha's had played in the Second World War was hardly mentioned. In fact, the brave men had been awarded more than two thousand awards for gallantry between them.

Maybe it was because of her lineage. Her father was a Ghurkha and had been killed in the early days of the war;

she had never met him but treasured the only photo of him that she had. This was the reason she felt so strongly about it and she hoped one day, that these selfless men would get the recognition they deserved.

Once inside we gave our summer jackets to a lady behind the counter who, in turn, gave us tickets so we could collect the garments on the way out. The cloakroom attendant was a grumpy, forty-plus woman who seemed to resent our presence but both Mary and I ignored her indifference and carried on walking into the main function room.

As we had correctly guessed there was more than a splattering of grey hair at the event. We both remarked at how much time and effort must have been put in to making the reunion a success. There were several men in a variety of military uniforms. Mary and I sat at a table close to the dance floor which was full of people talking rather than dancing, as the band had yet to begin. In no time at all, we had been supplied with drinks by admiring men and we both sat looking around as we enjoyed them.

Simultaneously my eyes met with a man who had dark hair that was streaked with grey, he was wearing an English army uniform. To my alarm I realised, too late, it was Edward Bromley, Susan's husband. I had stayed with them after Travis had tried to kill me and he had been very kind and considerate towards me.

As soon as he spotted me, he made a beeline towards me, shoving others out of the way in his race to reach me. Instead of the telling off that I had expected, Edward planted his pint of beer solidly onto the table and grasped me in a tight embrace as Mary looked on quizzically. I felt surprisingly weepy as I buried my head into Edwards comforting shoulders and listened as he told me how worried they had all been since I disappeared.

As Edward Bromley and I broke free from our embrace, I was further surprised to see Mr Pellow, or Ivan, as he told me to call him, striding towards us looking wonderfully smart in his uniform. I felt very proud of the two of them. I again, waited for Ivan Pellow to start remonstrating with me about the money I had taken and the fact that I had deserted my fiancée, who was also his brother-in-law. But I was wrong. He didn't mention it at all and his only concern was for me and all the time I had been missing.

It stuck me that, not for one minute, had I thought that anyone would be in the least bit worried about me, in fact I thought that they'd all be glad to see the back of me. Feeling overly emotional, I struggled to find words. Mary got up from her seat, walked around and wrapped her arms around her me as I began to tremble, and this immediately comforted me. Mary asked if I was alright and I nodded but I don't think she was convinced. I noticed both Ivan and Edward could not help but admire Mary's extraordinary beauty as she walked over to me, they could hardly take their eyes off her.

Just at that moment, the band struck up its first song and it was impossible to have a conversation. As the first cords of '*We'll meet again*' by Gracie fields sounded, Edward gestured for me to follow him.

All four of us picked up our drinks and headed for a small area known as the '*snug*' where we could chat. Conversation was a little awkward at first because of the nature of my departure, but after a while we forgot what had happened and the dialogue flowed with no one actually mentioning it. After a while, Edward asked me if we could talk alone for a few minutes.

I nodded and followed him outside the room into a draughty porch, on the side of the building. Edward now seemed ill at ease as he began to talk and I audibly gasped when he told me the reason why. Edward explained that Jimmy Fairly was present at the reunion. All at once I felt like a little girl. The child in me longed to meet my father but the adult was angry for the abandonment.

I couldn't think clearly, jumbled thoughts flew around my head as I struggled to digest what Edward was telling me. Finally, I asked Edward if he would introduce me to my father. Edward said that he would gladly but here was not the place or time, he suggested we meet for lunch at the Lyons Corner house the following day and I nervously agreed.

Once back at the table, I apologised to Mary but said I needed to go home. Mary rose immediately to accompany me and we said our goodbyes and left. When we got back to the flat Mary poured us both a generous amount of brandy and for the first time, since we had met, we really began to talk. Mary told me about her mother and stepfather. She showed me the ragged photo of a Junior Commissioned Officer called Jeevan Magar and revealed, with immense pride, that he was her father. I could now see where Mary had got her exotic features from.

Mary went onto tell me about the squalor her family lived in and what she had suffered at the hands of her mother's husband. I, in turn, told her about what I had suffered with Travis. Mary was stunned to learn that I had once been a married woman. Mary also told me about the money she sent home each week and she hoped that her mother used it wisely.

We talked late into the night. After drinking a little too much alcohol Mary confided in me that she was pregnant and that's was why she had been so down. She tearfully explained that the father was a married man, who no longer wanted to have anything to do with her. This explained Mary's sadness in the last few weeks and as my dear friend's tears fell freely down her cheeks, I held her close and promised that we would sort out her problem together while assuring her that she was not alone.

Mary offered to take the day off from work and come with me to meet my father the next day but I told her that I would be fine. I also reminded her that we needed her wages, as well as mine, to cover the rent. Mary reluctantly agreed, and the following day, she set off on a sunny Saturday morning to her job at the store.

Although I had hidden it well from Mary, I was feeling extremely nervous and anxious about meeting my father. I changed my outfit three times before deciding on a *Mary Quant*, white cotton mini dress with blue flowers and some low heeled white court shoes. I carried my white cardigan with me in case the weather turned cold then suddenly felt angry with myself. What on earth was I doing making an effort to impress a man who had abandoned me as a tiny baby.

I arrived at the pre-arranged meeting place and took several deep breaths before I nervously pushed the café door open. I immediately spotted Edward sitting in a booth to the left the room, I was very glad he was here. He was with another man sitting opposite to him, with his back to me. He wore a royal blue American airman's uniform and my heart began to beat faster in anticipation at meeting the man who was my actual father.

48

Jimmy Fairly told me, many months later, that he had never felt so afraid in his whole life. To him, meeting me, his only daughter, was more terrifying than the times he had sat in a plane, being shot at by the enemy. In his mind, this felt a whole lot more frightening. He heard the clang of the shop's bell as the door opened and looked up to see Edward gazing towards the door; Edward gave him a nod, so slight that he wouldn't have seen if he wasn't looking out for it. Jimmy told me his mouth felt as dry as sandpaper as he rose from his seat.

Slowly, he turned to face the door. He saw me and gasped and recalled that it was as though a young Susan was walking towards him. My build, stance and even the way I walked, reminded him so much of Susan and his heart yearned for the love that he had to let go.

As I approached, he nervously leant forward and looked as if he was about to kiss my cheek then, obviously, decided against it and he put out his hand instead. I leant forward and shook it. Jimmy took his hat off and asked me if I wanted to sit down, I nodded.

Edward offered to get some drinks and rose to go towards the counter. I sat in the seat he had vacated. I stared at the man who was my father. I was glad he hadn't hugged me, I hardly knew him and I didn't like to be hugged by strangers. I also found it oddly quaint that he took his hat off; it reminded me of what the American film stars did in the films.

I stared into Jimmy's bright blue eyes and they looked like mirrors of my own. I could see that I favoured Susan's looks but my thick dark blonde hair had, undeniably, been inherited from my father. Even saying the word 'father', in my mind, gave a warm feeling as though someone had put a thick coat over my shoulders.

Jimmy began to talk. He told me about his wife Maria, back home and his three sons, Donnie, Abe and Jimmy junior. Donnie an Abe had followed him into the military but young Jimmy was still in High School but wanted to train to be a lawyer, they all reckoned that he was the brains of the family. My father smiled as he said this, a sincere, friendly smile that put me at ease.

Before I met him, I had decided that I was going to be standoffish and a little cold but looking into his wonderful kind face threw all my stupid ideas to the wall. I began to tell him about my job and Mary. Edward arrived back at the table with tea, for himself and me and coffee for Jimmy. When he saw how well the two of us were getting on, he tactfully made his excuses and left us to get to know one another.

For me, it felt like the last piece of the jigsaw of my life had been put into place. From being an only child, I now had several brothers and sisters. I liked being part of a large, extended family. I listened as my father said that he would love me to come to America and meet his family. Jimmy told me that, as well as brothers, I had cousins, aunties and uncles who would love to meet me. I was swept away by his enthusiasm and listened happily as he told of his plans to tell his wife and children about me.

I watched his blue eyes light up when he recalled holding me as a baby and he told me that he thought about me all the time. We spent the entire day together getting to know each other; it felt like two halves of a circle coming together. We were both were very emotional when the time came for us to part. I promised I would visit him and that I would come to America to meet his family sometime in the future. We swapped telephone numbers and addresses and both tearfully held onto each other as we promised to never lose touch again.

As I ambled back to the flat I thought that, for the first time in my life, I felt like a whole person, not adrift as though something was something missing. There were no more skeletons in my family closet and to know the whole truth about my life was like a breath of fresh air. I promised that, as soon as I had time, I would visit Susan at Carmarthen farm and make my peace with her.

49

On Monday, at work, I made some tactful enquiries about getting rid of unwanted babies. No information was forthcoming so I tried to think of another way to sort Mary's problem. Adoption crossed my mind but how would Mary support herself while she was pregnant, her salary would not be enough for the both of them. It was all I could think about and I was disappointed that I would not be able to bring any good news home to Mary.

However, when I returned to my desk after the afternoon tea break, I found a hastily written note on a scrap of paper. It said 'baby person' and gave a name and address. I was so very grateful to whoever had written it but understood the girl's need for anonymity. I quickly stuck the note into my bag and headed home, feeling a little better now that I had something that may offer Mary a way out of her predicament. Mary was overcome with gratitude when I told her what had happened at work.

The two of us decided to visit the address on the following Tuesday which was Mary's day off, I would accompany her in my lunch hour. The day dawned and met up in Trafalgar Square and boarded the bus that would take us to the outskirts of the busy city. I could feel the tension running through Mary and held her hand tightly as the bus trundled onwards.

We got off at a bus stop in a small, narrow street. Small

houses lined both sides of the road, all identical with three windows and a low doorway. We walked slowly along; looking for the address we had been given. Both of us tried to make it look like we were merely out for a walk on the unusually warm October day. I could feel Mary starting to tremble as we walked, closely, beside each other. Simultaneously, we turned left and up a narrow lane that was supposed to lead to where we needed to go.

At first we thought we had been mistaken as there appeared to be no houses at the end of lane. I then spotted a small, scruffy caravan in an overgrown back garden of one of the properties. The static vehicle had obviously been white at one time but it was now stained green by the grass that climbed up the sides of it and almost reached the windows.

We both ventured curiously towards it. We were surprised to see the other side of the caravan was completely free of foliage and had a neat gravelled pathway leading to the door. I could hear Mary's heavy breathing and I linked her arm as we walked toward the door. I knocked loudly and we were both startled when a voice called out from somewhere behind us that she would be there soon.

A couple of minutes later a women appeared, it looked like she had walked through thorny hedgerow, bit of leaves and grass were hanging off her clothes and hair, she brushed herself off as she approached. She quietly introduced herself, as lily, and ushered us both through the door then pulled it quickly behind us; I guessed the woman to be around her late forties, she wore flowery wraparound overall covering all her clothing and was smoking a long, brown cigarette.

Without any preamble she asked which girl needed her

service, Mary stepped forward. Lily told her the cost and Mary fished the money out of her handbag and passed it to Lily with a shaking hand. The woman tucked the notes down the front of her apron and began to pull the tiny curtains over the two small windows so we were almost stood in pitch darkness.

In the monetary gloom, I felt Mary's terror, like it was almost palpable and my heart ached for my dear friend. A small eerie light then dimly illuminated the room, as lily switched on a lamp in the corner. She then dragged a rickety Formica topped table to the centre of the room and opened a flap at either end to make the table longer. She ordered Mary to remover her under garments and to lie on the table with her legs open.

Mary did as she was bid and pushed her pants into her handbag which she then handed to me. The table creaked and groaned frighteningly as Mary's full weight was rested upon it and I worried that it would collapse under the load. I stood facing Mary, stroking her face to calm her. I held her hand and looked away from the intimate operation going on behind me. I turned fleetingly to see Lily holding a large silver, stick-like item in her hand that could have been an unfolded metal coat hanger.

I took a deep breath and continued to stroke Mary's face reassuringly. I heard a watery sound then felt Mary's body stiffen as the object was jabbed inside her. A little time later Mary's face became contorted with pain. The procedure seemed to drag on and I asked how long it would be as I could see Mary was in obvious agony. I was given no answer. Some minutes later I heard a small popping sound and Mary cried out in agony. Lily said that the operation was over and told Mary to get dressed. Mary hurriedly did this as neither of us wanted to be in the place any longer than we needed to be.

Luck was on our side and we arrived back at the bus stop at the same time as the bus. Mary face was deathly pale and I had to hold her steady her as she mounted the vehicle steps. When we sat down Mary grabbed my hands tightly and thanked me wholeheartedly. Although she was very pale, I could see that Mary was also very relieved that the abortion was over and the problem had been dealt with.

On the journey home Mary developed a stomach pain that Lily had said would happen. Lily had advised Mary to get straight to bed as soon as she was home and to take any pain killers that she might need. By the time we were walking back to the flat Mary was almost doubled over with pain and it took a mammoth effort by the two of us to get in without anyone noticing what was going on.

Once we were inside, I helped Mary to bed and brought her a hot water bottle to put on her stomach. I also left a glass of water and some Beecham's powders for Mary to take when she needed. I then leant down and kissed Mary's warm cheek; I was glad to see that she looked so much less troubled than she had been for weeks, like a heavy weight had been lifted off her shoulders. I said goodbye to Mary, let myself out of the flat and hurried back to work, hoping I wouldn't be late.

I had not been at my desk for more than five minutes when I was summoned to James Sinclair's office by his ever-scowling secretary. I had arrived back from lunch five minutes late and was hoping no one had noticed but he obviously had. My heart was pounding as I knocked gently on the oblique glass at the top of the wooden door. James shouted for me to enter and I walked, tensely through the door and gave him what I hoped was my best smile.

James Sinclair looked down at his paperwork for a while without acknowledging me at all; finally he looked up and gestured for me to sit on the small chair facing him. When I sat down, he looked at me intently and I was surprised to hear him ask about Mary. I could see the sadness in his pale blue eyes and told him that Mary was doing very well. He eyes seemed to be far away, as if he was in another place, as he whispered that he had loved....did love Mary and mumbled something about complicated situations.

I sat, feeling a little awkward. At last Mr Sinclair became himself again; he regained his composure and was once again my boss, not the sad human being who was pining for my best friend. To my joy and delight he did not mention my lateness but offered me a promotion instead. He explained that his personal secretary was inadequate and had made one mistake too many and had sent an important document to the wrong client causing a few ructions that had been difficult to fix. The secretary was being dismissed at the end of the week. The job included a substantial pay rise and I could not contain my happiness as I gladly accepted the job.

The day seemed to drag; I enjoyed my work but I was eager to get home and tell Mary the great news. Finally the hooter rang out, spelling the end of the day. I quickly tidied my desk and said my goodbyes for the day. The weather was still very pleasant and I hummed to myself on the short walk home as I thought what I would spend my extra money on.

I bought a bunch of tulips from a lady on the corner of the street to celebrate my promotion. The smell of the flowers was sweet and reminded me of Cornwall. I let myself into the flat, filled the kettle then placed it on the gas hob. I felt around in the cupboard under the sink and found the only old, cracked vase that we owned. I arranged the blooms as prettily as I could before placing it on the coffee table in the lounge. Once the kettle had boiled I made a cup of tea for myself and one for Mary. I walked towards the bedroom, carrying both cups in one hand, anxious to share my news.

With my other hand, I knocked on the door then pushed the handle down and entered. A strange smell hit me and, at first, I wasn't sure what it was. The room was in darkness so I groped around for the light switch and put the two drinks down on the untidy bedside table. I could hear Mary's laboured breathing as I got nearer the bed. I softly called her name. Then, as though I had been hit with a lightning bolt, I recognised the smell. Many years ago I had gone to an abattoir with my auntie and uncle; I knew that the smell that hung around the entire room was stale blood.

Cautiously, I bent towards Mary and touched her hand. It was stone cold, I stroked her face. In comparison, this part of her body seemed to be burning up. I called Mary's name and tried to shake her awake; when she did not rouse I tried to pull her into a sitting position. As I did this, the blanket fell to the floor and I was so shocked I pressed my hand to my mouth to stop screaming.

The white sheet underneath Mary was no longer white but a vivid red. Blood began literally dripping from it onto the wooden floor. I screamed and was violently sick. I wiped my mouth and ran with lightning speed out of the door to the telephone box on the corner. I dialled 999 as I tried to still my trembling fingers. As soon as it was answered I screamed for them to send someone to help Mary. The kindly operator managed to calm me enough to get my address from me, I then ran back to the flat leaving the phone dangling in the red box.

I tried to breathe only through my mouth so the over powering smell would not make me wretch again. I could hear Mary moaning softly now and I rushed forward and knelt down beside her bed. I held Mary's hand in my own and kissed her hot cheek. Mary looked up at me and tried to raise her other hand. I caught hold of this one also and gazed back at her, telling her that help was on the way. Mary looked straight into my eyes and I moved closer and hugged Mary to my chest. As I held the limp body I heard a gentle sigh leave Mary's mouth then she breathed no more.

I held onto Mary, talking to her, begging her to stay strong until help arrived. Tears flowed from my eyes, unchecked, as I told Mary about my promotion and pay rise. I told her that the extra money would enable us to get a better flat and maybe even a television. As I carried on chatting it began to feel as though something was sitting on my chest, restricting my breathing but I continued to talk to Mary about the rosy future we had together.

I didn't know the ambulance had arrived until I felt a hand gently tap my shoulder, I quickly moved aside to let the ambulance men do their job. I watched as they gently they lifted Mary's lifeless body onto the stretcher and covered her with a blue blanket. I thought that was a good thing because I remembered very ill people sometimes shivered and went into shock so needed to be kept warm. I couldn't stop myself shaking.

As the ambulance drove to the hospital I sat beside Mary. I talked about all the things we had to look forward to. When we arrived Mary was stretchered into the hospital and I hurried after her. We came to a door which I was barred from going through, so I sat on a hard wooden chair, one of many placed along the hospital corridor to wait for the doctors to make Mary well again.

Very shortly, a tall man approached me wearing a white doctor's coat. He was carrying a clip board and wore a stethoscope around his neck. An unlit pipe hung out of the corner of his mouth as he told me with unnecessary abruptness that Mary was dead.

I stood rooted to the spot. Everything around me was a blur and directly in front of me stood this heartless monster. He was telling me that if Mary had not tried to kill her baby she would be alive today. He ranted on about flightiness and the young girls today who had no moral standing and deserved everything they got.

I was consumed with anger, so hot I was convinced I could kill the man in front of me. The closest person in the world to me had died and this excuse for a human being was going on about his bloody standards and principles. I screeched like someone demented and began pummelling at this condemnatory being that stood in front me. I could hear the screaming and ranting though I didn't know it was me but I felt every punch I landed.

Suddenly, I was being dragged along the corridor, still I screamed and fought. I still shouted out vile profanities at the shocked man, who now had blood pouring from his nose and was dropping onto his pristine white coat. The cold air hit me as I was hurled out of the double doors and thrown down the concrete steps. The coldness of the concrete on my face seemed to bring me to my senses and I sat on the floor panting from my exertions.

Slowly I climbed to my feel and began to walk. I felt as if something was trying to pull out my stomach and heart. The pain in my chest felt physical. I caught my reflection in a shop window and was shocked as I realised I looked like a mad woman. I was covered in Mary's blood and my hair was sticking up messily where I had continuously run my hands through it. I had a cut on my cheek, which must have happened on the concrete steps. Tears were falling from my eyes, I couldn't stop them nor did I want to. I found myself at the door of our flat. As I entered it felt as though I was not in control of my body, I felt as though I was floating past everything.

Once I was indoors, I didn't switch on the light but headed for the sofa; I then lay down and put my head on a cushion. The slight smell of Mary's Chanel perfume lingered on it. The aroma took me back to the previous Friday when we had been getting ready to go to the reunion. I remembered Mary happily trying on several outfits before she decided on a black mini skirt and white blouse. She felt so close that I reached out to touch her, only to see my hand suspended in mid-air.

A fresh rush of misery engulfed me and I cried until I fell into a fitful sleep where I dreamt that Mary was berating me for taking her to Lily, the abortionist, and I was begging for forgiveness.

50

Susan told me, many months later, how she arrived at the station to pick up Edward and Ivan when they arrived home from the reunion. Edward had taught her to drive many years ago and she loved the freedom it gave her. Both men emerged from the station wearing their military uniforms and Susan thought they looked very handsome. She beeped the car horn then got out of the vehicle and waved to the two of them, she then walked to the rear of her car and pulled open the boot.

Edward and Ivan shoved their bags into the small space then all three squashed into the car for the short journey home. Edward and Ivan talked excitedly, all the way home, about the reunion and how it brought back so many memories. Tactfully Ivan didn't mention me or Jimmy, preferring to leave that to Edward to do in private. Susan dropped Ivan off at his grocers shop and after a quick chat with Cissy she drove the rest of the way home.

Back in the kitchen at Carmarthen, Susan made them both a cup of tea then sat down to listen to Edward's news. He told her a bit about the reunion. Edward then held Susan's hand as he began to tell her about me… and about Jimmy. Susan told me she felt stunned, she was happy because I was safe and well but sad that she had not seen me herself, Regarding Jimmy, first she felt relief that that there had been no animosity between him and Edward and secondly, oddly enough, acute jealously that she had not been the one to see Jimmy again.

A long time ago he had meant everything to her; at one point she thought that she loved him. Watching Edward, as he chatted away happily Susan felt very proud and grateful to her husband. Thinking again, she decided she was glad that she had not met Jimmy; the past was best left alone. She was overjoyed when Edward told her that I intended to visit as soon as I could. This was the good news that she would focus on, nothing else mattered as long as she had her family around her.

51

I awoke in the early hours of the morning, stiff and cold. At first I couldn't recall what was causing me so much heartache then it all came back like oil gushing from a well and the tears began to fall again. The intensity of my grief was starting to frighten me, I felt as though I would go mad with it. Rising from the couch I went into the kitchen, making a superhuman effort to pull myself together. I boiled the kettle and made some tea then used the rest of the hot water to wash my face and body.

With each movement I felt as though I was being dragged towards the edge of a precipice and I knew if I fell into it, I would never get out. As the gentle light of dawn broke through the night sky, I felt totally lost and alone. There seemed to be no point in anything, I couldn't work out one good reason to carry on with my life. I dressed myself in clean clothes and walked out of the flat, now unable to be anywhere near to the place where Mary died.

Without knowing why, I found myself outside of the Royal British Legion where Mary and I had been to the reunion. I sat on a low wall close by. The tears continued to fall and I couldn't stop them. I was feeling frightened, bewildered and increasingly panicky. A kindly elderly man, who walked slowly, leaning on his stick arrived and shuffled towards me. Placing his hand on my shoulder he asked if there was anything he could do to help.

I shook my head then without knowing I was going to say it, I asked the man if he would be able to get in touch with my father, Sergeant James Fairly of the American Royal Airforce.

The man explained that he was the treasurer for the British Legion and if I would like to accompany him inside, he would do his very best. I sat in the very same room that I had been in previously with Mary as the man went to make some phone calls. The room looked bare and solemn, bereft of life and fun. Some of the banners still hung upright from the night of the reunion, others just clung on half-heartedly. I had no idea how long I waited, a one point, the kindly treasurer pressed a cup of tea into my hand which I gratefully accepted.

Then Jimmy was there, standing in front of me like a burning beacon of hope in a pitch black room. I stood up and he pulled me into his arms. For several minutes all I could do was sob pitifully while saying over and over again:

'Oh dad, please help me, I don't know what to do,'

Jimmy hugged me and stroked my back gently. He kept telling me that everything would be all right and that he would take care of me. Finally he guided me outside and we walked to the hotel that he was staying at, a short distant away. In his room, he led me towards a small sofa near the window and sat me down. Jimmy then knelt down and asked if there was anyone he could call. Without pause, I asked him to call Susan.

I knew that she was the only person who would be able to see me through this pain. I longed for her strength and kindness. When my tears finally stopped, I felt utterly exhausted Jimmy led me to the bed. I laid on it he pulled the blankets over me. I fell asleep almost immediately.

As Jimmy listened to my steady breathing and was sure I was

asleep he went down to the lobby and called Ivan Pellow. The two men had swapped phone numbers in order to be pen pals so this was the only way he could contact Susan.

52

Susan heard the rumble of Ivan's motorcycle as she prepared the evening meal on a chilly October afternoon. She told me how she shivered when she heard him but couldn't work out why; she just had a distinct feeling of unease. She was surprised that he had come to visit in the middle of a working day but quickly put the kettle on the hob in readiness. Ivan knocked and entered, she heard him stamp his boots on the door mat and remove his outer clothing. As Ivan entered the kitchen Susan handed him his tea and offered him a slice of cake.

Ivan refused the food and immediately started explaining to Susan what Jimmy had told him on the telephone. Susan's first thought was to drop everything and race off to be with me but she knew that there were things to organise. She quickly thanked Ivan as he had to hurry back to his shop. Firstly, Susan called Ethel and was greatly relieved when she agreed to come and stay at the farm while Susan came to London.

That evening, when they were both alone Susan explained everything to Edward, leaving nothing out, she wanted no more secrets or lies. She realised that she could have not loved her husband more when he insisted that she must prepare for her journey right away. As she went upstairs to pack some clothing Edward called the station to find out the time of the next train to London. He was informed that it would arrive at five in the morning. Edward went to help Susan pack and got the van out to drive her to the station.

Jimmy had organised a taxi to pick Susan up from the station to take her to the Imperial Hotel where he was staying. Unused to such luxuries, Susan would have felt quite grand if she was not feeling so exhausted and worried about me. It was a short journey to the hotel and, on arrival; a bell boy walked out to the car and opened the door for her.

Susan attempted to pay the fare but was told that this had all been taken care of so she followed the boy, who was carrying her bag, into the lobby of the lavish building. Jimmy appeared at the top of a sweeping staircase. Susan was worried that she wouldn't recognise him but she needn't have worried, he had hardly changed at all. He still had most of his dark blonde hair but it was now peppered with grey strands and his hairline started a little further back. Jimmy looked splendid in his blue air force uniform, even if the buttons were slightly strained around his middle.

He quickly ascended the stairs, and then stopped as he stood opposite Susan, looking ill at ease. As they looked at each other the years seemed to disappear. Susan remembered comforting the homesick Jimmy as they huddled together, listening to the explosions from the bombs, in a crowded air raid shelter. Jimmy had brought out Susan's maternal instincts back then and she had helped him through his fear. She even remembered the old smells of burning buildings and the rubber from the gas masks.

She told me how Jimmy held out a hand, awkwardly, which she took and shook then they were both heading back up the stairs with Jimmy filling Susan in on all that had happened. He explained, from when he had got the call from the treasurer of The Royal British Legion, he had been five minutes from leaving the hotel to catch his flight home. He had postponed his departure as soon as he seen the state I was in. He told Susan that he had felt entirely out of his depths with me as he had three sons and he was unused to girls and tears but that he had done the best he could.

Susan told me I was still asleep when she walked into the bedroom so she crept forward and stroked my hair gently so as not to wake me, Susan thought sleep was the best healer. When she returned to the main room, Jimmy had ordered coffee for them both. Tea was Susan's preferred drink but she thought it would be rude to say so and took the coffee gratefully. It did actually ease her tiredness a little.

Jimmy explained that although I was babbling mainly, he could just about make out that a friend of mine had recently died. Susan thanked Jimmy so much for calling her but neither of them talked about the past. Both had families and lives which they were happy with.

As they finished their drinks, I emerged from the bedroom and instantly ran over to Susan. She stroked my head as I sobbed. Susan allowed the tears to fall for a while then she held my head in her hands and looked her directly in my eyes. She told me that she was aware that I had lost a very good friend recently but that I must try and compose myself or I would become ill.

I nodded and sniffed. Susan pulled me onto the sofa beside her. It was mid-morning and Jimmy had ordered some toast. All three of us were surprisingly hungry and finished a second round before we began to talk. Now more in control, I explained about Mary and how it was my fault she was dead and how terribly lost and guilty I felt.

At this point Susan took charge. In order to keep my mind busy, she began to ask practical questions, like who needed to be informed and who was going to organise the funeral. We got a telephone directory from the front desk but there was no one called Magar in it and I confessed that neither of us talked too much about our lives before we came to London.

I said that Mary's employers should be told and also my own boss. I explained to Susan in sparse detail about the relationship between Mary and James Sinclair. Because of this relationship, Susan decided that she should go and see him personally to tell him, rather than call him on the telephone.

All the while, without me realising it, Susan was keeping me occupied so I could try and keep my sadness in check. Susan asked me if I would like to speak at Mary's funeral. I replied that I didn't think I would be able to. Susan told me to write a eulogy that she would read it for me. She then left me in Jimmy's capable hands as she went to tell Mary's former employer what had happened.

Susan was totally unprepared for the depths of James Sinclair's sorrow; she felt helpless, all she could do was hand him some tissues until his crying subsided. He then insisted that he would get his secretary to arrange the funeral and he would foot the bill. He told Susan that Mary was estranged from her family and had no idea where they were. Susan also dropped into the shop were Mary worked and told them the grim news.

Back at the hotel Susan was relieved to see me still in control and sitting with Jimmy going through the eulogy that I had written for Mary. As the three of us sat and ate dinner that evening, in the hotel restaurant, Jimmy guiltily informed us that he would have to leave in the morning; he explained apologetically that he had an early start. I told him not to worry and enjoyed being in the presence of both my mother and father, it probably wouldn't happen again.

Jimmy and I decided to say our goodbyes that evening and Susan stood tactfully stood outside the room. She heard Jimmy telling me to come to America and meet my step brothers and other relatives. I promised that I would, at some point in the future. She also heard him tell me that he loved me and would always be there if I needed him. Susan felt tears pricking at the sides of her eyes and wished everything could have been different.

Finally she heard the sound of my bedroom door closing and she re-entered the room. Jimmy was sitting on the sofa with watery eyes. He got up and poured himself a drink, he asked Susan if she would like to join him and she nodded. She held his hand as she promised Jimmy that she would take care of me and write to him to let him know how I was getting on. They both then finished their drinks and left to go to their subsequent bedrooms. When Susan woke the following morning Jimmy was gone.

She made sure I ate some of the breakfast that was served but was sad that she could not ease my pain a little. My tired face was deathly pale and the redness of my eyes was accentuated by my pallor. Keeping my grief under control was difficult but, with Susan's help, I was determined to try and stay strong.

Jimmy had paid for us to stay at the hotel for two more days. On the morning of Mary's funeral I was unusually quiet and subdued; a marked change from the weeping and wailing that I had been doing. Susan had bought us both black coats for the occasion. There were only two other mourners at the cemetery and I leant heavily on Susan as we followed the wooden coffin up the narrow aisle of a small church, on the outskirts of the city.

The grey October day only served to intensify my mood. The sky seemed low and was a very dark grey as rain threatened at any second. No birds sang above and the chill penetrated through our clothes. James Sinclair stood sedately at the back of the church trying intently to keep his emotions in check. The other person present was Miss Langdon, Mary's supervisor at the store where she worked. The small woman stood with sad dignity dabbing her eyes every now and then with a small white handkerchief, embroidered with dainty flowers.

Susan rose and walked to the front of the church, as she did, she patted my shoulder, reassuringly. I had written a truly beautiful tribute to my beautiful friend. Susan read that I hoped that Mary would be reunited with her beloved father and that they would be in a world of peace and joy where there was always laugher and bird song. I also asked for Mary's forgiveness and wrote that I would never forget my devoted friend.

The music began and the small party followed the coffin back out of the church. It was carried by kindly grave diggers and workmen who had volunteered to do this in the absence of any of Mary's family. As the clods of earth began to hit the, now lowered casket, Susan felt me begin to crumble. She hooked her arms underneath mine as I cried the most agonizing sobs Susan had ever heard. Susan held tightly even when her own arms began to ache, she did not let go, she needed to be there for me in my desperate time of need. As the last words were uttered by the clergyman, large drops of rain began to fall from the darkened sky.

James Sinclair opened a large black umbrella and walked away from the grave, he looked a large crow in his black attire. Miss Langdon drew nearer and told me how dear Mary was to her and what a beautiful girl she who was who taken too soon. These words made my sobs to rise to crescendo pitch. Susan thanked Miss Langdon and led me away. As I became louder Susan could see that I was on the verge of hysteria.

Hesitantly, Susan raised her hand and slapped my cheek. I immediately became silent and Susan was terrified that she had done the wrong thing. In actual fact, the action caused the opposite effect, the sting on my face had brought me, almost instantly, to my senses and I became embarrassed about the wailing sound that had, only seconds ago, screeched from my mouth. Susan and I made our way back to the Imperial Hotel to pack her few belongings and try and sort out the future.

53

The train thundered homewards and Susan told me how she was itching to be back at Carmarthen Farm. She and I had had a long chat and I had insisted on staying in London to work my notice and pay the final month's rent on my flat. I explained that I wanted to leave properly, not run away. I also needed time to come to terms with Mary's death and decide what do with my life. Susan respected my decision and told me that I would always have a home in Cornwall.

Before she left, Susan had phoned Lucy in London to tell her what had happened. Joyce had answered the telephone and asked Susan to pop in on her way home so she could talk to her about concerns for Lucy. Susan agreed but insisted that it had to be as flying visit as she didn't want to take advantage of Ethel's good nature.

Susan got a taxi from the station directly to Lucy's address; she was looking forward to seeing Lucy and Joyce again. She climbed out of the cab and took the lift up to the flat. She then knocked on the door only for it to be opened, almost immediately, by Joyce. The two embraced warmly and Joyce gestured for Susan to follow her into the kitchen, through the lounge.

As Susan walked after Joyce, she saw Lucy standing at the large window overlooking Clifton downs. Susan watched as Lucy twitched constantly and craned her neck as though she was looking for something specific. Once in the kitchen, Joyce closed the door. Joyce confided her worries about Lucy. She explained seemed to be getting worse rather than better.

Lucy's medication had been raised and she has attended sessions with a psychiatrist but nothing seemed to be helping. The doctors had asked Desmond to consider electric shock therapy but he was very unwilling and spent a lot of time trying to find alternative treatment. Susan returned to the room where Lucy stood. She gently tapped her on the shoulder, causing Lucy to start violently. Lucy apologised and asked how she was.

Susan told me that she tried to follow Lucy eye line to see what on earth she was looking at but could see nothing. She put her arm around Lucy's shoulder and asked if there was anything she could do to help her. Lucy shook her head sadly but not did move her eyes away from the window. Susan pulled Lucy into her arms, feeling so very sorry for the friend who had helped her in her moment of need but feeling helpless to return the favour.

As Lucy buried her head in Susan's chest, a slight movement out of the window fleetingly caught Susan's eye. She told me that it had unnerved her. It seemed to come from the right hand side of the Downs but it was so brief Susan wandered if it was her tiredness or her imagination playing tricks on her mind. To try and take Lucy's mind off whatever was troubling her, Susan invited her and her family, including Joyce to come and stay over Christmas. Lucy was visibly relieved and Susan actually felt Lucy's body become less tense as she held her.

With all the necessary arrangements made Susan left the apartment and headed back to the station to resume her journey home. Susan sat in the relatively empty compartment of the train as it chugged homewards. Her mind wandered back to the war years, when she would use the very same train line to visit Edith, Iris and Johnny as often as she could. They were all small children then and being looked after by Edward's parents, while they both worked towards the war effort.

Susan remembered how much longer the journey took back then, for several different reasons. The track might have been bomb damaged or one of the trains commandeered for military personnel. To hinder the enemy, if they should invade, there were no signs at any of the stations which made the journey perilous for new comers.

The movement of the train as it clicked over the rails seemed to be humming closer, closer as she travelled towards Cornwall and home. Finally it puffed into the station. Susan was so eager to be home that she almost tripped over her own feet as she stepped down from the train.

She quickly scanned the platform and spotted Edward striding towards her. Susan told me how overjoyed she was to see him and raced into his arms leaving her suitcase where it stood. Edward was thrilled that Susan was, obviously, so happy to see him and held her close until they both laughed and stood apart. Edward then retrieved Susan's battered suitcase and held her hand as they walked towards to his trusty van.

Edward cranked the vehicle in gear and they headed towards Carmarthen farm as Susan told Edward all about me and also Lucy. As he listened to his wife's voice, Susan could sense that Edward felt hugely relieved. She believed that this was because, in truth, he had not wanted her to go to London, purely because Jimmy Fairly was there, and he was terrified that Susan would leave him for the dashing American Airman. But he also knew that he needed to show Susan that he trusted her completely and in order to do that he had to support her decision to go and help me through my grief.

They both smiled warmly at each other and all was well in their world as they drove into Carmarthen farmyard. Susan said she had never felt happier than when she leaned over and kissed Edward gently on the lips, he took that as a signal that they were moving on and putting past mistakes behind them and she told me that she would be forever grateful to her husband and God.

54

I knew that it would be difficult returning to the flat, but I also knew that it was something I needed to do, in order to put the past events to bed. The key was tight in the lock, as usual, and the door caught on the mat forcing me to shove it open in order to enter. Everything instinct seemed to be telling me to leave and not enter, but I was determined to do it. As I strode into the tiny lounge my nostrils prickled at the smell of stale blood and when the tears formed in my eyes, I quickly swallowed them down.

There was still the very faint odour of Mary's Channel perfume and I knew then that I would miss my dear friend for the whole of my life and I would never forget her. After I had made myself a cup of tea I took some deep breaths and headed towards Mary's bedroom, to the task I had been dreading.

The curtains were drawn and I had to feel around for the light switch. The pungent smell of death was quite terrifying but it wouldn't stop me doing this final task for Mary. I pulled the curtains opened and wrenched the tight sash window up to allow the cold November air to penetrate the room. First, I gathered up all the blood stained sheets and bedding and put them into the large stone sink, adding cold water and salt in a bid to remove the stains. I then set about scrubbing the mattress vigorously to try and remove any trace of the pink blood stain.

It was hard work and took me a long time but I finally

managed it. I then dragged the mattress off the bed, over towards the open window, in an effort to get it dry. As I did this a small book dropped to the floor. I picked it up and a bundle of pound notes and five pound notes fell out. I quickly gathered them up then looked at the pages. I was amazed to see that it was Mary's diary as I thought Mary much too disorganised to write one.

As I flicked through the sheets I remembered some of the events that Mary had written about and I smiled, especially the story describing the angry wife who had forced her way into our flat to give me a thump. I remembered us laughing together, again the tears threatened.

On the inside of the back cover was written the name Mary May Bennett and an address in Southampton. As I read on I discovered this was Mary's actual name and that she had a mother, stepfather and four younger brothers. She had been sending money to her mother on a weekly basis. As I was reading, I felt as though I was intruding into Mary's life. It was difficult for me to comprehend being so close to another person but actually knowing very little about them.

I walked out of Mary's bedroom and into my own; sitting on the edge of the bed I tried to work out, in my own mind, where my future lay but nothing was forthcoming. I needed to stay in London until the lease on the flat ended in mid-December but I couldn't think of what I would do after that, London seemed empty with Mary.

I made the decision I would take Mary's money to her mother and explain about her daughters passing; I then set about cleaning the bedding and the flat, in general in the hope that an epiphany would come to me, and decide what I would do for the rest of my life. At the moment all I could see, in the future, was a black miserable tunnel leading nowhere.

55

A parcel arrived from my mother three days after she left London, I opened it curiously and realised it contained long letter, and I began to read;

My dearest Jane,

I feel I need to explain everything to you, in the hope that it will clear the air and eliminate any bad feelings between us. I admit, much to my shame, that when your actual parentage started to unravel, I felt immediately alarmed. When I saw, what I thought was, Johnny and you staring romantically into each other's eyes I was terrified. I, obviously, couldn't hide my distress and it seemed as if my worst dreams had come true.

The writing became a little messy as if she needed to write quickly, she continued,

I walked back towards the kitchen, weighed down with worry. I hadn't meant to sound so harsh but when I saw you and Johnny staring lovingly at one another, it had sent hot pokers of panic racing through me, making me feel physically sick. Back at the house I apologised to you for my harsh attitude and blamed a headache.

I thought back and remembered telling her she had nothing to apologise for and asked her if she would like a lie down. I was completely in the dark as to what had caused her outburst but, as always, I just wanted to keep the peace. She thanked me but insisted that there was far too much work to do. I carried on reading;

As soon as the coast was clear and I knew that I was alone, I phoned my dear friend, Cissy, who lived in the village with her husband Ivan, her brother Alan and their young daughter Linda, as you know. I felt so very desperate and hated the fact that the situation was no longer under my control. I asked, if she could spare any time to come and see me. Cissy, hearing the urgency in my voice, said she would walk to the farm with her baby Linda, to try and settle her to sleep and would arrive in a half hour.

I told her how extremely grateful I was, my work load meant I was unable to leave the farm but I desperately needed someone to talk to. I had known Cissy for many years, since she and Alan had been evacuated to the farm during the war. When she was older Cissy had come to work with me in Bristol and, although there was a twenty year age gap between us, we had become the very best of friends. That half hour, as I stood and waited, it seemed to last an eternity and I couldn't stand still. I was feeling so agitated that when I finally saw Cissy pushing open the farm gate, I put the kettle on the hob and raced out to meet her. Cissy's baby daughter, Linda, was sound asleep in her pram, her tiny chubby cheeks red with teething.

We left the pram in a sheltered part of the yard, near the porch, and then went into the house. Once the tea was made I fought to hold back the tears as I began to tell Cissy that my worst fears had happened and you and Johnny and had romantic feelings for each other. I remember that conversation word for word, as if it happened yesterday.

Unbeknown to both me and Cissy someone else was listening to our discussion. Edward, my husband told me, a few months later, exactly what he had heard. He had been mending a bit of Cornish hedging in one of their fields that had needed repairing for a while. He'd almost finished the job when his trousers caught on a sharp barb of wire almost exposing his modesty. Edward explained how he held the torn flap of clothing together then headed back to the house to change.

He pushed open the farm gate and walked into the large porch; as he entered he immediately heard the gentle voice of Cissy talking to me. He was about to push the door and go in when something in the tone of my voice stopped him, he stood very still and listened. He heard me telling Cissy that I had caught you and Johnny flirting in the milking shed. At first, Edward had smiled to himself and thought that son of his was a dreadful lady's man, and no doubt about it. He listened on as Cissy asked me if I thought it could turn into a serious relationship.

He heard me sigh deeply and something inside knew that he had to remain hidden and listen to what I was about to say. I paused a while before saying I didn't think so but I was afraid that something might develop if they stayed living in the same house. Edward heard the sound of a chair scraping the floor and imagined Cissy walking over to me, he then heard Cissy ask me if I would be able to tell Johnny the truth.

Now Edward's whole body was alert, he moved a little closer in order to hear what we were saying. Something deep inside, that he had buried many years ago, was stirring and he knew he had to keep listening even though he felt that he was intruding into a very private conversation, but he couldn't stop listening, he heard Cissy say,

'If you told Johnny that Jane was his sister, he would understand why you acted the way you did, but would he keep the secret from his father?'

I told Cissy that I no idea how Johnny would react if he knew that I had been unfaithful to Edward, no matter how long ago it was, as they were very close. I was frightened that my whole family would hate me if they knew that I had an illegitimate child and not only that, they all know who she was. The words reverberated in Edward's mind; he told me how he remembered the moment clearly, word for word.

He shook his head as though he was trying to deny what he had heard. He tried to work out exactly what he had been said; he also knew there was no unhearing it and he now realised that I had had an affair and that Jane was my daughter. The shock he felt took his breath away. Using Jane's age to calculate her birth date he concluded that his I must have had an affair while he was away fighting in the war.

He could hardly comprehend how I could do such a rotten, low thing. He clenched his fists tightly and fought the urge to storm in the kitchen and ring my bloody, cheating neck. Just then, Cissy's daughter, Linda, began to grizzle and cry in her pram. Edward knew that this would bring Cissy out and he would be discovered. He turned raced towards the nearest barn. Safely in his hiding place, he sat down on an upturned bucket and tried to digest the devastating revelation that his own wife had given birth to a child with another man and he found this almost incredulous. He was enraged with fury and disgust.

His humiliation seemed to be eating away at his pride. Edwards mind went back down the years to 1943. He recalled his mother saying, before she died, that I had been to Ireland, where Lucy had lived. At the time he had thought his aging mother was going a bit senile but now he pondered, could I have gone to Ireland to give birth? He remembered that Lucy hailed from Ireland and still had the hint of an Irish accent.

Had she adopted his wife's daughter? He thought back to the times that Lucy and you had visited the farm; Edward recalled thinking that we both had the same mannerisms and were very similar in build and appearance. All the nagging little snippets of niggling thoughts over the years now made sense. Edward, he later told me, was in an utter state of devastation. He had no idea how long he sat there but it must have been a while because he became aware that someone was calling his name. His dazed mind desperately tried to work out what he wanted do.

Edward asked himself, did he want to end a marriage that had been happy up until this point? He had not wholly faithful during the war because it was a difficult time. It was an unsettled period and no one was sure how long they would live so everyone each lived for the day and tried not to think too far ahead. He contemplated and struggled with his thoughts. After careful determination he came to his conclusion. Edward decided that did not want to lose me or break up his harmonic family life. It was a hard decision but one that he decided he would stick to. My secret would stay locked inside him for ever.

My mother explained how they continued to discuss how to remedy the situation, oblivious to the fact that someone was listening. Cissy then came up with an idea. She told Susan that the post office in the village was advertising for a new postmistress as the present one was retiring. Her idea was to suggest I that she applied for that job.

Cissy went onto say that because her home was opposite the post office she would ask me if I would like to live there with them. It was nice and close and they had plenty of room. My mother told me how she thought this was the perfect solution, so long as it was what I wanted. At that point Linda started bawling in the pram outside and Cissy jumped up and said she must dash; my mother thanked Cissy for her help and tried to put her mind to her work.

I smiled as I remembered how easily and unsuspectingly I had fallen in with their plans.

As I began to scrub at the pots and pans in the big earthenware sink my mind wandered back to when you were born. I felt dreadfully guilty when Michael died and Lucy and you began to visit for holidays. I also felt extremely lucky to be a part of your life.

For a terrible moment I thought I thought I had pushed my luck too far and that my past was about to be exposed, thanks to Cissy that may not happen. That's was the reason I encouraged you to apply for the job at the post office and move in with Cissy but all that really did was delay the inevitable. I am so glad that I was able to help you in your time of need and be with you for Mary's funeral.

On a lighter note I want to tell you about what happened when I stayed in Bristol when Lucy had baby Gertie. Lucy and her new daughter spent three days in hospital recovering from the birth. I spent the days pushing Mikey around Bristol in his pushchair. The Red Lion pub where I had spent many evenings, during the war, was still open. I gazed in through the window. The only thing different was the presence of a shiny juke box, standing in the corner, otherwise I was surprised to see that little else changed at all, although its clientele were a little different.

It was filled with young men in Teddy boy outfits and winkle pickers shoes. The girls wore black and white coloured mini dresses with zig zag patterns. Other wore bold outfit in psychedelic colours. Most outfits were made in the style of Mary Quant; the hairstyles ranged from enormous beehives to tiny, neat bobs the framed the face in a similar fashion to the singer, Cilla Black.

I walked across the town. As I stood there, time melted away and I was back in October of 1942. It seemed as though the air raid siren was screeching out and everyone was walking, in an orderly fashion, to the nearest shelter. I could hear the approaching planes and the desperate shouts of the ARP men who were hurrying people to safety then I saw Jimmy, your father. A lone airman, stood frozen to the spot as everyone rushed past him. I walked over, took his arm and led him to the nearest Morrison shelter.

The poor man was rigid with fear and shocked at how calmly the Bristolians remained with bombs dropping all around them. Jimmy had only arrived in the country a few hours earlier, coming from America to help Britain fight the war, and had become separated from the rest of his crew. There and then I felt something stirring inside for this vulnerable, petrified man.

Once inside, I could hear the bombs dropping and the shelter shudder. The smell of burning buildings tingled in my nostrils as I remembered the smoke wafting into the place, as we sat on tenterhooks waiting for the raid to end. Jimmy and I enjoyed a relationship that helped us through the darkest times of the war.

Eventually, my mind returned to the present, I glanced around. There were several courting couples, holding hands as they strolled around without a care in the world. My young life had been overshadowed by the war. My whole family spent years living apart and no one knew if they would still be alive the following day. I wondered where the time had gone.

I walked along the road to see the house that I had once lived in. It had now been turned into four flats and I longed to knock on the door and peep into the room that had been my home during the war years, but I decided against it. I walked on until I came to the spot where the munitions factory, where I had toiled for many long hours, had stood. The factory was no more, instead a very large cinema stood in its place. I found my trip down memory lane oddly disturbing.

As I walked along the Downs I saw a woman sitting on one of the benches, staring across the grassy panorama. The face was familiar and I thought back down the years until I remembered. Quickly, I started to walk towards the woman who turned and looked up at me. As recognition hit us both, we ran together and hugged fiercely.

The woman was my very close friend, Joyce, whom I had worked with during the war. We had managed to keep in touch for a while then lost contact in the early 1950's. Meeting Joyce again was wonderful; we both had so much lost time to make up for.

Joyce had obviously changed in the years since she and I had last met, in 1941. Back then Joyce was a bottle blonde twenty-something who enjoyed the company of various men. Now her hair was little more subdued. It was a soft hazel brown colour and the once brightly painted face was now without makeup. I was surprised to find that Joyce had never married.

As we chatted we began to feel the coldness seeping through our clothes and Joyce suggested meeting up in the Red Lion for a drink, for old time's sake. I thought that a marvellous idea and said I would ask Violet to join us. We arranged a time and went on our separate ways.

I telephoned Violet to tell her about the planned evening and Violet gushed that of course she would come and for me to bring Mikey to her place and one of her girls would watch him. I replaced the receiver and walked back to the flat, feeling really excited about the evening ahead.

We left Mikey who was now with Violet's daughter Daisy, and we linked arms as we made our way to the Red Lion. Violet told me that she had just been to visit Lucy and her new baby at the hospital and how the little girl was an angel and looked the dead spit of Mikey. Violet stopped walking as she confided that she thought Lucy was looking so much better now that the baby had been born. Violet told me that she worried a lot about Lucy at times and even wondered whether the pregnancy was affecting the balance of her mind because she was always convinced that someone was watching her.

I kept quiet, I didn't like to mention that I, too, sometimes had the feeling that I was being watched, when I left Lucy's flat some days.

It struck me too, that I sometimes had the same feeling when I was at the flat but I put that down to the ordeal I had suffered with Travis. I continued to read.

In no time at all we had reached the pub and were delighted to see Joyce sat at our 'usual' table at the corner of the bar room. We all laughed at the thought of their 'usual' table because we hadn't sat at it for more than twenty years.

As the three of us sat sipping at our port and lemons, the years seemed to melt away I asked if Joyce and Violent remembered the hours we spent working in the factory, making parts for aeroplanes, Edith and Iris were little girls then and were convinced that I was actually building the whole plane I told Violet and Joyce.

We all agreed that we were glad we came though the war unscathed, it was terrifying sitting in the air raid shelter waiting for the next bomb to land on us, Joyce recalled, shuddering at the thought.

Not everyone was that lucky though, I told them how Michael,

God rest his soul, had hung himself in 1953 and how he had been suffered with his mind since he left Burma in 1942 and how every time he slept, he thought he was back in the prisoner of war camp and would lash in confusion.

Joyce nodded with understanding as she told us how there were so many men she met, during the war, that suffered from the same thing, screaming nightmares and sweats. I'm guessing that, for most of them it eased with time but for some, like Lucy's husband, it must be a living nightmare, to never get any peace.

I asked Joyce what she was doing with her life. Joyce told me that she had met a man towards the end of the war who was ten years older than her. At first she had thought that it was her usual 'sugar daddy' routine but then she found she had fallen in love with him, and he with her. Unfortunately, he was married with four young children and promised her that they would be together once they had all flown the nest.

At that point someone got up from the table, next to us, a little too quickly their chair tilted backwards then clattered onto the floor noisily. Joyce was so startled she almost fell off her seat. I remembered when the air raid siren went off years before and we would all quickly make our way down to the cellar below the pub. Joyce was always terrified, once having been trapped in a collapsed building.

Violet and I used to hold Joyce's hand to try and comfort her; everybody would be waiting, on edge, for the raid to end. I watched as Joyce retained her composure and concluded that the men weren't the only people left scarred by the war.

Joyce continued, saying that Will, her boyfriend, had bought her a lovely flat in Somerset where she had been living since the beginning of 1950. Sadly their plans for the future were never to be realised. Her man friend was struck down by a heart attack at the young age of fifty one. Joyce told them of her shock because he was such a fit man and she continued to say that the saddest part was that she could not attend his funeral and had to look on from a distance, hidden in the shadows.

Her face clouded over at the memory. She hurriedly cleared her throat and said that she had sold the flat in Somerset as there were too many memories for her to cope with and had bought a place in Bristol.

I asked how she lived and Joyce explained that she had enough money to keep her going for the moment but was looking for work and hoped that she would find something that suited her. That's how I managed to bring her and Lucy together and it turned out to be a wonderful thing. Violet and I talked about our own lives and I was surprised to realise that Joyce knew about you.

Joyce explained that it was the way I had protected you when we were all trapped under a wall, which had caved in after a bombing raid. I apologised for not sharing my secret, as Joyce was one of my very close friends but Joyce understood, the fewer people that knew about your existence, then, the better. Joyce was glad that Edward and I remained happily married and that life was going well for us

We all left to go our separate ways sometime later, with Joyce and me vowing not to lose touch again. As I walked back to Lucy's flat I thanked God that I still had my family. I didn't think I was made to live alone as Joyce was doing and hoped that my old friend was not lonely.

On the train home, I was feeling very glad that I had helped Lucy and her family in some small way. I knew also that Lucy was glad to have Joyce's help and company and they both got on well together. Desmond was a thoughtful, kind man and totally devoted to his wife. In the last few days that I had been at the flat I couldn't help but notice how jumpy Lucy was. She seemed to be constantly looking around her, jerking her head from side to side like a tiny bird on the lookout for a lurking cat.

I really hoped that the medication would help Lucy. Joyce had promised to keep me informed of the family's progress. As the train arrived in Truro, I smiled to myself. I had enjoyed my trip to Bristol but always adored coming home to my family. Edward arrived to pick me up in his trusty van and we chatted on the small journey back to the farm.

I told him about my concern over Lucy's anxiousness and Edward suggested that I invite them all down to the farm for a holiday soon. I kissed him on the cheek, I was so happy to be with my darling husband.

Ethel was waiting for us when they arrived and helped me carry my things inside. I sensed, almost right away, a difference in my friend. Ethel smiled as she talked and went about her work in a cheery fashion. Once inside Ethel turned to face me. She was grinning broadly and I noticed that she had a light in her eyes that I hadn't seen for years.

Ethel gushed as she told me that her son's wife was expecting twins. I began to congratulate Ethel when the bombshell came. Cyril and his wife wanted Ethel to come over to New Zealand to live so she could help them bring up her grandchildren.

I now knew this was the reason for the change in Ethel. Instead of just living her life, Ethel was now going to begin to enjoy it again. I thought that Ethel looked younger and more animated than she had in a long while. We both hugged and cried tears of joy and sadness all at once. The joy was for Ethel and the sadness because we would be living in different countries.

I had never so felt completely content, as I stood in kitchen after my visit to London. Edward carried my luggage upstairs as I put on my apron and began to peel potatoes for the families evening meal. Johnny is engaged to Dulcie Dunstan's daughter, Sharon, and I couldn't be happier.

When they were not working on the farm, Johnny and Edward were building a bungalow for Sharon and Johnny to live in on the grounds at Carmarthen; this arrangement made my heart to sing. It means I can share in my son and his wife lives and help them in any way I can. Fortunately, I get on very well with Sharon; I can even call her my friend.

I love nothing more than having my family around me and with Edith and her family living only a few miles away also, I feel so very lucky. There was a letter waiting on the dresser on my return. It was from Iris, who wrote that she had been given leave over Christmas and would be coming home. I realised, that with all the people I had invited for the festive season, I am going to have a very full house indeed and am very much looking forward to it.

I hope that you are not finding life too unbearable without Mary. I know how hard it is to lose someone close to you and it seems as though the pain will never end. I know it won't seem like it now but time will lessen your feelings of grief and you will be able to remember Mary fondly and look back at your time together with happiness. I will always be here for you if you need me.

With all my love

Susan x x x x x

The letter made me feel closer to her and I knew I would treasure it forever.

56

I looked at the stunning scenery as my train from London made its way to Southampton. There was an early morning frost covering the buildings and roads that gave them a ghostly affect but also made them look much prettier than the usual grimy soot covered places they usually were. As I left London behind, I whispered a silent and final goodbye to Mary.

The scenery changed from urban to rural and the lush green fields were dotted with snow and ice as the grey clouds skittered across the sky. It was a cold and uncomfortable journey and I was glad to arrive at my destination. I left my luggage in a locker at the station and took a cab to the address I had found in Mary's diary. The taxi turned into an estate of houses that all looked in a state of disrepair, some looked close dereliction. Stopping outside one of the scruffiest houses of all, I asked the driver to wait for me to return.

In order to reach the door of the property, I had to squeeze my way through a tiny strip of concrete that was all that remained of the pathway. The small garden was a tangle of overgrown weeds and grass. I then had to negotiate some huge nasty looking thorns that clung to my clothes as I attempted to pass. The door had no discernible colour as most of the paint had come away and the letter box was hanging on by a single screw. I knocked nervously and waited.

A few minutes later the door was pulled open by a young

lad. I thought he looked around eleven or twelve years old and I asked if I could speak to his mother. The child explained that she was unwell and asked if he could help. For a child so young, I found he had a very mature attitude so nodded. The boy beckoned me in and I followed him up a narrow hallway that lead passed the stairs and into a tiny kitchen.

Wedged in the middle of the filthy room were a rickety table and a couple of wooden chairs. The boy pulled one out for me and introduced himself as Robbie Bennetts. Before I could say anything he asked if my visit was to do with Mary. I nodded and gazed at the child. He looked skinny and undernourished and in a good need of a wash, just like the house did. Robbie tilted his head to one side and said:

'She dead ain't she?'

I nodded and questioned how he could know that. Robbie sniffed and wiped a tear from his eye:

'When the money stopped comin', I knew something 'ad 'appened to our Mary, she was kind through and through.' He sighed and looked down to the floor as he struggled to compose himself. I walked over to him, pulled him into my arms and waited until he began to speak again:

'My dad walked out soon after Mary left, he had thing about her, I tried to stop 'im getting to her but he was crafty, used to put a chair under the door handle so I couldn't get out to 'elp her.'

'Has the money that Mary's been sending helped?' I asked:

Robbie scoffed.

'Has it hell, she bin spendin that on bloody gin, all she ever does is get 'ammered, I earn what I can to keep us altogether, I work as a delivery boy for the bakery.' He finished proudly.

I could hardly hide my astonishment and realised he must be a lot older than he looked. I was about to speak when the kitchen door was flung wide and an enormous woman shuffled in through it. Her hair was greasy, grey and matted and the folds of her skin were encrusted in dirt. She wore an old grey overall, tied around her whole body that was covered in food stains.

She mumbled something unintelligible; as she turned I caught the unmistakeable smell of gin, not only from the woman's breath but from every pore in her body. I crinkled my nose in disgust at this excuse for a mother. I suddenly felt very guilty at the way I had ignored Lucy, the lady who had raised me, for many years. Turning to Robbie I explained that I needed to leave as I had a car waiting and told Robbie how sorry I was about Mary.

Robbie thanked me and followed me to the door, once out of ear shot of Mary's mother, I took the money I had found and handed to Robbie. The little lad was over whelmed with gratitude and could not stop thanking me. I gave him a quick hug then fought my way back down the overgrown path and back to the taxi. As I was driven back to the station I pondered why God would allow women to have children for them to neglect and not care for. I felt so very sorry for Robbie and his siblings and struggled to work out why some people had so much and others so little.

57

Susan smiled as she told me how she recalled thoroughly enjoying the Christmas preparations at Carmarthen Farm. A warming fire crackled in the grate as she, Iris and Edith's three younger children decorated the large Christmas tree with coloured tinsel and glittering baubles. The smell of pine needles brought back memories of many Christmas's past when her children were younger.

She told as she watched nervously as Iris climbed a ladder and hung colourful paper chains across the ceiling. When they had all finished decorating the room it was a myriad of colours and light and looked very festive. The only thing missing, for her, was me.

A sprinkling of soft, powdery snow began to fall as she drew the curtains, making the room seem all the more cosy and inviting. She told me, the unexpected knock at the door startled her as she was not expecting any visitors. She pulled the lounge door behind her to keep the warmth in the room and headed towards the front door.

Pulling it open she found me standing on the step while the taxi driver unloaded my cases. To say that she was overjoyed would be an understatement; she felt that her prayers had been answered. She eyed the amount of luggage I had bought and thought it indicated that I would like to stay a while and she felt deliriously happy and blessed.

She pulled me into her arms and I, shyly, hugged her back. At that moment Johnny and Edward arrived back in the yard and more hugging and laughter followed. They all carried my baggage up the stairs. I was shown into the large room at the front of the house that I had previously slept in and overlooked the bustling farmyard below. Susan explained to me that she must leave me to feed the workers but told me to take my time to settle in and to join them for dinner when I was ready.

I smiled as Susan hurried out of the room. The night stars sparkled in the velvet black sky as I drew the heavy curtains across my window. All at once I, too, was overcome with a feeling of contentedness and for the first time in a long while I felt truly at home.

58

Joyce phoned the farm and we all listened in as she gabbled excitedly to Suzy that Desmond and herself were packing up the necessary items for their stay at Carmarthen Farm. Lucy was looking a lot better than she normally did, her trembling had virtually ceased and she was playing snap with Mikey, as Gertie looked on curiously.

Suzy relayed the conversation to us all as we sat having breakfast the morning before their arrival. The family were due in Cornwall the following day and we were all were looking forward to seeing them, especially the children. It would be wonderful seeing the joy of Christmas through a child's eyes.

I knew that both children adored all the farm animals, from their previous visits, and the fuss everyone made of them and Desmond enjoyed the rest from his stressful job. He was also hugely relieved that Lucy seemed so much calmer and happier than she usually was when they were at home in Bristol.

He had written to Susan to tell her this and Susan had showed me the letter and expressed her relief that Lucy may actually be on the mend. The doctors wanted to treat Lucy with electric shock therapy but he did not want his wife to have to suffer that, he just hoped she would improve with time. He decided to put it out of his mind until after their holiday.

Desmond wrote of his joy at the simple things in life. He loved it when Joyce and Lucy put the children to bed together while he cooked the three of them dinner. He could hear Lucy reading Little Red Riding Hood to Mikey and laughed at the way she made up the voices of the big bad wolf

He wrote how, sometime later, when all was quiet in the bedroom and the three adults sat enjoying a drink. All of them chatted happily about the forthcoming Christmas and how they were all looking forward to it. He explained that, if only for a short time, Lucy seemed relaxed and at ease with life. As they ate dinner, he couldn't help but look lovingly at Lucy. As she and Joyce chatted, he noticed that Lucy looked radiant. As she spoke, her eyes sparkled and her face became animated and he, like Susan, began to think that, maybe, Lucy was going to get better.

He continued to write in his letter how he longed to ease her daily torment. The thought of her constant suffering almost brought tears to his eyes. He thanked God, and Susan, every day for sending us Joyce. She is such a wonderful woman, so kind and patient with Lucy and she obviously loves the children as much as Lucy and I do.

He wrote on to say that, sadly, the normality vanished as soon as the evening came to a close. Lucy wandered toward the spot where she always stood by the window and ever vigilant, she peered through a crack in the curtains. She then turned to face the room. Without warning she screamed. He rushed over to her and she told him she was overcome by a terrible feeling that she would never see this room or any of her home ever again.

He shuddered and held her tight and blamed her irrational thoughts on the cocktail of drugs the doctors kept prescribing her, to keep her calm; he knew it made her feel like she was constantly in a zombie-like state as she had told him several times. There must something that could soothe her battered mind and he longed to know what it was.

Both Susan and I were a little tearful as we finished reading Desmond's letter. We wished, as Desmond did, that something could be done to help Lucy. All we could do was hope that time would heal her and Desmond would have the ordinary family life he craved.

59

Cissy shouted 'hello' as she banged on the door of Carmarthen Farm then pushed it open. Shivering, she stepped into Susan's warm kitchen and took the cup of tea Susan handed her, gratefully. Linda, Cissy's daughter, had started school and this made life a whole lot easier for Cissy.

I lingered outside the kitchen door and listened as Cissy discussed Susan's grocery order. I heard the chairs scraping as they sat at the table and went through a list of farm produce that Cissy needed for her and Ivan's shop. The two women sat down for a natter once they sorted out the more serious business. I silently agreed as I heard Cissy exclaim to Susan, as she had done several times before, that she didn't think that she had a maternal bone in her body and although she loved her daughter, she would be her and Ivan's only child.

As they chatted I decided that I had to face Cissy sometime and it was pointless hiding away from her. I walked into the room and poured myself some tea from the still warm pot. Cissy glared at me while Susan asked if I would like some breakfast. I thanked her and informed her that I was ravenous. As Susan tuned to the stove to fry some eggs and bacon, Cissy turned to me and hissed:

'I don't know what the hell you're doing back here but keep away from my brother!' She spat, 'He's married to a lovely girl now so keep out of his bloody way.' She finished.

I saw Susan roll her eyes despairingly. She had often told me Alan was a grown man and didn't need Cissy sticking up for him. She turned around as I walked over and stood very close to Cissy:

'I won't go near your precious bloody Alan, Cissy but only because I choose not to: it's got nothing to do you so mind your own bloody business!' I told her, then I fished into my pocket for some cigarettes, I lit one up and told Susan not to bother with breakfast and stomped out of the kitchen.

To say that Cissy was taken aback was an understatement, Susan told after she had left. This was not the meek, mild mannered girl that had left Cornwall some years earlier. I noticed Susan smile to herself as she took frying pan off the hob. She and Cissy then continued to talk about the groceries Susan would need for Christmas and tactfully avoided mentioning my name.

60

The following day, Desmond and the family arrived at Carmarthen Farm. Joyce and Susan embraced each other; Susan then filled the teapot with hot water and mashed the tea leaves so everyone could have a hot cup of tea. Desmond and Lucy hastily took both children to the bathroom to avert an accident.

When Lucy and Desmond were out of earshot, Joyce whispered to us about her amazement as she realised that the nearer the family got to Carmarthen Farm, the more relaxed Lucy seemed. Desmond, Joyce, she and the children all sang songs and played I-spy and this made the journey fly by.

They were still laughing, when, what seemed like no time at all, they were pulling into the farmyard, trying to avoid the geese and ducks and any other animals that maybe wandering around the yard. Joyce laughed as she said that the doctors should prescribe Lucy with a daily dose of Carmarthen Farm and she would be right as rain in no time at all.

Iris, Jack and I all helped carry in the luggage. As Desmond brought in the last bag, snow began to flutter from the sky, looking like little tiny flies shining in the outside lights. It began to settle on the hedgerows and grass. The farm was quickly transformed into a scenic, winter wonderland.

As Joyce, Lucy and Suzy chatted; Iris and I took the children into the lounge to show them the Christmas tree. Both Gertie and Mikey's eyes were wide with excitement at the spectacular sight of the large tree and several presents piled around the base. Carmarthen was alive with chatter and laughter, just as Susan liked it to be.

Christmas day came and went in a flurry of activity and fun. It was now the day after Boxing Day and the farm was back at full working strength. We had all said a tearful goodbye to Ethel the evening before, as she began her journey to New Zealand. Edward and the rest of the workers had managed to get most of Christmas day off, doing only the vital jobs like the milking and feeding the animals. The festive season had tuned out to be truly magical, as it often was when there were young children present.

Susan told me she was sure that everyone had had a wonderful time. She had driven Iris to the station very early that morning so she could catch the train that would get her back to her barracks in time. She now needed to drive into the village to stock up on groceries.

She laughed as she said she had literally been eaten out of house and home. Both Mikey and Gertie were fussing and whining, fed up at being stuck in the house for two days, so Susan offered to take them into the village with her.

Both children obviously liked the prospect of this by their excited squeals and were hurriedly dressed for the outdoors. A large stonewall was in need of repair in one of the upper fields so I listened as Desmond volunteered to help Johnny and Edward with that. I watched the three men chat amiably as they headed out of the yard. All were warmly dressed to fend off the December frostiness.

This left just Lucy, myself and Jack at the farm. Jack was, as usual, up in his bedroom with his nose stuck in a book. I was just putting the kettle on to boil when Lucy walked into the kitchen. The whole time that we had been at the house, neither of us had been alone together, now an awkward silence hung over the room as Lucy walked towards the table and pulled out a chair to sit on.

As I spooned the tea into the pot I heard Lucy faintly mutter, barely above a whisper that she was sorry. I turned to see Lucy sat looking down at the well-used wooden table with tears spilling from her eyes. I felt a little teary myself, seeing the woman, who had taken care of me since I was a baby, looking so sad and desperate.

I dropped what I was doing, walked over to Lucy and put my arms around her trembling shoulders. I then kissed her on the head and told her that everything was all right, it was all in the past and that we must all move forward. I knelt in front of Lucy as I spoke. Lucy kissed my cheek and stroked my hair. I laid my head onto her lap and let the tears fall.

Lucy told me to let it all out, get rid of the hurt so that we could truly move on. I felt it gently seeping from my body then I muttered the words that Lucy had so badly wanted to hear. I looked up and whispered... 'I love you mum', and I did.

61

Susan laughed when she told how the children loved the fuss the villagers in Treruth made of them. Dulcie's mother came out from her shop with a stick of liquorice for them both and Cissy handed them both a juicy orange. Gertie and Mikey both sat on the bench beneath giant Oak Tree, munching their sweets, while Susan loaded up the van with the necessary supplies.

She shuddered when she recalled that, out of nowhere a large crow appeared and squawked loudly, frightening all in the vicinity and making Gertie cry with fear. Susan calmed the child and told her that the bird would not harm her.

Dirty white clouds thundered across the greying sky and without knowing why, Susan trembled violently. For no reason she could think of, she felt an urgent need to be back at Carmarthen and rushed to load up the van. At the far end of the field I imagined that Desmond was being a great help to Edward and Johnny. Susan told me they would all be piling stones on top of each other, to fix the hole in the Cornish hedge.

Desmond later said they had just began to secure the barbed wire, across the top of the hedge, when a sound reverberated around the open countryside, it sounded like a gun firing but not like the hunting rifle that normally rang out in rural areas.

Edward told me how he dived to the ground for cover when

he heard the noise. The sound made him think he was back in the war, for a moment, and he lay on the floor covering his head for a moment before quickly pulling himself up.

Instinctively, Desmond related to me much later, he knew something was amiss and started to run back to the house with Johnny and Edward following, closely, behind him. Joyce also remembered how she been enjoying a walk in the snow-covered Cornish countryside, heard the noise, with curious caution, she headed back to investigate.

62

Back in the kitchen at Carmarthen, I had poured the tea but then realised that no one had remembered to bring a pail of milk in. This was probably because Christmas had messed up the orderly routine of the farm so I offered to walk to the barn to get some. Lucy put the woollen tea cosy over the teapot to keep the tea warm then reached into the larder for the large Christmas cake so we could both enjoy a slice with our tea.

Jack later told me, when he had popped into kitchen for some cake, how the room seemed to darken for a moment as he stood, and he watched as Lucy went to peer out of the window. He didn't know what she saw and made a hasty retreat back to his bedroom and the book that he had started reading that morning. What Lucy must have seen, I imagine, would have terrified her to the core. She probably couldn't believe her eyes when she saw Travis marching after me across the farm yard. I was, then, totally oblivious to his presence and unaware of the danger I was in.

I felt so much lighter, emotionally, now that I had cleared the air with Lucy and I hummed as I walked. The grey skies held the threat of another snowy night and I was looking forward to sitting in front of the roaring fire with my family later on that day. The milk was in an aluminium bucket at the back of the milking stalls and I walked over to fetch it. I then bent to pick it up and screamed in fright as, almost simultaneously, it was kicked violently from my hand. I turned and looked up into the hate- filled eyes of Travis Parkin.

Travis had changed quite a lot over the years. He looked older than he actually was, with a fleshy, ruddy face and reddening nose. His once manicured hair was a greasy, overgrown mess and his eyes belonged to those of a mad man. I knew that he had come to kill me. Not right away though, I realised as he started pulling roughly at my clothing.

I began to fight, like a wild cat, catching Travis off guard. I managed to floor him with a kick in the genitals only for him to yank at my ankle as I tried to flee. I punched out, spat, screamed and kicked but all to no avail. Insanity had strengthened Travis. Although he was a man of small stature, I was a slightly built girl with none of Travis's long-suppressed anger.

As I fought, frantically, with Travis I saw a movement behind his shoulder and was hugely relieved to see Joyce run into the barn. She immediately ran towards Travis and pulled at his hair in an effort to pull him off my struggling body. With a callousness of a man, devoid of human, feeling Travis reached into his inside pocket, pulled out a revolver and shot over his shoulder without turning his head.

Joyce raised her hand to her head, her face paralysed with shock. Hot, sticky blood ran down her face before she collapsed onto the floor, motionless. I now realised that I could no longer fight the man. Travis was obviously deranged and enjoying what he was doing, I was just stoking the flames by struggling so I stopped fighting and lay limp like a rag doll.

Travis was not happy with this and began slapping me violently across the face in an effort to make me fight. I did not respond. Travis began to fiddle with his belt buckle and

I closed my eyes and prayed my ordeal would be over soon. Travis bent over me and I was puzzled and relieved as I felt his body slump, as though lifeless on top of me. Opening my eyes, I saw Lucy, standing behind Travis, hitting him over and over with a garden rake. Blood began to seep down Travis's face and his eyes turned almost black with rage.

The next minute he was up on his feet, wrestling the implement from Lucy, this done he hurled the fork towards the side of the barn and walked purposely back to Lucy. He took the gun from his pocket and placed the barrel between Lucy's eyes. Lucy stared at Travis defiantly, showing no fear. Without taking her eyes off Travis, Lucy told me she loved me before the shot rang out and Lucy dropped to the ground.

I scrambled up to try and go to her aid but, as I knelt down beside her, I knew it was too late. Lucy was dead; her wide open, sightless told me that. Travis dropped the gun to the floor and walked back to me, to continue his assault, happy in the knowledge that he would not be interrupted again. He knocked me onto my back. His nostrils flared and his eyes were wide, he looked like the devil. I waited for death to free me.

Suddenly Travis's body was lifted off mine and I swear he flew a couple of feet into the air, he was hit by a blow so hard and it almost knocked him senseless. I watched, as sixteen year old Jack began to pummel into Travis relentlessly. Jack may have been a book worm but he had the stocky Penhaligan stature that he had inherited from his dead grandfather. As Travis realised he stood no chance against Jack, he tried to feel around with his hand for his discarded gun. Once he felt the coldness of the steel in his hand, he grinned as if he knew he was about to win the fight.

The combat continued until another shot rang out and I was sure my high pitched scream could have been heard for miles around. For one terrifying moment I thought that Travis had shot Jack as both their bodies seemed to be merged into one as the fight continued. I hardly dared breathe as I watched the two bodies separate and saw Jack pull himself from under Travis's lifeless form. I pulled myself up and ran towards Jack, sobbing with a mixture of relief and fear. I looked over to where Travis lay, blood was oozing from a chest wound and was mixing with the mud and hay. Travis's sightless eyes were dead and so was he. I felt overwhelming relief that my nightmare was finally over but still I could not stop trembling as Jack held me tightly in his arms.

63

Susan and I chatted much later, after I had married Alan, about the sixth sense she felt as she collected the groceries from the village. She didn't know why but it terrified her and she drove like a mad woman, back to Carmarthen Farm. She explained how she tried not to drive too fast, with the two children in the car, but the urgent compulsion, to reach home, almost overwhelmed her.

Finally, when she rounded the bend, the scene before her sent her memory spiralling back some twenty years earlier when a German bomb had landed on the house injuring her mother-in-law and baby son, Johnny. She first saw there were two ambulances parked outside the gate and four blue and white police cars, with lights still flashing, but obviously hastily abandoned.

Susan climbed out of the van and took the precaution of locking it, she said she was unsure why but she still felt an ominous feeling of foreboding so maybe that was the reason. Half of her wanted to race into the farmyard to find out what was happening the other half was telling her to flee. Cautiously, she walked through the already open five bar gate and habitually shut it behind her. There seemed to be a lot of activity in the milking shed so this is where she headed. As she approached she could see that the two doors were wide open.

I was now sitting on an upturned bucket while the police

spoke to Jack. An ambulance man was dabbing gently at my facial wounds with some cotton wool. I watched as Susan walked into the barn and hesitated for a moment as peered in and saw two bodies covered with blankets.

She was almost knocked over by two stretcher-bearers, racing past with an injured woman. She put her hands to mouth; I saw the shocked expression register on her face as she gazed at the lifeless body of Joyce. Blood was oozing down one side of Joyce's face and it was partially covered with a heavy white bandage.

I could see her steeling herself for what she was about to see as she ventured forwards and looked around the corner of the milking stalls. There were several police personnel, some in uniforms and others in suits. She grasped the side of the milking pen, to steady herself, as she almost collapsed with relief when she saw Jack, standing talking to a man in a tweed suit. The man was writing, in a note pad, everything he was saying. I was sitting to the left of Jack. The view was partially blocked by police officers and Susan was struggling to see who was sitting there.

She finally pushed her way through and stood in front of me. She gasped loudly, with relief, when she realised I was alive, then horror on seeing my horribly battered face. She rushed forward and dropped to her knees.

I protested that it was worse than it looked but Susan said she couldn't see how. One of my eyes were so swollen that it was virtually shut and the other one was ringed by a purple, mottled bruise. I had a puffy, cut lip and deep gouge marks on my chest. Susan looked at me questioningly and I spat one word, Travis. I then caught hold of Susan's hand and told her gently that Lucy was dead as was Travis, also Joyce who had been shot.

The more senior of the policemen turned to Susan and explained that Jack had saved my life when he had shot and killed Travis. Susan was struck dumb by what had happened could only shake her head in disbelief. Like all of us, she realised that Lucy had been telling the truth all along. Travis was watching her and that was what was making her ill and no one had believed Lucy.

64

A few days before Lucy's funeral, Desmond asked me if I would like Lucy's diaries and I said I would. An excerpt I read filled me with sadness as I imagined how alone Lucy must have felt when she wrote it:

I gazed out of the window and looked out on to the downs that stretched before me like a massive green carpet. I spotted him, almost straight away and immediately my body began to twitch; he no longer hides himself now but just stands watching me with an unsmiling smirk across his smug face. Joyce must have noticed me stiffen then begin to jerk, it feels as though electricity is passing through my body. I hear her put the iron she had been using, down onto the board and then she is behind me with her arms wrapped around my body.

I told Joyce that he was there, but when Joyce turned and looked out of the large bay window, the road and the Clifton Downs beyond it was empty. The lack of people was probably due to the rain that was pouring from the sky as if someone was emptying a bucket of water from it. I knew Joyce worried and wanted to ease my torment but he was far too clever to let anyone else see him, let them all think I'm mad. Joyce brought me a cup of tea, if only that was the solution to my problems, and then went to rouse Gertie from her nap.

My beautiful little girl is now a boisterous two-year-old and constantly wears me out, thank God for Joyce. Now that Mikey goes to nursery school five days a week, life is a lot less hectic. He is a wonderfully quiet and obedient little boy who does as he is told without complaint. I often wondered if, even at only three years old, he was aware that I am unwell and does not want to make things any worse for me, I hope not, he should be allowed the innocence of childhood.

Desmond is a devoted husband and father but I know he finds it hard to understand why I continuously seem to live on a knife edge. I take high doses of Valium and have talked to several psychiatrists, I tell them all the same thing but they don't believe me. They think I am suffering from psychosis that was triggered by the birth of Gertie.

I know that is not the truth and a small part of me thinks Joyce is not convinced. The times when we visit Susan and her family, in Cornwall, are the times when I am, if not wholly untroubled, a lot less. That is because he isn't there but I know I will have to return to Bristol, at some point, and the nightmare begins again.

Joyce asked Desmond about leaving Bristol and living in Cornwall but as much as he would have loved to, his job in Bristol is important and well paid. If he took a lower paid job then he would not be able to afford to pay Joyce for her help and both of us are quite sure I would not be able to manage on my own. I don't feel like I have the mental or physical strength to take care of my children, it's as though the energy drains out of my body from the moment I wake. All I can do is live through each day as best I can and try to create a loving, fearless environment for my two little children. Tomorrow is another day, God keep me and my family safe, thank you.

65

Lucy was buried in Treruth. All who loved her knew this was the place where she felt most at peace. Desmond, too, was devastated when he realised that Lucy had been telling the truth and that Travis had actually been watching her for years. She was not mad at all and he cried bitterly as he told me how it cut him to the core that he had not trusted her word and now she was dead. In his heart he knew he would never forgive himself, for as long as he lived, I told him that time would heal him and hoped this was true.

The small procession filed into the tiny church. The vicar said some very kind words about Lucy and expressed the sad loss of a mother for her very young children. I stood to read her eulogy. I took a very deep breath as I faced the congregation and told them what a wonderful, loving mother Lucy had been and how distraught I felt that she had come to such a violent end. Towards the end of the reading the tears began to pour down my cheeks.

Desmond and Susan together helped me finish my reading then led me back to the front pew, where we all sat. Joyce had managed to attend. The bullet that Travis had so callously shot, had glanced off the side of her head. She was permanently deaf in one ear but she told me how she felt that that was a small price to pay for her life.

66

As the chilly January wind blustered around the cheerless cemetery, I pulled my scarf snuggly around my neck. The clouds hung heavily in the sky as I walked along the gravel track towards Lucy's grave. A large, black crow stood silently on a swaying branch, seeming to watch me as I wound my way through the headstones. I reached Lucy's freshly-laid resting-place.

Sitting on the cold grey concrete, I began to arrange the roses I had bought into the stone the urn. The bright red colour was in startling contrast to the drabness that surrounded it. I noticed that Lucy's grave lay next to Betty Miners, who had died two years earlier. I was very humbled and upset as I realised both these women had saved my life at some point. I sniffed away my grief as I read the epitaph:

Lucy Masters, loving wife of Desmond
And devoted mother to Jane, Mikey and Gertie

I leaned forward and touched the words. Suddenly, I felt very alone. It was hard for me to believe that I had lost the two people, who were very dear to me, in just a few short months apart. I began to cry. I wondered if Lucy and Mary were comforting each other about their untimely deaths and hoped they were. I tried to work out some kind of future life for myself. In my heart, I longed to stay in the safe haven of

Carmarthen Farm with the Bromley family. Something inside told me that this was not going to be.

As I leant my head against the cold grave stone I felt someone touching my shoulder. I looked up and to see Alan standing above me. He picked me up and pulled me close into his chest. I clung onto in his warmth and strength. Alan held me, rocking me gently, until my crying ceased. He then took a folded, white handkerchief from his pocket and handed it to me.

Alan waited while I dried my face then asked if I needed a drink. I nodded, I felt very much in need and we both headed towards the village pub. Inside, the heat from the open fire, in the inn, was wonderfully inviting and comforting and we both headed for the table we had always used to sit at. I looked out of the window as the heavens opened and rain sheeted down from the sky like a waterfall.

After a while I began to feel much better and I thanked Alan for his kindness. I asked him who he had married and was he happy. Alan smiled, the reassuring, capable smile that I always loved so much, and told me that he had never married. When I told him what Cissy had said, he explained that his sister was a little overprotective and probably said it to save him from any further heartbreak. We both smiled and sat in the comfy haze of the ancient pub.

67

1968

The summer day in Ohio was peaceful and balmy now, with a gentle breeze blowing, making the heat bearable. Alan and I had got married the previous year and had moved to America to be with my father, Jimmy Fairly. I was absolutely amazed and overwhelmed at the wonderful welcome the family gave me, regarding the circumstance of my birth. My three wonderful step brothers were protective and loving as was my stepmother, Maria, who was overjoyed to have a daughter in her house full of men.

I know that we had made the right decision to start new a life in a new country, although I miss my English family very much. I am now in the eighth month of my pregnancy and there is no word to describe how happy I feel. I am holding a letter that I had received earlier today. It is from Desmond, he has written to say that he would like to marry Joyce, but felt it was too soon after Lucy's death. I intend to write back and tell him to do it at once. Life is too short to wait and it makes more sense to focus on the future rather than linger in the past.

Joyce loved Mikey and Gertie as though they were her own children, they would make a perfect family. I was quite sure that Lucy would not want Desmond to be alone and I was genuinely happy they had found each other, although it was from a tragic situation. I hugged my stomach once more and smiled.

Now my needs are few. I like to feel the warm body of someone who loves me, lying next to me in bed. I adore the coldness of the rain on my face after a hot day. I love to hear birdsong and laughter, family and belonging, to need and be needed.

Best of all, I am free. I am no longer afraid of waking up. I have found here everything I have ever needed in life, most of all I have found myself.

THE END